THE LITTLE BOOKROOM

ELEANOR FARJEON'S

SHORT STORIES FOR CHILDREN

CHOSEN BY HERSELF

Illustrated by

Edward Ardizzone

OXFORD

UNIVERSITY PRESS

OXFORD
UNIVERSITY PRESS

Great Clarendon Street, Oxford OX2 6DP
Oxford University Press is a department of the University of Oxford.
It furthers the University's objective of excellence in research, scholarship,
and education by publishing worldwide in

Oxford New York

Auckland Cape Town Dar es Salaam Hong Kong Karachi
Kuala Lumpur Madrid Melbourne Mexico City Nairobi
New Delhi Shanghai Taipei Toronto

With offices in

Argentina Austria Brazil Chile Czech Republic France Greece
Guatemala Hungary Italy Japan Poland Portugal Singapore
South Korea Switzerland Thailand Turkey Ukraine Vietnam

First published 1955
First published in this edition 2011

Poem to Edward Ardizzone taken from
'Morning Has Broken: Biography of Eleanor Farjeon'
by Annabel Farjeon and reproduced with permission
of the Eleanor Farjeon Estate

Data available

1 3 5 7 9 10 8 6 4 2

Printed in Great Britain

Paper used in the production of this book is a natural,
recyclable product made from wood grown in sustainable forests.

these stories are dedicated with love to

DENYS BLAKELOCK

who began to share my childhood

in the Little Bookroom

sixty years after

To Ted from Eleanor, September 1956

When all the fairy tales are told
And young and old go bedward,
Oh, what a debt both young and old
For ever owe you, Edward.

In darkness lit by dreams come true
The years revive their embers
And what the child's eye saw, through you
The ageing eye remembers.

The phoenixes of infant joy
And woe and all-desiring
Which time endeavours to destroy,
Arise from their first firing,

Reborn in images once born
Ere the dull brain retarded,
Picturing still our earliest morn
When words were unregarded.

So with my Picture book I lie
Among the old ones bedward
Knowing the unpaid debt which I
For ever owe you, Edward.

AUTHOR'S NOTE

IN the home of my childhood there was a room we called 'The Little Bookroom'. True, every room in the house could have been called a bookroom. Our nurseries upstairs were full of books. Downstairs my father's study was full of them. They lined the dining-room walls, and overflowed into my mother's sitting-room, and up into the bedrooms. It would have been more natural to live without clothes than without books. As unnatural not to read as not to eat.

Of all the rooms in the house, the Little Bookroom was yielded up to books as an untended garden is left to its flowers and weeds. There was no selection or sense of order here. In dining-room, study, and nursery there was choice and arrangement; but the Little Bookroom gathered to itself a motley crew of strays and vagabonds, outcasts from the ordered shelves below, the overflow of parcels bought wholesale by my father in the sales-rooms. Much trash, and more treasure. Riff-raff and gentlefolk and noblemen. A lottery, a lucky dip for a child who had never been forbidden to handle anything between covers. That dusty bookroom, whose windows were never opened, through whose panes the summer sun struck a dingy shaft where gold specks danced and shimmered, opened magic casements for me through which I looked out on other worlds and times than those I lived in: worlds filled with poetry and prose and fact and fantasy. There were old plays and histories, and old romances; superstitions, legends, and what are called the Curiosities of Literature. There was a book called *Florentine Nights* that fascinated me; and another called *The Tales of Hoffmann* that frightened me; and one called *The Amber Witch* that was not in the least like the witches I was used to in the fairy-tales I loved.

Crammed with all sorts of reading, the narrow shelves rose halfway up the walls; their tops piled with untidy layers that almost touched the ceiling. The heaps on the floor had to be climbed over, columns of books flanked the window, toppling at a touch. You tugged at a promising binding, and left a new surge of literature underfoot; and you dropped the book that had attracted you for something that came to the surface in the upheaval. Here, in the Little Bookroom, I learned, like Charles Lamb, to read anything that can be called a book. The dust got up my nose and made my eyes smart, as I crouched on the floor or stood propped against a bookcase, physically uncomfortable, and mentally lost. I was only conscious of my awkward posture and the stifling atmosphere when I had ceased to wander in realms where fancy seemed to me more true than facts, and set sail on voyages of discovery to regions in which fact was often far more curious than fancy. If some of my frequent sore throats were due to the dust in the Little Bookroom, I cannot regret them.

No servant ever came with duster and broom to polish the dim panes through which the sunlight danced, or sweep from the floor the dust of long-ago. The room would not have been the same without its dust: star-dust, gold-dust, fern-dust, the dust that returns to dust under the earth, and comes up from her lap in the shape of a hyacinth. 'This quiet dust,' says Emily Dickinson, an American poet—

This quiet dust was Gentlemen and Ladies,
And Lads and Girls:
Was laughter and ability and sighing,
And frocks and curls.

And an English poet, Viola Meynell, clearing her ledges of the dust that 'came secretly by day' to dull her shining things, pauses to reflect—

But O this dust that I shall drive away
Is flowers and kings,
Is Solomon's temple, poets, Nineveh . . .

When I crept out of the Little Bookroom with smarting eyes, no wonder that its mottled gold-dust still danced in my brain, its silver cobwebs still clung to the corners of my mind. No wonder that many years later, when I came to write books myself, they were a muddle of fiction and fact and fantasy and truth. I have never quite succeeded in distinguishing one from the other, as the tales in this book that were born of that dust will show. Seven maids with seven brooms, sweeping for half-a-hundred years, have never managed to clear my mind of its dust of vanished temples and flowers and kings, the curls of ladies, the sighing of poets, the laughter of lads and girls: those golden ones who, like chimney-sweepers, must all come to dust in some little bookroom or other—and sometimes, by luck, come again for a moment to light.

E. F.

Hampstead
May 1955

Contents

THE KING AND THE CORN

THERE was in the village a simpleton who was not the ordinary type of village idiot, by any means. He was the Schoolmaster's son, and had been one of those precocious children of whom everything or nothing may be hoped. His father hoped everything, and forced him to live in his books; and, when the child had reached the age of ten, saw the end of his hopes. It was not that the boy's bright wits turned dull, he lost them altogether. Well, but did he? He sat in the fields, smiling a great deal and talking seldom, until some chance loosed his tongue; then he talked without pause, till he came to his stop, like an old musical box that everybody thinks is out of order, and, unexpectedly kicked, plays out its tune. One never knew what chance kick would set Simple Willie going. In books he took no more interest at all. Sometimes his father put under his eyes one that had been his delight, but he glanced indifferently at the old tales and records, wandered away, and picked up the daily paper. He generally dropped it very soon; but occasionally his eye seemed chained by a paragraph, usually of a trifling character, and he would stare at it for an hour.

His father hated the name his boy had been given by the villagers, but it was spoken with affection, and Simple Willie was even pointed out to visitors with pride. He was singularly beautiful; tawny-haired, fair-skinned, gold-dusted with freckles, with blue eyes sly and innocent like a child's, and fine-cut lips which smiled with unusual charm. He was sixteen or seventeen when he was first pointed out to me. I was spending the month of August in the village. For a fortnight he only replied to my greeting with a smile; but one day, as I lay at the edge of a corn-field, three parts cut, and drowsily watched the centre patch diminish, Simple Willie strolled up and lay beside me. Without looking at me he reached out his hand, and fingered the scarab I wear on my watch-chain. Suddenly he began to speak.

When I was a boy in Egypt I sowed my father's corn. When it was sown I used to watch the field until the green blades began to grow, and then, as the days went by, I saw them turn from grass to grain, and the field from a green field to a gold one. And every year, when the field was gold with corn, I thought my father had the richest treasure in all Egypt.

There was at that time a King in Egypt who had many names. The shortest of his names was Ra, so that is what I will call him. King Ra lived in the city in great splendour. My father's field was outside the city, and I had never seen the King, but men told tales of his palace, and his rich clothes, his crown and his jewels, and his coffers full of money. He ate off silver plates, and drank from cups of gold, and slept under curtains of purple silk fringed with pearls. I liked to listen when men talked of Ra, because he sounded like a fairy king; but I could not believe he was a real man like my father, or that his gold mantle was as real as our cornfield.

One day, when the sun was very hot, and my father's field was tall, I lay in the shadow of the corn picking the grains from an ear, and eating them one by one. As I did so, I heard a man's laugh over my head, and I looked up and saw the tallest man I had ever beheld, looking down on me. He had a great black beard in curls upon his breast, and his eyes were as fierce as an eagle's; his head-dress and his garments glittered in the sun, and I knew he was the King. A little way off I saw his guards on their horses, and one held the bridle of the King's own horse, which he had left when he came to look at me. For a little while we only gazed at each other, he down, and I up. Then he laughed again, and said, 'You look contented, child.'

'I am, King Ra,' said I.

'You eat your corn as though it were a feast.'

'It is, King Ra,' said I.

'Who are you, child?'

'My father's son,' I said.

'And who is your father?'

'The richest man in Egypt.'

'How do you make that out, child?'

'He owns this field,' I said.

The King cast his bright eye over our field, and said, 'I own Egypt.'

I said, 'It is too much.'

'How!' said the King. 'Too much! It cannot be too much, and I am a richer man than your father.'

At this I shook my head.

'I say I am! What does your father wear?'

'A shirt like mine.' I touched my cotton shirt.

'See what I wear!' The King swept his gold mantle round him, so that it stung my cheek. 'Now do you say your father is richer than I am?'

'He has more gold than that,' I said. 'He has this field.'

The King looked dark and angry. 'How if I burn this field? What will he have then?'

'The corn again, next year.'

'The King of Egypt is greater than Egypt's corn!' cried King Ra. 'The King is more golden than the corn! The King will outlast the corn!'

This did not sound true to me, and I shook my head again. Then a storm seemed to break in King Ra's eyes. He turned to his guards, and cried harshly, 'Burn this field!'

And they set fire to the four corners of the field, and as it burned the King said, 'Behold your father's gold, child. It has never been so bright before, and will never be bright again.'

Not till the gold field was black did King Ra go away; and as he went he cried, 'Which is more golden now, the corn or the King? Ra will live longer than your father's corn.'

He mounted his horse, and I saw him go, his golden mantle blazing in the sun. My father crept out of his hut, and whispered, 'We are ruined people. Why did King Ra burn our field?'

I could not tell him, for I did not know. I went to the little garden behind the hut, and wept. When I opened my hand to wipe the tears away, I saw the half-empty ear of ripe grain stuck to my palm. It was the very last of our treasure, half an ear of corn, all that remained of thousands of golden ears; and lest the King should want to take it too, I stuck my finger in the earth, making holes, and into the bottom of each hole I dropped a grain. Next year, when the corn of Egypt ripened, ten lovely ears stood in my garden among the flowers and gourds.

That summer the King died, and was to be buried with great pomp. It was the custom for Kings of Egypt to lie in a sealed chamber, filled with jewels, rich robes, and golden furniture of all sorts. Among other things, he must have corn, lest he should be hungry before he arrived in heaven. A man came out of the city to fetch the corn, and he passed our hut, going and coming. The day was hot, and on the way back he came in to us to rest awhile, and told us that the sheaf of corn he carried would be buried with the King. Soon he fell asleep, from heat and fatigue, and while he slept his words rang in my head. I seemed to see King Ra again, standing above me, saying, 'The King of Egypt is more golden than the corn! The King of Egypt will outlast the corn!' And I ran out quickly to my garden, and cut down my ten ears, and thrust the golden blades among the corn the sleeping man had gathered for the King. When he awoke, he took up the sheaf and went on his way to the city. And when King Ra was buried in his glory, they buried my corn with him.

Simple Willie stroked my scarab softly.

'Is that all, Willie?' I asked.

'Not all,' said Willie. 'Hundreds and hundreds of years afterwards, last year indeed it was, some Englishmen in Egypt found King Ra's tomb, and when they opened it, there, among the treasures, lay my corn. The golden stuffs crumbled in the light of day, but not my corn. These Englishmen brought some of it to England, and passed my father's house and stopped to rest awhile, as the Egyptian had done, so long ago. They told my father what they had with them, and showed it to him. I handled it for myself, my very corn.' Willie smiled at me, his radiant smile. 'One grain stuck to my palm. I sowed it in the middle of this field.'

'Then, if it grew,' I said, 'it must be in that little uncut patch.'

I looked at the cutter, making its last revolution. Willie rose, beckoning me to follow. We looked carefully over the small remaining patch, and in a moment he pointed to an ear of corn which seemed taller and brighter than the rest.

'Is this the one?' I asked.

He smiled at me, like a sly child.

'It's certainly more golden than its fellows,' I said.

'Yes,' said Simple Willie. 'How gold's the King of Egypt?'

THE KING'S DAUGHTER CRIES FOR THE MOON

ONE night the King's Daughter looked out of her window, and wanted the Moon. She stretched out her hand to take it, but couldn't reach it.

So she went upstairs to the garret, and stood on a chair, and pushed up the skylight, and got out on the roof of the Palace. But still she couldn't reach it.

So she climbed up the tallest chimney-pot, and clung to the cowl, and still she couldn't reach. Then she began to cry.

A bat that was flying by stopped to ask, 'King's Daughter, why are you weeping?'

'Because I want the Moon,' said she, 'and I can't reach it.'

'Neither can I,' said the bat; 'and if I could, I am not powerful enough to pull it out of the sky. But I will tell the Night of your desire, and it may be she will fetch down the Moon for you herself.'

The bat flew away to tell the Night, and the King's Daughter continued to cling to the chimney-cowl, and look at the Moon, and cry for it. When morning came, and the Moon disappeared in the light, a swallow awoke in its nest under the roof; and she too asked, 'King's Daughter, why are you weeping?'

'Because I want the Moon,' said she.

'I prefer the Sun myself,' said the swallow, 'but I am sorry for you, and I will tell the Day, and perhaps he will be able to help you to your wish.' And the swallow flew away to tell the Day.

The Palace was now in a state of commotion, for the Nurse had gone to the room of the King's Daughter, and found the bed empty.

She rushed at once to the King's bedchamber and banged on the door, crying, 'Wake up, wake up! Someone has stolen your daughter!'

The King got out of his bed with his nightcap awry, and called through the keyhole, 'Who?'

'The Boy who cleans the Silver,' said the Nurse. 'Only last week a plate was missing, and he who steals a plate will steal a princess. Yes, that's who, if you ask *me*.'

'I *did* ask you,' said the King. 'Therefore, let the Boy be put in prison.'

The Nurse ran as hard as she could to the Barracks, and told the Colonel-in-Command that the Boy who cleaned the Silver was to be arrested for stealing the King's Daughter. The Colonel-in-Command put on his sword and his spurs and his epaulettes and his medals, and gave every soldier a week's leave to go home and say goodbye to his mother.

'We will make the arrest on the First of April,' said the Colonel-in-Command. Then he shut himself up in his study and began to draw up plans of attack.

The Nurse went back to the Palace, and told the King all that was being done; and the King rubbed his hands with satisfaction.

'So much for the Boy,' he said. 'Be sure not to let him get a hint of it till the moment of his arrest arrives. And now we must see about tracing the Princess.'

He sent for his Chief Detective, and put the matter before him. The Chief Detective immediately looked very clever, and said, 'The first thing is to find some clues and take some thumb-prints.'

'Whose thumb-prints?' asked the King.

'Everybody's,' said the Chief Detective.

'Mine too?' asked the King.

'Your Majesty is the First Gentleman in the Realm,' said the Chief Detective. 'We shall naturally begin with your Majesty's.'

The King looked pleased, and spread out his thumbs; but before the Chief Detective started taking thumb-prints, he sent for his full force of Under-Detectives, and told them to search for clues all over the city. 'And be sure you are all well disguised,' said he.

The Second Detective scratched his chin and said, 'I'm sorry, Chief, but last Spring Cleaning I found that the moth had got into the disguises, so I sold them to the rag-and-bone man.'

'Then order some more at once from the disguise-maker,' said the Chief Detective, 'and tell him to be quick about them.'

'May we choose our own disguises?' asked the Second Detective.

'Yes, what you like, as long as they are all different,' said the Chief; and the Detectives, of whom there were a round thousand, went home to think out their disguises, all different. But it took a lot of settling, because three wanted to go as Burglars, and five as Teddy Bears.

Meanwhile the Chief Detective had prepared a plate of black stuff, and the King was just rubbing his thumbs on it, when the Cook came up and gave notice.

'Why?' asked the King.

'Because do what I will, the kitchen fire won't light,' said the Cook, 'and if the kitchen fire won't light, I won't stay.'

'Why won't it light?' asked the King.

'Water in the flue,' said the Cook. 'It trickles down, and it trickles down, and I mop it up, and I mop it up, and it's not a bit of good, it only comes down faster. Nobody can be expected to cook without a fire, so I'm going.'

'When?' said the King.

'Now,' said the Cook.

'You must have your thumb-prints taken first,' said the King.

'Does it hurt?' asked the Cook.

'Not at all,' said the King. 'It's rather fun.'

The Cook had her thumb-prints taken, and went and packed her boxes. As soon as they heard that the

King's Cook had given notice, all the other cooks in the country gave notice too; for whatever happened in the King's home set the fashion in the Duke's, and the Earl's, and the Baron's, and the Mayor's, and in Mr and Mrs John Jenkinson's.

The Consequence was—

But there were such a lot of Consequences that they can't all be told in one chapter. If you want to know what they were, you must go on to the next.

II

The bat flew away to find the Night, and tell her that the King's Daughter was crying for the Moon. But Night was not easy to find, though her shadow was everywhere. At last, however, he found her walking in a wood, looking to see that all was well. If a flower was too wide awake, she touched its eye, and the eye closed; if a tree stirred in its sleep, she hushed it till it was quiet. If a wren cheeped in its nest, she stroked its feathers till it dreamed again. But the drowsy owl in the hollow trunk, or the moth clinging under its leaf, she wakened and sent flying. When the bat settled on her hand she said, 'Well, child, what are you come for?'

'I am come to tell you that the King's Daughter wants the Moon.'

'She must want, then,' said the Night. 'I can't spare the Moon. Go back and tell her so.'

'But, mother, she is crying for it.'

'Fie!' said Night. 'If we gave babies everything they cry for in the dark, mothers would get no rest at all. Tell me one good reason why I should give this one what she is crying for.'

The bat tried to think of a good reason, and at last said, 'Because she has grey eyes, black hair, and white cheeks.'

'What has that to do with it, foolish one?' said Night. 'Go, go, I am busy.'

She shook the bat off her hand and went on through the wood, and the bat hung himself upside down on a branch and sulked.

Out of a hole in the tree an owl popped its head and asked, 'Did you say grey eyes?'

'Yes,' said the bat, 'as grey as twilight.'

Up through a crack in the ground a mouse poked its nose and asked, 'Did you say black hair?'

'Yes,' said the bat, 'as black as a shadow.'

And a moth peered round a leaf to ask, 'Did you say white cheeks?'

'Yes,' said the bat, 'as white as starshine.'

The owl then said, 'She is one of us, and we must stand by her. If she wants the Moon, she ought to have the Moon. Night is in the wrong.'

'Night is in the wrong!' repeated the mouse.

And 'Night is in the wrong!' echoed the moth.

A small passing wind caught the syllables and carried them round the world. Up hill and down dale it went, whispering, 'Night is in the wrong! Night is in the wrong! Night is in the wrong!' And all the Children of the Dark came out to listen, owls and foxes, nightjars and nightingales, rats and mice, bats and moths, and the cats that prowl on the tiles. When the wind had said the thing three times, they too began to say it.

'Night is in the wrong!' barked the foxes.

'Night is in the wrong!' rattled the nightjars.

'Have you heard the news?' squeaked a mouse to a moth. 'Night is in the wrong!'

'Yes, she is in the wrong,' agreed the moth. 'I always said as much.'

And the nightingales trilled the words so loud and long that they reached the ears of the stars, who all began to shout at once, 'Night is in the wrong!'

'What do you say?' asked the Moon, from the middle of the sky.

'We say, and we say it again,' said the Evening Star, 'that Night is in the wrong; we will say it till all's blue.'

'You are right,' said the Moon. 'I have not liked to mention it before, but nobody knows Night better than I do, and without any doubt she is entirely in the wrong.'

Nobody stopped to ask why Night was in the wrong; it was enough that everybody was saying so. Long before morning the Children of the Dark had worked themselves into a state of fury against their mother, and decided to rebel against her.

'But, above all, concerted action is necessary,' said the Moon. 'It is useless for a moth to protest here, and a cat to howl there. If we mean to act, we must act together. At a given moment we must one and all refuse to support Night any longer.'

'Yes, we must act, we must strike, we must refuse to support the Night!' cried the bats and the cats, the moths and the owls, the stars and the nightingales, all in one breath.

'Hush!' said the Moon. 'She may hear you. Go on for a while as though nothing had happened; and on the First of April, when our plans are prepared, we will show Night once and for all that she is in the wrong.'

III

A few hours after the Children of the Dark had come to their great decision, the swallow was on its way to tell the Day that the King's Daughter was crying for the Moon. He found Day just stepping out of the sea, wiping his golden feet on the sand.

'Up with the lark, swallow!' said he. 'How come you to be out so early?'

'Because,' said the swallow, 'the King's Daughter is crying for the Moon.'

'Well, that's none of my business,' said Day, 'and I can't see, child, that it is any of yours.'

'Not my business, not my business!' twittered the swallow indignantly. He tried hard to think why it should be his business, and added, 'Why, father, how can you say it's not my business! The King's Daughter has blue eyes, gold hair, and pink cheeks.'

'Then she has her full share, and can do without the Moon,' said Day. 'What! would you have me fall out with my sister the Night in order to dry the tears of the King's Daughter? Get on with your work, silly twitterer, while I get on with mine.' And with a stride he stepped from the shore to the fields, gilding the grass as he went.

Up through a pool in the rocks a fish pushed his nose.

'Blue eyes, has she?'

'As blue as the sky!' said the swallow.

A daisy leaned over the cliff and asked, 'Gold hair?'

'As gold as light,' said the swallow.

A gull hung poised in the air, to ask, 'And pink cheeks?'

'As pink as morning,' said the swallow.

The gull slid down the wind, and screamed, 'Then she is one of us, and if she *wants* the Moon she must *have* the Moon. And if Day will not help her to *get* the Moon, down with Day!'

'Down with Day!' cried the daisy.

'Down with Day!' gasped the fish.

And a little wave that was running backward and forward on the sands heard the words, and flowed back into the sea murmuring, 'Down with Day! Down with Day! Down with Day!'

The big waves caught it up, like the chorus of a song, and they too thundered, 'Down with Day!' as they towered up and fell down with a crash; and soon the whole sea was heaving with the sound of the words, and the tides were streaming with it to all the shores of the earth. 'Down with Day!' roared every tide as it swept in; and all the creatures of the five Continents heard them, and echoed the cry in their own ways: the mocking-birds of America whistled it, the elephants of Africa trumpeted it, the hooded cobras of Asia hissed it, the laughing jackasses of Australasia shrieked it, and all the larks of Europe trilled it to the Sun.

'What's that you're singing?' the Sun asked the larks, who were his particular pets.

'Down with Day! Down with Day! We are singing, Down with Day!'

'By all means,' said the Sun. 'Down with Day, and high time too! Why did we never think of it before?'

As soon as the Sun had said it, all the Children of the Light began to wonder why they *hadn't* thought of it before, and to consider how they might bring it about.

'Leave that to me,' said the Sun. 'Each must do his share, but all must be done together. I will myself concoct a plan for effective action, and as soon as it is prepared you shall know your parts. Hold yourselves ready for the First of April; till then, the great thing to remember is that upon one point we are all agreed: Down with Day!'

'Down with Day!' shouted all things together, birds, beasts and fishes, grass, flowers and trees, stones, wood and water. 'Down with Day!'

They were all of them very determined, and none of them knew what about.

IV

As soon as the Detectives had got their disguises, they scattered themselves over the City to find clues by which they might discover the King's Daughter. Some looked in the broad streets, and some in the twisty ones; some searched the parks, and some searched the slums. Wherever they went, they found suspicious signs, and as soon as they found them they hurried with them straight to the Palace to tell the King. Detective A, for instance, disguised himself as a Park-Keeper, and in the very first hour discovered a ragged Tramp snoring in the grass under a tree.

'That's a suspicious character, that!' thought Detective A. 'It is written all over his face!' To test his theory, he stooped down over the snorer and shouted in his ear, 'Where's the King's Daughter?'

The Tramp half-opened one eye, muttered 'First to the right and second to the left,' and began to snore again. Detective A ran as hard as he could on the trail, and the first to the right and the second to the left

brought him to a public-house called the Hog's Head. In the bar nineteen Sailors were being served by the thin Innkeeper and his buxom Wife. Detective A pushed his way to the front, and ordered a pint of porter as a blind. The moment he had drunk it down he threw off all pretences, and seizing the Innkeeper by one hand and his Wife by the other, he demanded, 'Where's the King's Daughter?' 'How should *we* know?' retorted the Innkeeper. 'Wherever she is, she's not here.' 'Ah, you'd deny it, would you!' cried Detective A. 'Hands off, my lad!' said the Innkeeper's Wife, pulling her wrist away. 'Ah, you'd struggle, would you!' cried Detective A. Then he threw open his coat, revealed himself, and arrested them; and to make things safer he also arrested the nineteen Sailors, and ordered them to follow him to the Palace; and on the way, to make things *quite* safe, he stopped in the Park and arrested the Tramp. Then he took them all to the King.

'Who are these?' asked the King.

'These are doubtful characters, Your Majesty,' said Detective A. 'This one,' he pointed to the Tramp, 'says your daughter is at these ones' public-house,' and he pointed to the Innkeeper and his Wife. 'And these ones say that this one is mistaken,' and he pointed to the Tramp again. 'One of them is telling a story.'

'Oh, what a pity!' said the King. 'And who are all these?' And he looked at the nineteen Sailors.

'These were all in the bar at the time,' said the Detective, 'and probably in the conspiracy too. I thought it best to take no chances.'

'You did splendidly,' said the King, 'and you shall be promoted. Let the suspected persons be thrown into prison; and if they have not proved themselves innocent by the First of April, they shall die.'

While this was being done, the King promoted Detective A, and he had scarcely finished doing so before Detective B came in disguised as a Customer, and behind him came a Draper, forty-three Shopgirls, a Nurse, and a Baby in a pram.

'Who are these?' asked the King.

'These are suspicious persons, Your Majesty,' said Detective B. 'I noticed this Baby's pram standing for half an hour outside this Draper's shop, and the Baby was crying in a highly suspicious manner, but refused to inform me of what was wrong. So I went inside the shop, and there I saw the Nurse being served at the counter with a yard of something. "What's that?" I sez to her. "Mind your own business," she sez to me. "It *is* my business," sez I, and seized the object, which proved to be this.' And Detective B produced from his pocket a yard of blue elastic.

'What's that for?' asked the King.

'Ah, just what I asked *her*, Your Majesty! And she said I was no gentleman, and refused to tell me. So as she wouldn't confess, of course I arrested her, and to be on the safe side I also arrested everybody else in the shop, and the Baby into the bargain.'

'You did well,' beamed the King. 'Unless they can prove their case, they shall all be beheaded on the First of April.' And he had the Nurse, the Baby, the Draper, and the forty-three Shopgirls thrown into prison, and began to promote Detective B. He was only half-done when Detective C came in, disguised as a Postman, followed by four-hundred-and-two Private Householders.

'Who are all these?' asked the King.

'These are all suspectable individuals, Your Majesty,' said Detective C. 'They have all had letters sent to their houses with the wrong names and addresses on them, and to avert suspicion they have all written "Not Known!" on the envelopes and put them back in the pillar-box. So I gave each of them a double rat-tat, and as soon as they opened the door I arrested them, as you see, till they tell who the letters are for, and who they are from, and what is inside them.'

'Wonderful!' cried the King. 'If they have not told by the First of April, they shall perish. You too shall be promoted. Did ever a King have a Detective Force like mine?'

During the next hour Detective D, disguised as a Ticket Collector, came in with nine-hundred-and-seventy-eight Persons who had bought railway tickets, and were obviously trying to leave the city; and Detective E, disguised as a Public Librarian, brought in two-thousand-three-hundred-and-fifteen Novel-Readers, who had all asked for Detective Stories at the Public Library. There was no doubt of it that they were all suspicious characters, and they too were thrown into prison until they could explain themselves; otherwise, said the King, on the First of April they would all lose their heads.

So it went on till night; and just as the King was going up to bed, there was a great shout in the Palace, and the sound of scurrying feet, and into the Throne-room dashed the Housekeeper with an open penknife in her hand and a Second Housemaid at her heels. Gesticulating wildly, the Housekeeper rushed towards the throne, but before she could reach it the Second Housemaid tripped her up, gagged her, and handcuffed her.

'Bless my soul!' said the King. 'What's all this about?'

The Second Housemaid got up and took off her cap; her hair came off with it, and in its place the rather bald head of the Second Detective was disclosed. He pointed, panting a little, to the speechless Housekeeper struggling on the floor.

'This is a Highly Suspicious Person, Your Majesty,' said he. 'Disguised as one of Your Majesty's Second Housemaids, I went to search your daughter's room for clues. I stole in quietly when no one was looking, and immediately saw that someone had been before me. The carpet was strewn with bits of metal—every lock of the Princess's drawers and cupboards had been picked! Certain that all was not well, I continued my investigations. I looked stealthily behind curtains, and opened cupboard doors suddenly. At last I looked under the bed. There I saw a big black felt slipper, and in the slipper was a foot; beside it was a second foot inside another slipper. I dragged them out into the light, and found them attached to the body of Your Majesty's Housekeeper. She fled; I gave chase; and the end of the chase you saw.'

'Yes, but,' said the King, 'she *isn't* my Housekeeper.'

'*Not!*' cried the Second Detective. 'Worse and worse. She is probably a dangerous criminal who, having stolen your daughter, came back for loot. I think we can safely say, Your Majesty, that we are on the track!'

The King was delighted; the False Housekeeper was condemned to death on the First of April; the Second Detective was promoted; and the Court went to bed and to sleep.

But nobody else did; for by now everybody knew that a thousand Detectives in Disguise were let loose in the streets, and that at any moment you might be arrested by anybody. Before morning, half the people in the City were under lock and key, and the other half was running away as hard as it could from everybody else.

V

Master Johnny Jenkinson, who was the Drummer-Boy in the King's Army, went beating his drum up the path to his Mother's cottage-door. Instead of knocking, he beat a special tattoo that brought his Mother running. As soon as she set eyes on him she threw up her hands for joy, and then flung her arms round his neck, crying, 'It's never you, Johnny! it never can be you!' as though she couldn't believe her senses.

'Yes, Ma, it's me,' said Johnny. 'What's for supper?'

'Dad, Dad, come here!' cried Mrs John Jenkinson; and from the back-garden appeared Mr John Jenkinson with his spade, and seeing his son he sat down plump on the third stair and filled his pipe to hide his emotion.

'But, Johnny, what brings you here?' asked his Mother, 'when I thought you were twenty miles off in the City?'

'I've got a week's leave, Ma,' said Johnny, 'and so has every man Jack of us.'

'But for why, Johnny?'

'Ah!' said Johnny, looking important, 'that's what we haven't been told. But we can guess. There's something big afoot.'

'War, do you mean?' whispered Mr John Jenkinson.

'What else can it be, Dad?' replied Johnny. For what else *could* it be?

'War with whom, Johnny?' asked Mrs John Jenkinson.

'Well, it's being kept as dark as dark, Ma,' said Johnny; 'but who's to stop a chap thinking? Some of us think it's war with the King of the North, and some think it's war with the King of the South. But *my* opinion is—' He paused, because he hadn't made up his opinion yet.

'You don't mean to say, Johnny,' gasped Mrs John Jenkinson, 'you never mean to say it's war with *both*!'

'Why don't I?' asked Johnny, closing one eye. And from that moment he did.

'This is awful!' moaned Mrs John Jenkinson. 'We can never beat them both at once, never!'

'Trust *us*, Ma!' boasted Johnny, and did a tattoo on his drum. 'All we want is good vittles inside us, and then we can tackle anything. What's for supper?'

Mrs John Jenkinson threw her apron over her head, and wept aloud. 'Nothing's for supper, Johnny, nothing at all. The cook's given notice.'

'But here, I say!' cried Johnny, for the first time looking anxious. 'We haven't *got* a cook! *You* do the cooking in this house, Ma!'

'Well, and if I do!' retorted his Mother, drying her eyes and looking rather defiant. 'What I say is, the one that does the cooking is the cook, and I suppose I can give notice as well as another!'

'But why, Ma?'

'Because it's the fashion, Johnny. The King's Cook gave notice the day before yesterday, and every other cook in the country stopped cooking within twenty-four hours. It would be a sort of treason for us to go on cooking when the King's Cook won't. And there it is.'

Johnny sat down by his Father on the third stair. 'This spoils my leave, this does,' he said. 'And what's more, it will spoil every other chap's leave too. You wouldn't believe what a chap's meals mean to a chap on leave.'

'And not only to chaps on leave,' said Mr John Jenkinson puffing his pipe to conceal his feelings. 'There's others.'

'What do *you* do come dinner-time, Dad?' asked Johnny.

'I goes down to the Inn and smokes,' said Mr John Jenkinson.

'Let's get along, then,' said Johnny. And father and son went sadly down the path.

At the Inn they found every man in the village assembled. It was the only place for the Men to go now that the Women had stopped cooking. Feeling against the Women was beginning to run high. As the Men got hungrier and hungrier, they also got angrier and angrier; and the Women, on their part, got stubborner and stubborner.

'Nothing for breakfast? Nothing for dinner? Nothing for tea?' cried the Men, at meal-times.

'The King gets nothing for breakfast and dinner and tea!' retorted the Women. 'And what the King gets is good enough for *you*!'

So in all the Inns all over the land the men gathered and talked furiously about the Women: and they took a resolution, that as long as the Women wouldn't cook, *they* wouldn't work. 'United we stand, divided we fall,' said Johnny's Father. 'We'll all stop work together on the First of April.' The word flew like wildfire from Inn to Inn throughout the kingdom; and every man Jack of them agreed.

But it wasn't only Women that were talked of in the Inns; for now that the soldiers had come home on leave, they began to talk furiously about War as well. Like Johnny the Drummer-Boy, each soldier came back looking very important, as though he alone knew what it all meant; and some said they were going to war with the King of the North, and others with the King of the South.

'Nay,' said another, ''tis the King of the East.'

'Wrong!' said a fourth; ''tis the King of the West!'

'Guess again!' jeered a fifth; ''tis none of these at all, but the King of the Blacks, and I had it from the Lance-Corporal himself.'

'Then the Lance-Corporal may put his head in a bucket,' scoffed a sixth, 'for the Sergeant-Major told me, in strictest confidence, that 'twas the King of the Whites!'

The arguments raged high, for this King and that; every Monarch in the world was named by one soldier or another. And the Spies of the Monarchs heard what was said, and hurried back to their own countries with the news; and as soon as they heard it, all the Kings of the World gave orders for their armies to be mustered, and their ships to set sail, on the First of April.

VI

On the First Day of April:

The King sipped his coffee and said: 'This is the day for the Suspicious Characters to be beheaded.'

And the Colonel-in-Command buttered his toast and said: 'This is the day for the Boy who cleans the Silver to be arrested.'

And all the Men in the land said: 'The day has come for us to stop work.'

And all the Kings of the World said: 'The day has come for us to go to war!'

And the Sun called the Children of the Light and said: 'The hour is come to do Day down.'

And the Moon summoned the Children of the Dark and said: 'The hour is come to prove Night in the wrong.'

And now, terrible things began to happen all over the world.

First the Colonel-in-Command called out the Army to arrest the Boy; and the Army wouldn't come. So the Colonel went to the Army and flashed his sword at them, and asked, 'Why not?'

Then up spoke Johnny the Drummer-Boy. 'Because, Colonel, a soldier's a man as well as a soldier, and today every man Jack in the land has stopped work.'

'Ay, ay, every man Jack!' shouted the Army.

The Colonel clicked his spurs at them and asked, 'What for?'

'Because as long as the King's Cook won't cook for him, the Women won't cook for *us*, and no man can work on an empty stomach. As soon as the King's Cook goes back, and we've had a square meal, we'll do our jobs again.'

'Ay, ay, a good square meal!' shouted the Army.

The Colonel rattled his medals at them, and went to tell the King that he must get back his Cook at any price.

The Cook was sent for, looked at the kitchen grate, said the chimney was still dripping and the kitchen fire wouldn't light, and refused to come back till it did.

Then the King said, 'Send for the Plumber!' And the Plumber sent back word that a plumber might be a plumber, but he was likewise a man, and every man Jack had stopped work; and until his wife began cooking again, he wasn't going to plumb for anybody.

Then the King sent for the Second Detective, because the Chief Detective had entirely disappeared, no one knew where. When the Second Detective came, the King commanded him to arrest the Cook for not cooking, and the Plumber for not plumbing, and the Second Detective scratched his chin and said, 'I'm sorry, I can't.'

'Why can't you?' asked the King.

'It's like this, Your Majesty. A Detective may be a Detective, but he is also a man, and until my wife begins cooking again I can't go on detecting.'

'But what about all the people who were to be beheaded today?' cried the King.

'They'll have to keep their heads,' said the Detective, 'because the Headsman says it's all very well, but a headsman's a man, isn't he? and until his wife begins cooking again—'

The King put his fingers in his ears and burst into tears. But the next moment he took them out again and said, 'What's that?'

And no wonder! For the sound of cannons and trumpets was ringing through the air, and the Nurse rushed in to say that all the Monarchs of the World were marching on the City, and the coast was entirely surrounded with their ships.

'Help! Help! Call out the Army!' cried the King. But the Colonel shrugged his epaulettes at him and said, 'They won't!'

'Then we are lost,' groaned the King, 'and nothing can save us.'

Even as he said it, the Sun went out.

And the larks flew down instead of up, and the daisies turned black, and the dogs mewed like cats, and the stars came down and walked upon the earth, and a mouse came and pushed the King off his throne, and a seagull came and sat on his footstool, and the clocks struck midnight at noon, and dawn broke in the West, and the wind blew the other way, and the sea ran backwards at high tide, and the cocks crowed for the Moon to rise, and the Moon rose inside out, showing her black lining, and Day fell down flat, and Night was all wrong.

And in the midst of all the confusion, the door opened, and the King's daughter came in in her nightdress.

VII

The King flew at her and caught her to his heart, crying, 'My child, my child, where have you been?'

'I've been sitting on the chimney-pot, Daddy,' said the King's Daughter.

'Why did you sit on the chimney-pot, my darling?'

'Because I wanted the Moon,' said the King's Daughter.

The Nurse took her by the shoulders, shook her severely, and said, 'You've got your nightdress damp, you naughty little girl.'

'That was where I cried on it,' said the King's Daughter. 'I cried all day and all night, and I never stopped once. I cried all down me, and all down the chimney.'

'Did you indeed!' exclaimed the Cook; and she rushed to the kitchen. The chimney had stopped dripping, so she lighted the fire and began to cook as hard as she could.

At the same moment, the mouse and the seagull went hurrying to the Children of the Dark and of the Light, crying together:

'The King's Daughter has brown hair, brown eyes, and a brown skin!'

The children of the Dark turned in a body upon the bat, and shouted, 'You told us she had black hair, grey eyes, and a white skin!'

'I suppose I got mixed in the dark,' muttered the bat.

'And *you* told *us* that she had gold hair, blue eyes, and a rosy skin!' shouted the Children of the Light to the swallow.

'I must have got dazzled by the dawn,' twittered she.

The Children of both Light and Dark then said, 'This puts us in a difficult position. We have been supporting a creature who is not one of us. We must set Day on his feet again at once, and tell Night that she is entirely in the right.'

No sooner said than done. The stars went back to their places, the sea reversed itself, time straightened itself out, and everything did what it ought to do; and when, last of all, the Sun came out, he shone upon the Kings of the World sailing home in their ships as fast as they could. For they said they had never seen anything like it, and you couldn't go to war with everything as topsy-turvy as *that*, could you?

The good news was brought to the King in the Palace, and he clapped his hands and said to the Colonel-in-Command, 'Now they've gone we shan't want the Army for *them*, so let it arrest the Boy who cleans the Silver.'

'What for, Your Majesty?'

'For stealing the Princess.'

'But he didn't steal me,' said the Princess.

'Oh, so he didn't,' said the King. 'Then we must let him off. And I suppose we must let off all the people who were going to be beheaded too.'

'All but the False Housekeeper I found in the Princess's bedroom,' said the Second Detective. 'For she *was* a suspicious character.'

So he went and let out the Tramp and the Sailors and the Nurse and the Baby and the Draper, and the Shopgirls and the Householders and the Train-Travellers and the Novel-Readers, and all the others who had been put in prison. But the False Housekeeper he dragged by the hair into the King's Presence, and just as he got her there the hair came off, and the quite bald head of the Chief Detective appeared in its place. So they took the handcuffs off his hands, and the gag out of his mouth, and when he had done spluttering he said to the King:

'Wasn't my disguise a good one! Nobody recognized me, not even my Second Detective.'

'You shall be promoted!' said the King. 'But what were you doing in the Princess's bedroom?'

'I was searching for clues, of course; and I'd only just done picking the locks with my penknife, when I heard someone coming—'

'That was me!' said the Second Detective.

'So naturally I got under the bed.'

'And *I* found you there!' boasted the Second Detective.

'Ah, but *I* found something else there!' said the Chief Detective. 'This!' And from under his big black skirts he produced a Silver Plate.

'There!' cried the Nurse. 'That's the very one that was missing; and if it hadn't been missing I'd never have suspected the Boy of stealing the Princess. So it was your fault, every bit of it,' she said, turning to the Princess. 'What did you take it for, you naughty little girl?'

'Because it was so nice and round and bright,' said the Princess, 'and I wanted it. And I *do* want it.'

'You shall keep it,' said the King, 'as long as you promise me one thing.'

'Yes, I promise; what is it?' asked the Princess.

'Never to cry for the Moon any more.'

'I should just think I wouldn't!' said the little Princess. 'The Moon is horrid. I've seen her inside. It's all black. That's why I came down. What's for dinner?'

And 'What's for dinner?' they were asking all over the country; and the Women stirred the pots, and the Men went back to work, and the Sun rose in the East and set in the West; and the world forgot in less than no time everything that comes about when the King's Daughter cries for the Moon.

A LONG time ago old Miss Daw lived in a narrow house on the edge of the town, and Young Kate was her little servant. One day Kate was sent up to clean the attic windows, and as she cleaned them she could see all the meadows that lay outside the town. So when her work was done she said to Miss Daw, 'Mistress, may I go out to the meadows?'

'Oh, no!' said Miss Daw. 'You mustn't go in the meadows.'

'Why not, Mistress?'

'Because you might meet the Green Woman. Shut the gate, and get your mending.'

The next week Kate cleaned the windows again, and as she cleaned them she saw the river that ran in the valley. So when her work was done she said to Miss Daw, 'Mistress, may I go down to the river?'

'Oh, no!' said Miss Daw. 'You must never go down to the river!'

'Why ever not, Mistress?'

'Because you might meet the River King. Bar the door, and polish the brasses.'

The next week when Kate cleaned the attic windows, she saw the woods that grew up the hillside, and after her work was done she went to Miss Daw and said, 'Mistress, may I go up to the woods?'

'Oh, no!' said Miss Daw. 'Don't ever go up to the woods!'

'Oh, Mistress, why not?'

'Because you might meet the Dancing Boy. Draw the blinds, and peel the potatoes.'

Miss Daw sent Kate no more to the attic, and for six years Kate stayed in the house and mended the stockings, and polished the brass, and peeled the potatoes. Then Miss Daw died, and Kate had to find another place.

Her new place was in the town on the other side of the hills, and as Kate had no money to ride, she was obliged to walk. But she did not walk by the road. As soon as she could she went into the fields, and the first thing she saw there was the Green Woman planting flowers.

'Good morning, Young Kate,' said she, 'and where are you going?'

'Over the hill to the town,' said Kate.

'You should have taken the road, if you meant to go quick,' said the Green Woman, 'for I let nobody pass through my meadows who does not stop to plant a flower.'

'I'll do that willingly,' said Kate, and she took the Green Woman's trowel and planted a daisy.

'Thank you,' said the Green Woman; 'now pluck what you please.'

Kate plucked a handful of flowers, and the Green Woman said, 'For every flower you plant, you shall always pluck fifty.'

Then Kate went on to the valley where the river ran, and the first thing she saw there was the River King in the reeds.

'Good day, Young Kate,' said he, 'and where are you going?'

'Over the hill to the town,' said Kate.

'You should have kept to the road if you're in anything of a hurry,' said the River King, 'for I let nobody pass by my river who does not stop to sing a song.'

'I will, gladly,' said Kate, and she sat down in the reeds and sang.

'Thank you,' said the River King; 'now listen to me.'

And he sang song after song, while the evening drew on, and when he had done, he kissed her and said, 'For every song you sing, you shall always hear fifty.'

Then Kate went up the hill to the woods on the top, and the first thing she saw there was the Dancing Boy.

'Good evening, Young Kate,' said he. 'Where are you going?'

'Over the hill to the town,' said Kate.

'You should have kept to the road, if you want to be there before morning,' said the Dancing Boy, 'for I let nobody through my woods who does not stop to dance.'

'I will dance with joy,' said Kate, and she danced her best for him.

'Thank you,' said the Dancing Boy; 'now look at me.'

And he danced for her till the moon came up, and danced all night till the moon went down. When morning came he kissed her and said, 'For every dance you dance, you shall always see fifty.'

Young Kate then went on to the town, where in another little narrow house she became servant to old Miss Drew, who never let her go to the meadows, the woods, or the river, and locked up the house at seven o'clock.

But in the course of time, Young Kate married, and had children and a little servant of her own. And when the day's work was done, she opened the door and said, 'Run along now, children, into the meadows, or down to the river, or up to the hill, for I shouldn't wonder but you'll have the luck to meet the Green Woman there, or the River King, or the Dancing Boy.'

And the children and the servant girl would go out, and presently Kate would see them come home again, singing and dancing with their hands full of flowers.

THE FLOWER WITHOUT A NAME

ONE day a Cottager's child, whose name was Christie, went into the meadows beyond her Mother's garden and picked a flower. This happened long ago, yet not so long ago as all that; that is to say, it did not happen today, nor did it happen on the first day of all, but on some day in between.

Christie was delighted with her flower, for it was very beautiful, and she came running to find her Mother, who was watering the pinks in the round bed.

'Mother,' cried Christie, 'look at my pretty flower I've found!'

Her Mother was never too busy to look when Christie asked her to, so she put down her jug of water and took the flower in her hand.

'There's a pretty flower now!' she said.

'Yes, Mother, isn't it?' said Christie. 'What is its name?'

'Why,' said her Mother, 'it is a—it is a— Dear me, to think I don't know its name! You must ask Father.'

Christie ran to the Cottager, who was mending the fence, and she held up her flower. 'What is its name, Father?' she asked.

'Let me see now,' said the Cottager, laying down his hammer. He looked at the flower for a minute or two, and then he scratched his head. 'Well, well!' said he. 'I've forgotten its name, if ever I knew it. But give it to me, for I'm to see my Lord's Keeper about some mole-traps, and maybe he'll know, being woodwise.'

When Christie's Father had had his talk with the Keeper, he showed him the flower. 'What's the name of this here?' asked the Cottager.

The Keeper looked at it, and sniffed at it, and thought a bit. But at the end of his thinking he said, 'I never saw its like before, in wood or field or marsh or hedge. I don't know its name. However, I'm just about going up to the Manor, so I'll take it along and ask my Lord's Clerk, for he's a clever young man, and has to wear spectacles along of reading so many books.'

Now my Lord's Clerk had studied most things, and flowers not the least of them. He had indeed in his Lord's library all the books about flowers that ever were written. So when the Keeper sought him out and said, 'I've a flower here I'd like to know the name of,' the Clerk answered, 'Show it to me, and I'll tell you its name.'

But when he set eyes on it he knew he had spoken too soon.

'That's a queer thing!' said my Lord's Clerk. 'For I know the names of all the flowers in the world, by both their court and country names, yet I don't know the name of this one. Leave it with me, and I'll see if I can find out.'

The Keeper left the flower with the Clerk, and the Clerk pressed it and dried it, and spent a whole year trying to find out something about it. He put the question to the wisest scholars in the kingdom, and the matter spread abroad till wise men in lands over the sea were all puzzling their wits about the name of the flower. But in the end they could not find one for it.

So after a twelvemonth the Clerk came to the Keeper and said, 'That flower you brought me has no name at all.'

'What flower's that?' asked the Keeper, who had forgotten all about it. The Clerk reminded him of it, and said:

'The wisest men in the world have but one opinion, and it is this. We know that Adam gave names to all the flowers created, and as this flower has remained unnamed since the days of Eden, it is doubtless one which was forgotten at the Creation, and the Lord has only just remembered to make it. But as it was never named by Adam, it has no name now; therefore, the wise men have destroyed it—for how can anything be without a name?'

'I'm sure I couldn't say,' said the Keeper. 'I expect you're right.' And the next time he met the Cottager he said, 'That there flower of yours hadn't any name at all.'

'What flower?' said the Cottager, who had a short memory. The Keeper reminded him of the flower, adding that the wise men had destroyed it.

'Well, no harm's done,' said the Cottager; and that night at supper he said to his little daughter:

'Seemingly your flower had no name of its own after all.'

'But where *is* my flower?' asked Christie.

'The wise men destroyed it,' said the Cottager. No more was said, and from that day no one except Christie remembered that such a flower had ever been.

But all her life, and when she was quite an old woman, Christie would sometimes say to herself and others:

'When I was a child I found such a pretty flower.'

And when they asked her what flower it was, she smiled and answered, 'Only our Lord could tell you; it hadn't got a name.'

HERE was once a Goldfish who lived in the sea in the days when all fishes lived there. He was perfectly happy, and had only one care; and that was to avoid the net that floated about in the water, now here, now there. But all the fish had been warned by King Neptune, their father, to avoid the net, and in those days they did as they were bid. So the Goldfish enjoyed a glorious life, swimming for days and days in the blue and green water: sometimes low down close to the sand and shells and pearls and coral, and the big rocks where the anemones grew like clusters of gay flowers, and the seaweed waved in frills and fans of red and green and yellow; and sometimes he swam high up near the surface of the sea, where the white caps chased each other, and the great waves rose like mountains of glass and tumbled over themselves with a crash. When the Goldfish was as near the top as this, he sometimes saw swimming in the bright blue water far, far above him a great Gold Fish, as golden as himself, but as round as a jellyfish. And at other times, when that distant water was dark blue instead of bright, he saw a Silver Fish such as he had never met under the sea, and she too was often round in shape, though at times, when she seemed to swim sideways through the water, he could see her pointed silver fins. Our Goldfish felt a certain jealousy of the other Gold Fish, but with the Silver Fish he fell in love at sight, and longed to be able to swim up to her. Whenever he tried to do this, something queer happened that made him lose his breath; and with a gasp he sank down into the ocean, so deep that he could see the Silver Fish no longer. Then, hoping she might descend to swim in his own water, he swam for miles and miles in search of her; but he never had the luck to find her.

One night as he was swimming about in very calm water, he saw overhead the motionless shadow of an enormous fish. One great long fin ran under its belly in the water, but all the rest of it was raised above the surface. The Goldfish knew every fish in the sea, but he had never before seen such a fish as this! It was bigger than the Whale, and as black as the ink of the Octopus. He swam all round it, touching it with his inquisitive little nose. At last he asked. 'What sort of fish are *you*?'

The big black shadow laughed. 'I am not a fish at all, I am a ship.'

'What are you doing here if you are not a fish?'

'Just at present I am doing nothing, for I am becalmed. But when the wind blows I shall go on sailing round the world.'

'What is the world?'

'All that you see and more.'

'Am I in the world, then?' asked the Goldfish.

'Certainly you are.'

The Goldfish gave a little jump of delight. 'Good news! Good news!' he cried.

A passing Porpoise paused to ask, 'What are you shouting for?'

'Because I am in the world!'

'Who says so?'

'The Ship-Fish!' said the Goldfish.

'Pooh!' said the Porpoise. 'Let him prove it!' and passed on.

The Goldfish stopped jumping, because his joy had been damped by doubt. 'How can the world be more than I can see?' he asked the Ship. 'If I am really in the world I ought to be able to see it *all*—or how can I be sure?'

'You must take my word for it,' said the Ship. 'A tiny fellow like you can never hope to see more than a scrap of the world. The world has a rim you can never see over; the world has foreign lands full of wonders that you can never look upon; the world is as round as an orange, but you will never see how round the world is.'

Then the ship went on to tell of the parts of the world that lay beyond the rim of things, of men and women and children, of flowers and trees, of birds with eyes in their tails, blue, gold, and green, of white and black elephants, and temples hung with tinkling bells. The Goldfish wept with longing because he could never see over the rim of things, because he could not see how round the world was, because he could not behold all at once all the wonders that were in the world.

How the Ship laughed at him! 'My little friend,' said he, 'if you were the Moon yonder, why, if you were the Sun himself, you could only see one half of these things at a time.'

'Who is the Moon yonder?' asked the Goldfish.

'Who else but that silver slip of light up in the sky?'

'Is that the sky?' said the Goldfish. 'I thought it was another sea. And is that the Moon? I thought she was a Silver Fish. But who then is the Sun?'

'The Sun is the round gold ball that rolls through the sky by day,' said the Ship. 'They say he is her lover, and gives her his light.'

'But I will give her the world!' cried the Goldfish. And he leaped with all his tiny might into the air, but he could not reach the Moon, and fell gasping into the sea. There he let himself sink like a little gold stone to the bottom of the ocean, where he lay for a week weeping his heart out. For the things the Ship had told him were more than he could understand; but they swelled him with great longings—longings to possess the Silver Moon, to be a mightier fish than the Sun, and to see the whole of the world from top to bottom and from side to side, with all the wonders within and beyond it.

Now it happened that King Neptune, who ruled the land under the waves, was strolling through a grove of white and scarlet coral, when he heard a chuckle that was something between a panting and a puffing; and peering through the branches of the coral-trees he beheld a plump Porpoise bursting its sleek sides with laughter. Not far off lay the Goldfish, swimming in tears.

King Neptune, like a good father, preferred to share in all the joys and sorrows of his children, so he stopped to ask the Porpoise. 'What tickles you so?'

'Ho! ho! ho!' puffed the Porpoise. 'I am tickled by the grief of the Goldfish there.'

'Has the Goldfish a grief?' asked King Neptune.

'He has indeed! For seven days and nights he has wept because, ho! ho! ho! because he cannot marry the Moon, surpass the Sun, and possess the world!'

'And you,' said King Neptune, 'have you never wept for these things?'

'Not I!' puffed the Porpoise. 'What! Weep for the Sun and the Moon that are nothing but two blobs in the distance? Weep for the world that no one can behold? No, Father! When my dinner is in the distance, I'll weep for *that*; and when I see death coming, I'll weep for *that*; but for the rest, I say pooh!'

'Well, it takes all sorts of fish to make a sea,' said King Neptune, and stooping down he picked up the Goldfish and admonished it with his finger.

'Come, child,' said he, 'tears may be the beginning, but they should not be the end of things. Tears will get you nowhere. Do you really wish to marry the Moon, surpass the Sun, and possess the world?'

'I do, Father, I do!' quivered the Goldfish.

'Then since there is no help for it, you must get caught in the net—do you see it floating yonder in the water? Are you afraid of it?'

'Not if it will bring me all I long for,' said the Goldfish bravely.

'Risk all, and you will get your desires,' promised King Neptune. He let the Goldfish dart through his fingers, and saw him swim boldly to the net which was waiting to catch what it could. As the meshes closed upon him, King Neptune stretched out his hand, and slipped a second fish inside it; and then, stroking his green beard, he continued his stroll among his big and little children.

And what happened to the Goldfish?

He was drawn up into the Fisherman's boat that lay in wait above the net; and in the same cast a Silver Fish was taken, a lovely creature with a round body and silky fins like films of moonlit cloud. 'There's a pretty pair!' thought the Fisherman, and he carried them home to please his little daughter. And to make her pleasure more complete, he first bought a globe of glass, and sprinkled sand and shells and tiny pebbles at the bottom, and set among them a sprig of coral and a strand of seaweed. Then he filled the globe with water, dropped in the Gold and Silver Fishes, and put the little glass world on a table in his cottage window.

The Goldfish, dazed with joy, swam towards the Silver Fish, crying, 'You are the Moon come out of the sky! Oh see, how round the world is!'

And he looked through one side of the globe, and saw flowers and trees in the garden; and he looked through another side of the globe, and saw on the mantelpiece black and white elephants of ebony and ivory, that the Fisherman had brought from foreign parts; and through another side of the globe he saw on the wall a fan of peacock's feathers, with eyes of gold and blue and green; and through the fourth side, on a bracket, he saw a little Chinese temple hung with bells. And he looked at the bottom of the globe, and saw his own familiar world of coral, sand, and shells. And he looked at the top of the globe, and saw a man, a woman, and a child smiling down at him over the rim.

And he gave a little jump of joy, and cried to his Silver Bride:

'Oh Moonfish, I am greater than the Sun! For I give you, not half, but the whole of the world, the top and the bottom and all the way round, with all the wonders that are in it and beyond it!'

And King Neptune under the sea, who had ears for all that passed, laughed in his beard and said:

'It was a shame ever to let such a tiny fellow loose in the vast ocean. He needed a world more suited to his size.'

And ever since then, the world of the Goldfish has been a globe of glass.

THE CLUMBER PUP

I

WHEN Joe Jolly's father died, his fortunes were almost at their lowest ebb. Not quite, for he had at least the chair he sat in. But the hut the Jollys lived in was not theirs; it was lent them, as part wages, by the Lord of the Manor whose wood John Jolly chopped. For the rest, he got three shillings every Friday. Even the axe he chopped with was not Mr Jolly's own.

Joe grew up in the woods with little education beyond the use of his hands, and a love of animals; and much in the same way he loved his father, whom he often helped with the chopping, though neither the Lord of the Manor nor his Steward knew of his existence.

Old Mr Jolly was taken ill of a Thursday evening, when last week's wages were spent. He sat down in his old chair and said, 'Joe, I see a better world ahead of me.' Next day he couldn't get up, so Joe did a man's day's work, and at the end of it went to the Steward for his father's shillings. The Steward asked, 'Who may you be?' and Joe replied, 'John Jolly's son.'

'And why doesn't John Jolly come himself?'

'He's sick.'

'And who'll do his work till he's well?'

'I will,' said Joe.

The Steward counted out the three shillings, and left it at that. In the back of his mind was the thought that if, by the grace of God, John Jolly died, he might put in his place an old uncle of his wife's who was considered by the Steward both a nuisance and an expense, as he was obliged to keep him under his own roof. But John Jolly lasted a month, during which time Joe tended him like a woman, and did all his work besides. As three shillings did not go far, with sickness in the house, he sold up their sticks, bit by bit, to get his father extra little comforts. By the fourth Thursday everything was sold but the chair and his mother's brass wedding-ring, John Jolly lay at peace under the grass, and Joe, for the first time in his life, considered his future.

He did not consider it for long; here he was, at the age of eighteen, a fine upstanding young chap, as limber as a squirrel, with a skin like the red tan on a pine tree, and no trade to his hands except the power to chop wood. So he decided to put in for his father's job.

When he went as usual on the Friday evening for his pay, he said to the Steward, 'Dad'll not be cutting timber for you any more.'

'How's that?' asked the Steward, hoping for the best.

'He's gone to a better world,' explained Joe.

'Ah!' said the Steward. 'Then the post of Lord's Woodcutter falls vacant after fifty years.'

'I'd like to put in for it,' said Joe.

But the Steward's chance to rid himself of his uncle had come; so he pursed his lips, scratched his nose, shook his head, and said, 'It wants a man of experience.' Then he counted out three shillings, wished Joe well, and sent him away.

Joe was not one for arguing; he knew he was experienced by craft, but not by years, and if the Steward thought one way, it was no manner of use his thinking another. He went back to the hut, looked at his father's chair, and thought, Well, I can't take it with me, and I don't want to sell it, and I'd never chop it up for firewood, and the next woodcutter will want something to sit on, and over and above that it'll like to stay where it has always been, as much as I should do. But it can't be helped, goodbye to you, old chair! And so, with three shillings and a brass ring in his pocket, Joe left the only home that he had ever known.

II

It was quite a new experience for Joe to be walking along a highroad many miles from his dwelling. Loving his wood better than most things, he had seldom seen reason to go out of it; but within forty hours of his father's death he was strolling through the world, with a bright eye and a quick ear for anything he might see and hear. Not minding which way he turned, he told himself to follow the first sound he heard. He had no sooner cocked his ear than he heard, very faint and distant, the familiar tapping of the axe-stroke on the tree. It was so far away that it might have come from another world. However, Joe heard it clear enough, and let it lead him on his way.

About noontime on the Saturday he heard a sound far more disturbing, the whining of a dog in distress. Joe quickened his pace, and turning the end of a lane he found himself in view of a village pond. A group of youths stood around it, one of whom had a puppy in his hands, which he was trying to hold under water; but the puppy's mother, a beautiful Clumber spaniel, was whining and worrying him so that half his attention had to be given to kicking her off, while the rest of the youths looked on, taking neither side, amused by the contest between the boy and the dog. As Joe appeared on the scene, the puppy-drowner lost patience, and, with a final kick at the spaniel, was about to toss the puppy into the middle of the pond. Before he could do so, Joe caught his arm, and said, 'None o' that!'

The youth turned on him roughly, but seeing somebody both taller and stronger than himself, instead of looking fierce looked sulky, and said:

'Why not? Puppies were born to be drowned, weren't they?'

'Not where I am,' said Joe, 'and you shan't drown this one.'

'Will you buy it?' asked the youth.

'What do you want for it?' asked Joe.

'What have you got?' asked the youth.

'Three shillings,' said Joe.

'Agreed!' said the youth. He handed the Clumber pup to Joe, snatched the three shillings, and ran off, followed by the other lads, who were shouting with laughter, he who had taken the money laughing louder than any. The spaniel stood on her hind legs, placed her forepaws against Joe's chest, and licked the hands that held her pup so gently.

Joe looked into her melting brown eyes and said, 'I'll see to your baby, lass; run you after your master.'

One of the boys then bawled over his shoulder, 'He's not her master! 'Tis a strange dog he found with the pup on his father's straw rick this morning!' And with a last guffaw of triumph over the simpleton who had parted with his money for nothing, they scampered out of sight.

'Well,' said Joe, 'it's no such bad bargain that's got me a fine little pup and a beautiful bitch to boot. So now you can both join my fortunes, mother and child together.'

He cuddled the pup inside his jacket, and as it settled there he knew, with a pang of joy, that this dog was *his* dog as no other ever could be again. He resumed his road with an empty pocket, and the Clumber spaniel running at his heels.

III

As Joe had no money, he had to walk hungry for the best part of the day. Towards evening, when the tapping of the distant axe which had never ceased to call him had become very near, he came to a wood. It was the first he had struck since leaving his own green forest, and he entered its shade with delight, feeling himself at home again. He had not been walking long when he heard the sound of mewing, a mew as tiny as the squeak of his pup. Following the sound, he soon found a scrap of a kitten, as gold as sunlight dappling a running stream, with eyes as clear as swung honey. It trembled on its four tottering legs, and was evidently pleased when Joe stooped and picked it up; he could almost hide it from sight by shutting his big fingers over its morsel of a body, soft as down. It was very cold, so he buttoned it under his jacket alongside the pup, where it lay purring with bliss.

The night was advancing; and now the sound of the axe hewing timber, which to Joe was better than music, was within a hundred yards of him. He stood still to listen to it for sheer pleasure. All of a sudden came the crash of a tree, followed by a groan. Now he stood still no longer, but hastened to the scene of the accident. Under the fallen tree a man lay pinned, an old man in shape so like his father that in the dusk Joe almost took him for John Jolly himself. But how could that be? Running to him, he saw that this old woodcutter merely resembled his father as one old man will resemble another, when they are much of a size, and have followed the same calling for a lifetime.

'Are you hurt badly?' asked Joe.

'I can't rightly tell till I'm unpinned,' said the old man. A great limb of the tree lay across the woodcutter's right arm. Joe found the old man's axe, and chopped him free. Then he felt the limb tenderly and skilfully, and found that it was broken; but he had too often set the broken legs and wings of hares and jays not to know what to do. In a few minutes he had made the old man comfortable, and lifting him from the ground asked where he might take him.

'My hut's not fifty steps from here,' said the old man. Under his direction, Joe bore him there. It was just such a dwelling as he was used to, but rather better furnished. A narrow bed with a gay coverlet stood in one corner, and on this Joe laid the old man down. Then, without asking questions, he set about brightening the fire, boiling the kettle, and preparing the old man's supper. He looked in the cupboard and on the shelf for food and crocks, and in no time had the teapot steaming, and the bread-and-dripping spread, while the old man lay and watched him with eyes as shrewd as a weasel's.

As soon as the sick man's meal was ready, Joe undid his jacket and took out the pup and the kitten. The Clumber spaniel settled herself by the hearth and suckled them both; and her eyes, following Joe's actions, were as bright as those of the old man.

Then Joe said, 'Where might I find water and scraps for the bitch?'

'There's a pump outside, and a bone on the shelf,' said the old man.

Joe found the bone, and fetched a pan of water, and set them beside the spaniel.

'Now,' said the old man, 'fetch cup and plate for yourself.'

This Joe did, and ate his bread and drank his tea with the relish of hunger.

'If you care to stretch out on the hearth,' said the old man, 'you're welcome to sleep here; further, if you will stay till my arm is mended, you can take care of my job for me.'

'What is your job?' asked Joe.

'That of King's Woodcutter.'

'And how do you know I'm fit for it?'

'Didn't I see you handle the axe, when you chopped me free?' said the old man. 'I've no doubt as to your fitness. But in the morning you must go and tell the King you are doing my work.'

IV

Joe slept sound on the hearth-rug, and was up betimes. He saw to the old man, the animals, and the hut; and, when all was in order, asked his way to the King's palace. The old man told him it was in the heart of the city, which lay three miles due north; and he advised Joe to take with him the royal axe, with the crown burned into the handle, as a sign that his tale was true. So Joe set out upon this new adventure.

At the end of the first mile, hearing a tiny mewing, he looked behind him and saw that the honey-coloured kitten had followed him; not wishing to go back, he buttoned the pretty creature under his jacket again, and pursued his way. The end of the second mile brought him out of the forest, and at the end of the third he saw for the first time the capital city of the country he lived in. As he drew near, amazed at the sight of so many houses and shops and churches, towers, temples, and turrets, domes, spires, and weathercocks, he saw that the whole place was in a commotion. The streets were packed with people running about, or stooping and crawling, as they poked their noses into every corner, grating, and cranny. At the gates a tall sentinel barred Joe's way, demanding, 'What is your business?'

'Does that matter?' asked Joe.

'Not at all,' said the sentinel, 'for whatever it may be I have strict orders to let nobody in and nobody out.'

'Very well,' said Joe, supposing that this was the way it was in cities; whereas in the woods you came and went as you pleased. But as he turned to go the sentinel caught him by the shoulder and cried, 'How come you to be handling the royal axe?'

Joe told his story briefly, and the sentinel opened the gates. 'Your business is the King's business,' he said, 'therefore you *must* come in. If anybody questions you, show him the axe, and it will be as good as a passport.'

Nobody questioned Joe's right to be in the city, however, all being much too concerned with their peeping and poking and prying; the nearer Joe approached to the palace, the greater became the fuss; and on arrival he found the palace in such a state of confusion, with nobles and pages running hither and thither and wringing their hands in despair, that once more he passed unheeded through the courtyards and corridors, until he reached the throne-room itself. Here he found nobody at all but a lovely girl in tears. In her white dress, with her lemon-coloured hair, she reminded Joe of his Clumber pup. He could not bear to see her in trouble, so he approached her and said, 'If it's a hurt, show me, and perhaps I can heal it.'

The girl checked her sobs enough to answer, 'It is a very bad hurt indeed.'

'Whereabouts?' asked Joe.

'In my heart,' said she.

'That's a hard place,' said Joe. 'How did it happen?'

'I have lost my kitten,' said the girl, and began to cry again.

'I will give you my kitten in its place,' said Joe.

'I only want *my* kitten.'

'This is a very pretty kitten, picked up in the woods overnight,' said Joe. 'She's marked like the flower in oak, and her eyes are as gold as honey.' And he took it out of his jacket.

'That *is* my kitten!' cried the girl. She stopped crying again, and caught the little ball of gold fluff from his hands, and kissed it many times. Then she ran and pulled a golden chain that rang a golden bell hanging in the middle of the hall. Instantly the room appeared to overflow with people, as everyone, from the kitchen boy to the King, came running to see what had happened. For the bell was only rung on great occasions.

The Princess, for it was no other, stood up on the throne, holding up her kitten in full view, and cried, 'This boy has found my Honey!' The joy was overwhelming; the news ran like wildfire from the throne-room to the courtyard, and from the courtyard to the streets. In five minutes, everybody had returned to his business, the city gates were opened, and the King was asking Joe Jolly what he would like for a reward.

Joe would rather have liked to ask for the Princess, for she would have matched so nicely with his Clumber pup; her hair was just the colour of his ears, and her soft brown eyes were looking at him as meltingly as any spaniel's. But of course she was out of the question, so he answered, 'I should like the Royal Woodman's job, till the Royal Woodman is whole again.'

'That won't be in *your* lifetime,' said the King; a remark that puzzled Joe greatly, but he was too diffident to ask the King what he meant, for Kings, he

supposed, had the right to talk as they pleased, even in riddles.

'Hand me that axe,' said the King, 'which I see is the royal axe, and kneel down on both knees and bow your head.'

Joe hoped the King was not going to cut his head off, for any reason or none; but he obeyed, knelt down, and felt himself touched between the shoulder-blades with the axe head. 'Rise, Royal Woodman!' commanded the King. 'Come once a month to the Forester's Lodge for orders, and let it be your first care to cut the choicest firing daily for the Princess's chamber.'

No order could have pleased Joe better; he pulled his forelock, with a smile at the Princess, but she had turned away, and with her nose in her kitten's fur was whispering things into its ear. So he pulled his forelock again to the King, returned on his traces, and found all in the hut as he had left it.

'Well?' asked the old man.

'Very well, indeed,' said Joe Jolly. 'The kitten was the kitten of the Princess, in consequence of which the

King has made me Royal Woodman till you are whole again.'

'Did he say so?' asked the old man, with a curious smile.

'It's how I understood it,' said Joe.

'Then so we will leave it,' said the old man. 'And since we are to bide together for a bit, you shall call me Daddy, for once I had a son who was a good son to me, and for his sake I like the ring of the word.'

V

Daddy took longer to heal than Joe would have supposed possible. Month after month went by, and the fracture in his arm would not set; moreover, he seemed to have been so shaken by his accident, that he never left his bed. Gradually Joe grew accustomed to stretching out on the hearth without thinking that it would soon be for the last time; the new job turned into an old one, and the days mounted until a year had passed. The Clumber pup was now a dog as beautiful as his mother, but Joe continued to think of him as the pup, if only to mark the difference between them. The old dog lay mostly indoors by the hearth, or out of doors in the sun; but the Clumber pup followed Joe daily to his work, and was the joy and delight of his heart. Since the day of his appointment Joe had stuck to the woods, and gone no nearer to the city than the Lodge of the King's Forester on the outskirts of the trees. He put in an appearance early in the morning on the first day of each month, and more often than not found the Forester chatting with a pretty chambermaid from the palace, whose name was Betty, and who evidently fancied a stroll in the morning dew before the duties of the day.

When she had gone, the Forester gave Joe his orders for the month; and wherever he might be cutting, he had each day to bind the special faggot of firing for the room of the Princess. He made the faggot of the sweetest smelling wood he could find, and with it he always bound up a little posy of whatever the season might offer. In spring there were the primroses and violets; in summer, harebells, wild rose, and honeysuckle; in autumn he found the brightest leaves and berries; and even winter had her aconites.

On Joe's nineteenth birthday, which fell on the First of June, he went as usual to the Forester's Lodge, and there found Betty in her striped silk frock, gabbling away a little faster than her habit.

'Yes,' she was saying, 'that's how it is, and no other! There's something she wants, and nobody knows what, for she won't say. Sometimes she mopes, and sometimes she sings, sometimes she pouts and sometimes smiles, as changeable as the quarters of the year, and she won't tell her father, she won't tell her mother, she won't tell her nanny, and she won't tell *me*! And the doctor says if she don't get it soon, whatever it may be, she'll fall into a decline and die of longing.'

'What's to be the end of it?' asked the Forester.

'Why, this; the King says that whoever can find out what the Princess is thinking, and give her what she wants, shall have whatever *he* wants, no matter whatso! On the last day of the month there's to be an Assembly at the palace, so that everybody can offer his opinion, and— Oh la! There's the eight o'clock bell ringing! Don't keep me gossiping any longer, or I'll be sure to be dismissed.'

The Forester kept her just long enough to give her a kiss, for which she boxed his ears, and then ran off as fast as her heels could carry her. The Forester laughed and said, 'That's something like a wench!' and turned to Joe and gave him his orders for the month. Joe went back, his head so full of them, except for one corner that was full of being sorry for the Princess, that for some time he did not miss his Clumber pup. But it was no longer gambolling about him, and even when he whistled did not come bounding and bouncing as usual; a thing any dog that loves his master must do when he hears the whistle, whether he wants to or not. So by then the pup must have got a long way off.

However, half through the morning he appeared, in the highest of spirits, where Joe was working; though when they got home that evening he would not touch his supper. This would have worried Joe, if the pup had not been so unusually boisterous.

That night Joe had a curious dream, as he lay stretched on the rug before the dying fire: one of those dreams we get when we are half awake, that seem to take place outside instead of inside us. In this dream, Joe saw, as plain as if he was waking, his Clumber pup lying nose to nose with the spaniel his mother, who lay with her head sunk flat on the floor between her two silky paws, and opened one beautiful brown eye to look at her child. And in his dream Joe seemed to hear how dogs make known their thoughts to each other, and the talk went this way between them. The spaniel said:

'What's the matter, son? Off your feed?'

'Not me, mother! I've had my fill today!'

'Where, then?'

'In the King's yard.'

'What were you doing in the King's yard?'

'Meeting a friend of mine.'

'What sort of a friend?'

'A cat.'

'Be ashamed of yourself!'

'Not me, mother! It was my foster-sister.'

'Oh, *that* cat.'

'Yes, the Princess's cat.'

'What is she like now?'

'Gold as honey.'

'Does she spit?'

'Yes, secrets.'

'What secrets?'

'She tells me what the Princess is thinking.'

'How does she know?'

'The Princess cuddles her into her neck, and tells her in her ear.'

'Whose neck and whose ear?'

'The Princess's neck and the cat's ear.'

'Well, and what is the Princess thinking?'

'She's thinking it's time she had a love-letter.'

'Oh,' said the spaniel, and suddenly went to sleep; and Joe's own sleep must have deepened, for he dreamed no more.

But in the morning he remembered his dream, and it seemed so real that he fell to puzzling. Was it a dream after all? His puzzle showed in his eyes, and Daddy from his couch asked, 'What's bothering you?'

'A dream I had,' said Joe. 'I don't know whether to act on it or not.'

'Would it be a good thing to act on it?' asked Daddy.

'It might save a damsel from a decline.'

'And would it be a bad thing to act on it?'

'Not that *I* can see,' said Joe.

'Then act on it,' said Daddy.

So before he went to work that morning, Joe sat down and wrote a love-letter. He was not very good at writing, so he did not make it a long one, and therefore made it as much to the point as he could.

He wrote:

'MY LOVE!

'I love you because you are lovely like my Pup.

'JOE JOLLY.'

It was rather straggly and blotted by the time he had folded it, but it was quite readable, which, after what is in it, is the best thing about a love-letter; so Joe, quite satisfied, took it with him to his work, and put it inside a bunch of pink campions which he tied to the Princess's faggot. Then he thought no more about the matter till the First of July, when, going to the Forester's, he found Betty taking her leave with these words:

'So that's the end of it, thanks be! For when the folk came yesterday to say in Assembly what they thought she wanted, the Princess just laughed at them all and said, "No need to guess, because I've got it!" But what it was she still wouldn't say; not that it matters, since now she's as gay as a lark, and the doctor comes no more.'

VI

Another year went by in peace and content. The work was good, the dogs thrived, the hut was comfortable, and there was always enough to eat; though, as Daddy still lay on the bed, Joe still lay on the floor. And on the First of June, his twentieth birthday, he went once more through the wood with the pup at his heels, to find Betty before him at the Forester's Lodge. Who wouldn't, thought Joe, be glad to be out at such an hour, with the birds singing in the leaves, and the dew on the flowers in the grass? But today Betty looked less glad than usual, as she gabbled her news.

'Yes!' she was saying. 'There we are, just where we were a year ago, and it's all to do again. And she's no more help now than she was then; there's only one thing she wants in the world, what, nobody knows! Though her father asks what, and her mother asks what, and her nanny asks what, and *I* ask what! The doctor comes daily to change her physic, all to no purpose, and he says if she doesn't get it soon she'll die of longing. So the last day of the month there's to be another Assembly, to say what the Princess wants, since she won't say herself, and he who gives it her shall have anything he names, no matter whatso, and— Bless me, Forester, there's the eight o'clock bell! Out upon you, keeping me here a-talking and a-talking when it's time for the Princess's chocolate!'

Off she ran, but not before the Forester had given her a hearty kiss, for which she smacked his face; and he only wagged his head saying, 'An excellent wench!' Joe took his orders, and went away very much troubled. If the Princess wanted a second love-letter, he couldn't think of anything else to say; yet the first one had plainly ceased to serve her purpose. In his bother, he failed once more to observe the absence of the Clumber pup. Later in the day he turned up, barking and jumping and wagging his tail, so that Joe had to throw down his axe and have a rough and tumble before he would be satisfied. Yet that night he never touched his supper at all, a thing that had only happened once before, just a twelve-month since, now Joe came to think of it. It brought it all back so strong to him, that as he lay on the mat before the fire and dozed off into his first sleep, he even dreamed that he heard the spaniel and her pup talking as they had talked a year ago.

'Now, pup, what's wrong that you can't gnaw your bone? Don't tell me you've distemper!'

'Not me, mother! I'm fed full of King's meat.'

'Where did you get King's meat?'

'In the King's kitchen.'

'What were you doing in the King's kitchen, then?'

'Calling on a friend.'

'What friend, indeed?'

'A cat.'

'Go drown yourself!'

'What for, mother? It was your foster-daughter.'

'Ah, *that* one! How's she grown?'

'Gold as honey.'

'But spits, no doubt?'

'Yes, secrets.'

'Still what the Princess is thinking?'

'Still. The Princess tells her what she tells no other.'

'And what's she thinking now?'

'That it is time she had a ring.'

'Oh,' said the spaniel. Her ear flopped over her eye, and she was asleep; and Joe's dream passed out of being.

But in the morning it revived in his mind, as clear as if it had happened. And had it not? He could not decide; and Daddy from his bed asked, 'What's the puzzle!'

'A funny sort of dream I had last night. I don't know whether to do aught about it, or naught.'

'If you did aught, what then?'

'It might save a damsel's life.'

'And if naught?'

'She might die.'

'I say, do aught,' said Daddy.

So when he had bound the day's faggots for the Princess, Joe slipped his mother's brass wedding ring over the stems of a wild-rose posy, and tied it carefully among the branches. Then, having done his best, he dismissed it from his thoughts, until a month later he heard Betty chattering volubly on the Forester's doorstep:

'Yes, clouds will pass on the darkest day, and butter come after the longest churning, and yesterday at the Assembly, before anybody could so much as open his mouth, the Princess laughed as happy as a child, and said, "Don't put yourself to the trouble of guessing, for what I wanted I now have!" Never a word more, so we're still all at sea, but there, no matter; doctor's stopped coming, King and Queen stopped worrying, and the Princess goes singing all over the shop!'

VII

Alas! a year later, on Joe's twenty-first birthday, the chambermaid had her sorry tale to tell again. That morning, when he reached the Lodge, she was relating, full of woe:

'Eat she won't and sleep she won't! She's white as a new pillow-slip! She weeps in corners, and stares at the sky, and says "no thank you" to all our offers; but sits by the hour with her honey cat in her arms, while doctor tears his hair, her father is distracted, her mother is distraught, and her nanny says nothing but "Lawks-a-mussy me!" Even *I* can't get out of her what she wants. But this much I do know, if she doesn't get it soon, they'll be digging her green grave. The King has ordered another Assembly on the last day of the month, and whoever can give her what *she* wants may have whatever *he* wants, no matter whatso! Eight o'clock, eight o'clock, there goes eight o'clock, and me oughting to be at my work: give over gossiping, Forester, do!'

Away she started, but the Forester pulled her back to give her a kiss, for which she tugged his hair and ran; and he nodded his head remarking, 'What a wench!' and gave Joe his orders. But the thought of the Princess's green grave was such a grief to Joe that he did not observe the absence of the Clumber pup till he was well at work. After a bit, the pup sneaked up, with his tail between his legs. Nothing Joe could do put him in spirits, and Joe being out of spirits himself it was not a happy day. They both went home depressed that night, and neither of them touched his supper. As Joe stretched out on the hearth, Daddy, who noticed everything, said, 'Off your feed?'

'Yes, somehow,' replied Joe; and fell into an uneasy sleep, in which he thought he heard the spaniel repeat the question to her son.

'Off your feed, pup? What's up? A canker in your ear?'

'Something like it, mother.'

'No doubt you've been overeating again at the palace.'

'Not a bone. Not a scrap. I just went there to see a friend.'

'Oh, you've a friend there?'

'A cat.'

'Give yourself a bad name, and hang yourself!'

'Why, mother? It was our honey cat.'

'Our honey cat! How is she?'

'Gold as honey.'

'Spits, though, I fear.'

'Only secrets.'

'Whose secrets?'

'The Princess's.'

'And what does the Princess want now?'

'She wants me.'

'You! What does she know of you?'

'The honey cat took me to her boudoir.'

'The minx! I disown her! You in a boudoir, a kennel dog like you!'

The spaniel put her paws over her eyes, and Joe heard no more talking in his fitful dreams.

But were they dreams, he asked himself in the morning, or had he been awake? Dream or no dream, he had a hole in his heart and Daddy could not but be aware of it.

'What is it, son?' he asked.

'I had a dream last night that's left me torn two ways.'

'If you went one way, what then?'

'There might be no need to dig a green grave.'

'And if you went the other?'

Joe fondled the Clumber pup's lemon ears, and said, 'That way might break my heart.'

'Should we dig *your* grave then?'

'I expect I'd get over it.'

'You'd not be the first,' said Daddy, 'to go through life with a mended heart; but once a grave is digged, it's digged.'

'All right,' said Joe.

He went out to his work, whistling to his pup to follow him, and when the day was done he made for the Princess a better faggot than he had ever made before, and tied his pup to it. The Clumber looked at him with mournful eyes, and tried to follow Joe home, dragging the faggot behind him. But Joe Jolly said, 'Stay there!' and went away quickly through the forest.

VIII

That was the saddest month Joe ever lived through. He tried to be cheerful for Daddy's sake and the spaniel's, but Daddy himself was extra quiet, the spaniel moped for her pup, and Joe had to bear his own broken heart. On the last day of the month, when June was at her zenith, and the forest was rich with sunshine, Daddy said, 'Joe, a man can't work all the year round all his lifetime. Take a holiday!'

'What would I do with it?' asked Joe.

'Go to the city and see the sights.'

Then it occurred to Joe that among the sights of the city was his own sweet pup. The mere thought of looking into his brown eyes and hearing his gay excited bark again made Joe's heart as light as a feather. He decided to follow Daddy's advice; his work was well in hand, and he could spare the day.

So off he set, and once out of the forest was amazed at the crowds on the road, until he remembered that this was the day of the Assembly. He allowed himself to be swept along on the stream towards the palace; for everybody had a right there on this day, and there, if anywhere, he would see his pup. It was with an eager heart he passed, for the second time, under the royal gateway, and entered the throne-room with the rest of the crowd.

The court was all assembled; from the middle of the crush, Joe could just manage to see the heads of the King and Queen, and the tops of the soldiers' pikes. A trumpet sounded, and a herald cried for silence. When this was obtained, he shouted:

'If any man present knows what the Princess wants, let him say so!'

But before a word could be spoken, the voice of the Princess called out, as gay as sunshine in the leaves, 'There is no need, for what I want I have!'

'What is it?' asked the King.

'Who gave it to you?' asked the Queen.

'I will neither say what it is nor who gave it to me,' said the Princess. 'Let everybody go.'

The herald blew his trumpet and dismissed the crowd. As it dispersed, Joe was left standing in the middle of the floor, in view of the great double throne, with the Princess seated at the King's feet, the honey cat in her arms, and crouched against her knee the Clumber pup. Suddenly there was a yelp of joy, the pup leapt into the air, bounded across the floor, placed his gleaming paws on Joe's two shoulders, and licked his face, whining and barking as though his heart would burst. Joe hugged him, and wept.

Then what a commotion in the court! Everybody asked, 'What is it? Who is it? What is happening?' The Princess rose, looking over the head of her honey cat, half smiling and half crying, and the King demanded, 'Who are you?'

'I'm your Royal Woodman,' said Joe.

'Why, so I remember! But the dog goes to you as to his master.'

'He was his master,' said the Princess, 'but now I am. This boy gave him to me, because what I wanted was the Clumber pup.'

'Then I can at last make good my word!' said the King. He beckoned Joe nearer. 'What do you want, Woodman? Name it, and it is yours.'

The Princess looked at Joe, and he looked at the Princess, with her white dress and her lemon-coloured locks. But he knew he must not ask for what he wanted most. So he put it out of his mind, and said, 'I would be glad of an extra mattress, so that I could lie on it instead of on the floor.'

'You shall have the best in the kingdom,' said the King.

But the Princess cried quickly, 'He must have something besides, for last year he also gave me what I wanted!' And she held up the old brass wedding-ring.

The King, being as good as his word, turned again to Joe, and asked, 'What else do you want?'

Joe clasped the Clumber pup to his heart, but of course he could not ask for it, for the Princess would die of longing if he took his dog away. So he put the thought from him, and said, 'When I came to this place, I left behind me, in my dwelling far away, my father's old chair. I should like to have that chair to sit in of a night, if it was doing nobody a bad turn.'

The King smiled graciously, and said, 'The chair shall be brought to you this very night, and in its place we will leave the best chair in the kingdom.'

He made a sign that the audience was ended, but the Princess cried still quicker than before, 'No, father! He must ask for a third thing, because two years ago he gave me this.' And she pulled out of her dress the old blotted love-letter, which was now older and more blotted than ever. The King took it from her, opened it curiously, and read aloud for all the court to hear:

'MY LOVE!

'I love you because you are lovely like my Pup.

'JOE JOLLY.'

The Princess hid her face in her honey cat.

'Are you Joe Jolly!' asked the King.

'Yes, sir,' said Joe.

'Did you write this?'

'Yes, sir.'

'And is it true?'

Joe looked from his white pup, with its lemon head, to the white-robed Princess with her lemon hair, and said for the third time, 'Yes, sir.'

'Then,' said the King, 'you must ask for the thing you want most in the world.'

Joe looked longingly at the Clumber pup, and kissed it hard between the eyes. Then he looked at the Princess, but she wouldn't look at him. He had to say something, and at last said slowly, 'As I can't have my pup, I'll have the honey cat.'

'Oh!' cried the Princess quickly. 'You can't have my cat without me!'

'Then,' said Joe, quicker still, 'you can't have my dog without me!'

'So let it be!' said the King. 'One half of the year you shall live in the Woodman's hut, and the other half in the palace; and wherever you live, the dog and the cat must live with you.'

That very evening Joe Jolly took his bride back to the hut, the honey cat purring in her arms like an aeroplane, and the Clumber pup leaping round them, being a happy nuisance. A bright fire burned on the hearth, supper was spread on the table, a soft mattress lay on the bed, and by the fire stood old John Jolly's armchair. But the Clumber spaniel had disappeared for ever, and Daddy was gone too. When Joe came to enquire about him, he was told that the old Royal Woodman had died a month before Joe Jolly had come that way, and that the post had been left vacant till the right man appeared to fill it.

THE Queen had a Pleasure Island, a little out to sea. When she wanted to make merry, she sailed there from her palace on the mainland, in a gilded barque, with silk flags flying. Her Court accompanied her, there were musicians on deck too, and she came to her Pleasure Island amid flowers and music. There she spent her days picnicking and dancing under the trees. Everything that could make her island rich and prosperous was brought there in abundance from the mainland.

Further out to sea lay a poor fishing-island. Here there was no abundance, and life was a hard battle. It was barren ground, stony or marshy, where grass scarcely grew, no trees or shrubs, and no flowers. Yes, there was just one flower, a small white rose-bush which belonged to little Lois. Her father's hut lay in the lee of the church that stood in the middle of the stony isle. He had scraped together a little soil, and the day he was married he brought the rose-tree over from the mainland, and set it by his door. His young bride tended it with so much care that it could not help growing; and when she died, Lois, who had known the rose as long as she had known her mother, tended it as her mother had done. It did not grow very big, its flowers were few, and sometimes bitten by the salt wind, but it was the only flower on the island, and the islanders were proud of it. Lois took care of it, but it seemed to belong to them all; it was the Island Flower.

Dangerous rocks surrounded the Poor Island, and its position exposed it to the roughest storms. Sometimes for days together the boats dared not put out from it, and those on the mainland could not approach it. The islanders were too poor to keep much store of food by them, nor could they grow it; so when the fishing-boats could not put out, the hard times were still harder. In fair weather the men lost no opportunity of getting fish. Most of it the women salted down for their own use; the rest they took to the mainland to sell for a little money, and they came back with flour and salt and materials to mend their nets with. But the men, who shared in common the few boats on which their trade depended, could hardly spare time to take their wives over and back, so the women waited till the tide went out. For there was in those parts an unusual tide, which once a month, at the full moon, receded far back into the ocean, leaving bare all the sand between the mainland and the island. The sea-bed lay exposed for a long time, long enough for the women to hurry over the sand with their creels of fish, and sell them to the merchants on the beach, and buy the few things that they needed most. Then the women trooped back across the patches of rock and stretches of ribbed sand, reaching the Poor Island just before the tide flowed in and cut them off. Sometimes they had to hurry, and had not time to complete their purchases, for they dared not be caught in the mouth of the rolling tide.

One evening, when the tide was out, the Queen looked from her Pleasure Island, and saw the band of women hurrying home. She had hardly noticed or thought of them before, but tonight the sight of them struck her heart. On the bare sand, where small pools gleamed with colours of the sunset, her own little isle lay like a glowing jewel; her summer palace, her gardens, fountains, and pavilions shone in the sun, and she herself, in her silk and silver gown, was like a Queen of Fairyland. While yonder, over the waste, the bare-legged women in their faded gowns, with their baskets on their backs, trudged to the Poor Island, which lay like a stone in the distance; not like a precious stone, but a common pebble. Yet perhaps, thought the Queen, there was something precious on it. How sorrowful, how sorrowful to live on the Poor Island! she thought. And suddenly she put her hand to her heart and sighed; for Queens have sorrows too, and perhaps even the poor folk had none greater than hers.

She looked across, and wondered; and little Lois, standing far away on the Poor Island, looked across and wondered too. Even at that distance she could see the Pleasure Island like a jewel, she could see the small bright spires and domes and towers of the palace bathed in light, and on the breeze that blew towards her she could hear faint strains of music, and even smell sweet flowers. How lovely, how lovely it must be to live on the Pleasure Island, thought Lois. And suddenly she stooped to smell her rose, for even the Queen, she thought, had no sweeter flower than this.

The Queen sent for her Chamberlain and said, 'I wish to go and visit the Poor Island.'

'That will be a new diversion for Your Majesty,' said the Chamberlain. 'When will you go?'

'The day after tomorrow,' said the Queen.

Next day the Chamberlain sent word to the Poor Island that the Queen was coming. She had not intended him to do this, but he thought it fitting that the Islanders should have a chance to prepare for the honour that was to be bestowed upon them. An honour indeed they held it. Such a thing had never happened before. The Queen herself was coming! How could they welcome her? Where could they receive her?

'We will receive her in the church,' said the Pastor.

And how could they entertain her? Should not the church be adorned for the Queen? The men and women met together to consult. They had nothing with which to adorn the church. There was the rose-bush, the Island Flower with its white blooms, but could they use that? No, said the father of Lois, if we do so we shall have nothing to show the Queen when she asks us, 'And what is the most beautiful thing on your Island?' But now we can all take her to see the rose bush, and that will please her.

Little Lois was abed when the consultation was held. Her thoughts were full of the morrow and the coming of the Queen.

The day dawned, and the people gathered on the beach. The Pastor was with them, but Lois stayed behind to wipe the steps of the church porch, for it had rained in the night, and the step was spattered with mud. Then she started to run after the others, fearing she would be late, and as she did so—splash! she was ankle-deep in a big puddle right in the middle of the path. She looked with dismay at her wet feet, not that she cared for herself, but this was the way the Queen must walk, and the muddy place was too wide to step over. How could even the Poor Island let the Queen tread in the mud? And look, there was her golden barque coming over the water already. Something must be done quickly, for she would soon be here.

It was only after the Queen had come ashore that Lois joined the people on the beach. The Queen was talking to the Pastor, and kissing the children as he told her their names. Some of her courtiers were with her, and followed her up the rough road to the church. 'What a Godforsaken place!' Lois heard one say to another, when their fine shoes stumbled on the stones. Her heart beat painfully as they approached the marshy spot which she had done her best to mend. Would her means hold good? Yes, the Queen passed over dry-foot.

Inside the church the people stood up and sang. There was no organ, but the Pastor gave the note, and they lifted their voices in a song of praise. When the song was over, the Pastor spoke a few words of thanksgiving to God who had sent the Queen to see them. Lois, who could not take her eyes off the Queen's beautiful face, saw that her eyes were as wet as the wet place on the ground, from which Lois had tried to protect her. But who can protect even a Queen from her tears?

When the people had sung one more song, they all went outside again. The Queen then said, 'May I see your homes and how you live? Is living very hard here?'

The Pastor was about to answer, Yes, but the father of Lois stepped forward, and spoke with sturdy cheerfulness, 'Life is hard everywhere, I take it,' said he. 'But no life is so hard that it has not something beautiful to show. And so it is with us on the Poor Island.'

'What is your beautiful thing?' asked the Queen. 'May I see it?'

'Gladly, Madam. It is a rose-bush.'

The folk pressed round her eagerly explaining, 'Yes, madam, it is such a rose-bush as you never saw! White roses, madam! It is the Island's only flower. It is in bloom now, madam; there are nine roses on it, and three more coming. It is the Island's happiness, madam. Let us show it you, it is only a few steps just behind the church.'

The poor folk bore the Queen around the corner, the fine folk following after. And when the proud excited crowd had reached the place, and the father of Lois led the Queen to his door to show her the rose-bush, there was nothing to see. Only a little scattered earth, where the rose-bush had been pulled up by the roots. The poor folk gasped, the courtiers tittered a little; and round the corner Lois knelt and wept. She wept beside the green leaves and white blossoms of her rose-bush, where she had strewn them that the Queen might not wet her feet.

The Queen sailed away in her golden barque, the visit was over, and life went on in the Poor Island as before. The Queen had gone away full of resolves. She would give an organ to the church, she would have good roads made, she would rebuild the poor huts, cartloads of soil should be carried over, and everyone should have a little garden. She would do all these things. Before she could do any of them, she died.

News reached the Poor Island that she had died suddenly of a secret pain; when she was buried, they buried her with the tears that had filled her heart and eyes in the Poor Island. No one else had shed these tears, they were her own; no one else, when she was dead, was concerned with their cause. Surely the Queen's tears were dried now. What had moved her to them was forgotten, what she had meant to do was left undone. Life went on in the Poor Island as before; only, it had lost its flower.

Nobody blamed Lois for what she had done. She had done right, they said; any of them would have done the same. When the Queen came to visit them, they could not let her walk in the wet, and now she was dead they were glad she had not had to do so. But Lois mourned; she mourned for her rose and for the Queen. To comfort her, her father promised her another rose, cost what it might.

The full moon came round again. Once more the sea ran back into itself, once more the women went in long procession to the mainland over the bared sand. This time the father of Lois went too, a hard-saved coin in his pocket. They sold their fish and made their purchases; and Lois's father bought a tiny rose-bush, another white one, which might with time become the Island's joy. While he was making his bargain, one of the women ran and tapped him on the shoulder, 'Come quick!' she said. 'The sky looks threatening.'

He looked at the sky and answered, 'Yes, we must hasten. I only saw it look so once before, when the tide rushed in and took the women unawares.'

All the women were flocking over the sand. The fisherman hurried after them; their one thought was to reach the Poor Island before the sea rushed in.

On the Island there was nobody but one or two girls, the children, and the Pastor. The men were out at sea on the other side. Those on the Island saw the darkening sky, and felt the breath in the air that presaged danger. They came down to watch for the return of the women. Lois came too, straining her eyes for her father. Far off on the dark wet stretch of sand the children saw their mothers coming like little ants—they were already far from the mainland, and they still had far to come. Then, swiftly, what all feared most took place. The tide rushed in and surrounded the Poor Island; and it surged on, with waves that raced each other like wild horses, on towards the little band of people in the distance. There was no hope, no help, no refuge. Before they could turn back, the tide must take them.

The Pastor knelt upon the rocks and prayed, and all the children knelt with him, praying and crying. Only Lois stood upright among them, gazing. For the deserted Pleasure Island of the Queen was streaming with pale light, that no one except Lois seemed to see; and in the light the Queen herself was standing. Distant as she was, like someone in a dream, Lois saw her as plainly as she had seen her in the church, when the people were singing; but her eyes were wet no longer, and a lovely smile was on her face. She was smiling straight at Lois, and in her hands were nine white roses with their green leaves. And as the wild green waves with their white caps rolled to the very feet of the Poor Islanders, the Queen cast leaves and flowers upon the water. The tide rolled on, covering all the space between the islands. But oh wonder! It was covered not with the green-and-white sea, but with a heap of green leaves and white flowers. The tide of roses reached from isle to isle, and on it the women walked dry-foot to their children, and Lois's father came safe with her new tree.

The people talk of the miracle to this day. If you do not believe it, go to the Poor Island for yourself, where the rose is growing still.

At Linguaglossa in Sicily there once lived a little peasant girl called Marietta. It was a country full of fruit trees, peach, and apricot, and the bright persimmon; there were almond-trees whose delicate pink flower came first of all in the year, and olive-trees whose leaves were always green, and vineyards full of white and purple grapes in their season. The peasants' life depended on their fruit trees, the fruit trees were their fortune.

The fruit country lay spread out at the foot of a big mountain with a heart of fire, and a hole in the top. Sometimes the mountain was angry, and spat fire and red-hot stones into the air through the hole, and if it was *very* angry it went on for days pouring out a fiery river of molten stone, that flowed away over the top of the hole like porridge boiling over the pot;

and flames leaped into the air, hundreds of feet high; and glowing lumps of rock were hurled through the flames, to fall where they would. All the while the fiery river streamed down the mountain-side, destroying everything in its course, and making a desert of the pleasant land; and where it passed the air became so hot that no one could live or breathe in it. So the peasants who tilled the earth in the shadow of the mountain always lived in fear of the hour when the mountain should begin to mutter in its anger; and when it did, they prayed to Saint Anthony to appease the mountain's anger, and save their fruit trees from ruin.

The great anger did not come very often, and Marietta was seven years old before she heard the mountain mutter in one of its real tempers. There came a morning when Giacomo, her big brother, happened to be home for a day or so, and she was playing by herself on the plot of ground where her own little peach-tree grew. This plot lay in the furthest corner of her brother's lands, and of all the fruit trees in those parts it grew closest to the mountain. Giacomo had planted it for her the day she was born, and she loved it better than anything else in the world. She would talk to it as if it were a friend, and Giacomo would sometimes tease her, and ask her how her playfellow was today.

'The little girl is feeling very happy,' Marietta would answer, when the peach-tree was in blossom; or perhaps, when the tree had peaches on it, she might say, 'The little girl is very strong today'. But later on, when the fruit was stripped and eaten, Marietta sometimes answered, 'The little girl has gone away, she won't come out and play.'

'What is she like, the little girl?' Giacomo would ask.

'So, *so* pretty; she laughs and sings, and dances all the time. She has a green dress and flowers on her head. She has gone to stay with the King of the Mountain, but she didn't want to go.'

Then Giacomo would laugh a little, and pull Marietta's black curls, but old Lucia the grandmother, who lived in the house and cooked, would shake her head at him and mumble, 'It may be so, it may be so, who knows?'

On this day when Giacomo was from home, while Marietta was picking flowers and chattering to her peach-tree, she felt a sort of tremble in the earth, and heard a sort of grumble in the air. It was no more than she had heard and felt at other times, and all she said to herself was, 'The King of the Mountain is angry about something'. But that sound brought men and women to a standstill at their work among the trees; and they gazed at the mountain with the fear in their hearts.

After a while they knew that the thing they most feared was upon them. It might last a long while or a short while, but the fiery river had begun to pour over the mountain-top, and presently it would reach the fruitful plain.

That evening old Lucia said to Marietta, 'Come.'

'Where are we going?' asked Marietta.

'To the village, to pray to Saint Anthony. Bring flowers with you.'

Marietta filled her little apron with the flowers she had gathered in the morning, and went with Lucia to the village. The peasants young and old were flocking there from all sides, and those who lived in the village had left their houses and were already in the church upon their knees. Nearly all had brought flowers, which they put at the feet of the figure of Saint Anthony.

Marietta, too, emptied her lapful before him, and then knelt down beside Lucia, and prayed.

'What shall I ask, Mamma Lucia?' she said.

'Ask that the fire may not descend upon us.'

So Marietta prayed as she was bid, until she grew tired of kneeling; then she got up and found some of the village children playing in the black shadows behind the tall pillars in the church. She played with them, and presently fell asleep for a while, and then woke up again, and saw more peasants coming into the church, peasants from the mountain-side, women in shawls, and men in old red cloaks lined with fur, bringing their children with them. Some had bundles of clothes and household goods, hastily got together before they fled from the fiery river which was descending on their homes.

All through the night the people stayed in the church, praying that the river might stop, or turn aside in its course, and in the early morning they went out and gazed towards the mountain. At the first glance they knew that their prayers had not availed, and that the fiery river was coming down on their lands. Already the air was scorching hot with its approach.

Old Lucia threw up her hands and wailed, and so did many others. Then the priest said, 'Have faith, my children!' and bade some of the men bring out the statue of Saint Anthony, and place it in the open air in the path of the fiery river. The men went into the church, and came out carrying the statue; and they bore it through the village, and set it on the road where the priest directed. The women and children followed with the flowers, and they heaped the flowers about the figure of the Saint, and gathered more to cover his feet.

Then in the clear dawn, with the hot breath of the mountain rolling towards them, the people all knelt down in the road, and the priest lifted his hands and prayed again to heaven to turn the course of the fire aside.

And still the fire streamed on.

At last the priest turned to the people and said with tears in his eyes, 'My children, a miracle may still happen, but I cannot let you stay here any longer. The danger is too great. You must leave your homes and your trees to heaven's mercy, and go.'

The peasants rose up full of sorrow. They went to their houses and got a few things to carry with them, and before they left, they went out into their orchards and kissed their fruit trees. Then in a great crowd they went out on the roads, and hurried away from the homes they never expected to see again. On every road was a stream of men flying from the stream of fire. Lucia and Marietta went with the rest.

Presently Lucia felt her dress tugged. 'Mamma Lucia! Mamma Lucia!' said Marietta.

The grandmother looked down. 'What is it, my little one?'

'Mamma Lucia, why did they kiss the trees?'

'To bless them, and save them, if it is God's will.'

'Mamma Lucia, I did not kiss my peach-tree.'

'The poor little peach-tree!' sighed old Lucia. 'It will be the first to go.'

'I must go back and kiss it, Mamma Lucia.'

'No, no, that is impossible now. It cannot be helped. Only feel, the air grows hotter. We must go as fast as we can.'

And old Lucia went as fast as she could, in the crowd that pressed about her—and in the press one little body at her side was like another little body, and she felt a child clinging to her skirts and thought no more about it. She only thought of the need to hurry on, until she heard her own name being called out loud along the road. 'Mamma Lucia! Mamma Lucia! Where are you? Are you there? Where is Mamma Lucia?'

'Here I am, here I am,' said the old woman, and 'Here she is!' cried a dozen voices, and many hands pushed her forward, till she was face to face with Giacomo, who on his way home had seen the great crowd coming towards him, and the fiery stream upon the mountain which would eat up his house and lands. But he was not thinking at that moment of his house, he was thinking of his little sister Marietta. When he saw Lucia his brow cleared, and he said, 'Heaven be praised! Where is the child?'

'Here she is,' said the old woman, and pulled forward the little one who clutched her skirts—and it was not Marietta; it was Stefano, the hunchback's child.

'Why, what is this?' exclaimed Lucia in bewilderment. 'Where is Marietta?' And she called Marietta's name, and the crowd called too, but in vain, Marietta was not there.

Suddenly Lucia threw up her hands and cried, 'I know! I know! The Saints have mercy! She has gone back to kiss her peach-tree.' The grandmother turned hurriedly and stumbled through the crowd, that made a way for her and Giacomo, whose heart was beating heavily with fear. Scarcely noticing the heat like a furnace into which they were hastening, the big man and the old woman went with all their speed along the road to the mountain. They passed the village, they passed the figure of Saint Anthony among his flowers, they passed many orchards and vineyards belonging to their neighbours, and at last they came to their own place at the mountain-foot. They did not stay to look inside the house; in spite of the heat they went across the lands to the far corner where Marietta's peach-tree grew.

And there lying under it they found her, her arm around it, her cheek pressed against it, her eyes fast closed. Beside her was a tiny image of Saint Anthony, which always stood in Mamma Lucia's room, and which Marietta had set in front of the tree, with a handful of flowers at his feet.

Giacomo stooped down over his little sister, and said, 'She is asleep. Her skin is cool.'

'Heaven be praised!' said Mamma Lucia. 'And the air is no hotter, too.'

They looked once more towards the mountain, and saw to their amazement that at the foot the fiery flood had turned aside, and after creeping a little way along the border of their lands, had ceased to flow.

'It is the miracle,' said old Lucia.

Marietta stirred, opened her eyes, and saw her big brother bending over her. She jumped up and flung her arms around his neck.

'Giacomo! Oh, how glad I am to see you! Giacomo, what do you think happened while you were away? The King of the Mountains got angry and sent down a river of fire, and I went to the church and gave flowers to Saint Anthony, and I was in the church all night, Giacomo, with the others! And in the morning we went out and put Saint Anthony on the road, and knelt down till it was too hot, and then everybody kissed the trees and ran away, but I forgot to kiss my peach-tree, Giacomo, so I came back and brought Saint Anthony to protect her, and then I kissed her and it was so hot I was frightened, but the little girl said, "Don't be afraid, Marietta, the King of the Mountains will go back if only I go back with him, and I *will* go back because *you* came back to kiss me, so go to sleep, go to sleep, Marietta, don't be afraid." So I did go to sleep, and where is the King of the Mountain?'

Giacomo said, 'He has gone back, Marietta,' and he hugged her close and looked at Lucia over her head. And the old woman looked at him and at Marietta, and at the peach-tree and the mountain, and she mumbled, 'It may be so, it may be so, who knows?'

I

As the young King of Workaday finished writing the last word of his poem, Selina the Housemaid knocked on the door.

'What is it, Selina?' called the King impatiently.

'Your Ministers want you,' said Selina.

'What for?' said the King.

'They didn't tell me,' said Selina.

'I'm busy writing,' said the King.

'At once, they said,' said Selina.

'Well, go and tell them—'

'I've got my stairs to do.'

The King groaned, put down his pen, and came out. As he went downstairs Selina said, 'While you're seeing the Ministers, I could do your room, I suppose.'

'Yes, but don't touch the desk, *please*. I always have to tell you.'

Selina only said, 'Oh, all right. Mind the stair-rods.'

'How can I? They aren't there.'

'That's why,' said Selina.

'Sometimes I think Selina has no sense,' said the young King to himself; and he wondered, as he often did, whether he oughtn't to give her notice. Then he remembered, as he always did, that she was a Waif and Stray, who had been found at the age of one month on the steps of the Orphanage, where they had brought her up and trained her for service. When she was fourteen, she had come to the palace with a tin box of clothes, and there she had been for the last five years, working her way up from the Scullery to the Best Bedrooms. If the King gave her notice she would never get another place, and would have to go back to the Orphanage for the rest of her life; so he gave her a cross look instead, and trod carefully down the stair-rod-less stair-carpet to the Stateroom.

The Kingdom of Workaday wanted a Queen, and his Ministers had come in a body to tell the young King so. And of course, said they, she must be a Princess.

'What Princesses are there?' asked the young King, whose name was John, because, as the old King his father said when he was born, as a name John had always worked well, and no nonsense about it. They did not believe in nonsense in Workaday, and they kept their noses so close to their jobs that they couldn't see anything beyond them. But they did their jobs very thoroughly; and it was part of the Ministers' job to see that their King married a Princess, and part of the King's job to marry her. John had been brought up to understand this, so he made no fuss when it came to the point, and just asked:

'What Princesses are there?'

The Prime Minister consulted his list.

'There is the Princess of Northmountains, the country which lies to the top of Workaday on the map. And there is the Princess of Southlands, which lies at the bottom. And there is the Princess of Eastmarshes, which lies on the right-hand side. Your Majesty might woo any of these.'

'And what about Westwoods, that lies on the left?' asked John. 'Is there no Princess of the West?'

The Ministers looked serious. 'We do not know, your Majesty, what lies in the West, for no one within man's memory has ever passed the fence that stands between us and the country beyond. For all we know, Westwoods is a desolate waste, inhabited by witches.'

'Perhaps it is a rich green land, peopled by lovely Princesses,' said the King. 'Tomorrow I will hunt Westwoods, and find out.'

'Sire! It is forbidden!' the Ministers cried in alarm.

'Forbidden!' repeated John thoughtfully; and then he remembered what he had forgotten since he grew up, how in his childhood he had been warned by his parents against ever venturing into Westwoods.

'Why?' he asked his mother.

'They are full of danger,' she had told him.

'What danger, Mother?'

'That I can't tell you, because I don't know,' said she.

'Then how do you know there *is* any danger, Mother?'

'Everyone knows it. Every mother in the land warns her child of it, as I am warning you. There is something very strange in Westwoods.'

'Perhaps it isn't dangerous, though,' said the Prince, as he then was; and the strange thing in Westwoods that nobody knew stayed in his thoughts, and he longed for it. So much, that one day he ran away and tried to get into the woods; but when he reached them he discovered a tall wooden fence, too high for a child to see over, and too close for a child to peep through. It hid the whole of that side of Westwoods which touched his father's kingdom. All along this fence, which looked as old as time, children were prying and peeping, stooping low, and standing on tiptoe, trying to find a crack, trying to be taller. The little Prince, too, stooped and peeped, and strained and peered. But all in vain—the fence was built too high and knit too close. He went back to the palace full of bitter disappointment, and sought his mother.

'Who put the fence round Westwoods, Mother?' he asked.

'Oh,' she cried in dismay, 'have you, too, been there? Nobody knows who put the fence up, or when. It is out of man's memory.'

'I want it pulled down,' said the Prince.

'It is there to protect you,' said she.

'Protect me from what?' asked the little Prince.

But as she did not know, she could not tell him; so she shook her head, and put her finger on her lips.

In spite of this protection of the fence, the mothers of Workaday had always warned their children of the dangers that lay beyond it; and the children had always run at once to try to find cracks to look through. No

Workaday child ever lost its wish to get into Westwoods until it grew up and got married and had a child of its own. And then it warned its own child of the dangers it had never seen.

It was no wonder, then, that when John declared he would go hunting in Westwoods, the Ministers were afraid for their children. They cried out again, 'It is forbidden!'

'So my mother told me when I was a boy,' said John. 'We will hunt Westwoods tomorrow.'

'Your Majesty! All the fathers and mothers in the land will rise against you if you pull down the fence.'

'We will jump over the fence,' said the young King, 'and we will hunt Westwoods tomorrow.'

He went to tell Selina to put out his things, and found her leaning on her broom over his desk, reading what he had been writing. 'Don't do that!' said the King sharply.

'Oh, all right,' said Selina. She moved off, and began dusting the mantelpiece.

The King waited for her to say something else, but as she didn't he had to. He said rather coldly, 'I'm going hunting tomorrow. I want you to put out my things.'

'What things?' asked Selina.

'My hunting things, of course,' said the King; and thought, She really is the stupidest girl I know.

'All right,' said Selina. 'So you're going hunting, then.'

'Didn't I *tell* you so?'

'Where are you hunting?'

'In Westwoods.'

'Never!' said Selina.

'I wish,' said John, in a great state of exasperation, 'you would understand that I mean what I say.'

Selina began to dust the desk, and a flick of her duster sent the King's writing on to the floor. The King picked it up angrily, hesitated, got rather pink, and at last said:

'So you read this, did you?'

'U'm-h'm!' assented Selina.

There was a rather long pause. 'Well?' said the King.

'It's a bit of poetry, isn't it?' asked Selina.

'Yes.'

'I thought it was,' said Selina. 'Well, I think your room's about done now.' And she took herself out of it.

The King felt so cross with her, that he crumpled his bit of poetry into a little ball, and threw it into the waste-paper basket, just to pay her out.

II

The morrow came, and the Hunt set forth, for Westwoods.

The eager young King rode first on his white horse, and his company of huntsmen and courtiers followed after. Presently the tall fence came in sight, but to the King it did not look so tall as it had done when he was a child. All along it children still crouched or stood in vain on tiptoe, trying to see through or over it.

'Stand aside, children!' cried the King, and put his horse at the fence. Over it went like a big white bird, and behind him clattered his courtiers. But not one followed where he had led the way. Some of them were fathers, who had warned their little ones of such dangers that now they were afraid of them themselves; and some of them were sons who, men though they were, had been warned anew that morning by their parents, when the word went round that the King was hunting in Westwoods. So one and all, fathers and sons, turned back their horses at the wooden fence; and only the King, being an orphan and a bachelor, took the leap and rode into the woods alone.

When he alighted on the other side, his first feeling was one of disappointment. His horse stood pastern-deep in withered leaves, and in front of him was a barrier of brushwood; dry twigs and branches, dead ferns and grass, all piled and mingled together, covered with white lichen and black rot. Caught in the barrier was a medley of all sorts of broken rubbish—torn pictures and broken dolls and tea-sets, rusty trumpets, old birds'-nests and faded wreaths of flowers, bits of ribbon in rags, glass marbles chipped and useless; books without covers, their pages scribbled over with pencil-marks; and battered paint-boxes, with few paints left in them, and those so cracked that they were past painting with. A thousand other things too, all as past use as one another. The King handled one or two—a humming-top with a broken winder, and the fragments of a kite without a tail. He tried to spin the top and fly the kite, but without success. Rather annoyed, and greatly puzzled, he rode through the barricade of rubbish to see what was on the other side.

It was nothing but a waste of flat grey sand, as flat as a plate, and like a desert in size. Flat as it was, he could not see the end of it, and though he rode across it for an hour he came to nothing different, near or far. Suddenly he was seized with fear of riding on for ever in this nothing, and looking behind him found that he could only just discern the barrier he had left, as faint as a shadow in the distance. Suppose he lost sight of that too! He might never find his way out of the waste again. In a panic he turned his horse's head, rode for the barrier as hard as he could, and in another hour had landed, with a sigh of relief, on the Workaday side of the fence.

The children plastered against it saw him coming, and shouted with glee.

'What did you see? What did you see?'

'Nothing but an old rubbish heap,' said John.

The children looked at him doubtfully.

'But what's in the woods, then?' asked one.

'There aren't any woods,' said the King. The children looked at him as though they did not believe him, so he rode to the palace where his Ministers hailed him with joy.

'Thank Heaven you are safe, sire!' they cried; and then, just like the children, they asked, 'What did you see?'

'Nothing and nobody,' answered John.

'Not a single Witch?'

'Nor a solitary Princess. So tomorrow I will go to Northmountains and begin my wooing.'

He went upstairs, and told Selina to pack his trunk.

'Where for?' asked Selina.

'Northmountains, to see the Princess,' said the King.

'You'll want your fur coat and your woolly gloves,' said Selina, and went to see about them. The

King thought his poem might come in useful too, but on looking in his waste-paper basket he found that Selina had emptied it. This made him so cross, that when she brought him his glass of hot milk the last thing, he wouldn't say 'Goodnight' to her.

III

When John arrived in Northmountains, he was surprised to find that nobody came out to meet him. Word had been sent in advance, and Kings' visits were not so frequent as to be taken for granted, thought John. It was very cool; it was more than cool, it was chilling. Some people were going about their business in the streets, and he saw others in the shops and houses as he passed, but nobody so much as glanced at him, or if they happened to, their expressions did not change. Not that they have any expression *to* change, thought John; I've never seen such stiff cold faces in my life. They sent a shiver through him. And so did the air, as still as frozen snow. It was not a very encouraging beginning.

However, the young King pushed on to the palace; which stood upon a glacier on a mountain-top, and was as bright as though it had been built of ice. It was a long and difficult climb for his horse, and by the time he reached the summit his hands were red and his nose was blue.

A tall and silent porter took his name at the door, and motioned John to follow him to the Throne-Room; John did so, feeling that he was not looking his best. The Throne-Room was hung in white, and felt exactly like a refrigerator; John looked for a fire, and saw a great fireplace, filled with blocks of ice. At the far end of the room the King of Northmountains sat on his throne, and his courtiers stood in rows as stiff as statues down the two sides. The women were dressed in white, the men in glassy armour, and what the King wore could not be seen for the great white beard which flowed like a cascade from his chin and cheeks, and hid the rest of him beneath it. At his feet sat the Princess of the North, completely covered with a snowy veil.

The Porter paused at the door, and whispered:

'King John of Workaday.'

The sound scarcely broke the stillness in the Throne-Room. Nobody stirred or spoke. The Porter withdrew, and the young King stepped into the room. He felt exactly like a piece of mutton being put into cold storage. However, there was no help for it, so he plucked up his courage, and slid to the foot of the King's throne. He did not mean to slide, but the floor was iced, and he was obliged to.

The old King looked coldly and enquiringly at the young one. John cleared his throat once or twice, and managed to whisper:

'I have come to woo your daughter.'

The King made the least gesture of the head towards the Princess sitting at his feet; it seemed to signify, 'Woo her, then!' But for the life of him John couldn't think how to begin. If only he could remember his poem! He made a desperate effort to do so, but with poets the first inspiration is everything; if the poem is lost, they can never do it quite the same again. However, he did his best, and kneeling before the silent figure of the Princess, he whispered:

'You're whiter than snowflakes,
You're colder than ice;
I can't see your face,
And perhaps it's not nice.
I don't want to marry
A lady of snow,
But I've come to propose,
And I hope you'll say no!'

Such a complete silence followed his proposal, that John began to think he must have got his poem wrong. He waited about five minutes, bowed, and slid backwards out of the Throne-Room. When he got outside he slapped his arms round his chest, said 'Whew!' several times, jumped on his horse, and rode back to Workaday as fast as he could.

'Is all settled?' asked his Ministers.

'Quite settled,' said John.

His Ministers rubbed their hands with glee. 'And when will the wedding take place?'

'Never!' said John; and went up to his room, and called for Selina to light the fire. Selina was good with fires, and had a splendid one burning in a jiffy. While she was tidying the hearth she asked:

'How did you like the Princess of the North?'

'Not at all,' said the King.

'Wouldn't have you, wouldn't she?'

'Learn to know your place, Selina!' snapped the King.

'Oh, all right. Anything more?'

'Yes. Unpack my bag, and pack it up again. Tomorrow I'm going to see the Princess of Southlands.'

'You'll want your straw hat and your linen pyjamas.' said Selina, and prepared to leave the room.

But the King said, 'Er—Selina—er—er—'

She paused at the door.

'Er—by the way, Selina! do you remember how that—er—bit of poetry went that you read of—er—mine?'

'I've got too much to do to trouble myself to learn poetry,' said Selina.

She went out; and the King was so cross that when she returned with a really hot hot-water-bottle for his bed, he never said so much as 'Thank you'.

IV

The next day the young King set out for Southlands, and to begin with he found the journey so pleasant that he was filled with hope and pleasure. The sky was blue, the air was still, and the day was sunny. But as he went on the sky grew bluer and bluer, the air stiller and stiller, and the day sunnier and sunnier; till, by the time he arrived, his pleasant feelings were overcome with languor. The land was heavy with the scent of roses, and the sun burned so fiercely that it was painful to gaze at the glaring sky, while the heat rising up from the baked earth melted the very shoes upon his horse's hoofs. The horse itself could scarcely move its limbs, and the perspiration streamed down its glossy flanks, and down the forehead and cheeks of its master.

As before, a messenger had gone ahead to announce his coming, and, as before, nobody came to meet him.

The royal city was as silent as sleep, the windows stood with all blinds drawn, and nobody stirred in the streets. However, there was no need to ask the way; the palace, built of burnished gold, with golden domes and spires, glittered a mile off as brightly as the sun itself; the King's horse dragged itself to the gates, and sank exhausted on the ground. It was as much as the King himself could do to stagger from his saddle, and give his name to the big fat Porter in the hall. The Porter merely yawned and took no notice, so John had to find his own way into the Throne-Room. There on a magnificent golden couch reclined the King of Southlands, with the Princess lolling on a mass of golden pillows at his feet. All round the room lounged the courtiers, on gilded ottomans, piled high with cushions. They all wore cloth of gold, and John could hardly tell among their tumbled heaps which were the people and which the golden pillows. But there was no doubt about the King and his beautiful daughter—for she *was* beautiful, thought John, only very, very fat. Her father was still fatter. He smiled a slow, fat, drowsy smile as John drew near, but made no other effort.

'I have come to woo your daughter,' murmured John.

The King's smile grew a little fatter and a little drowsier, as though he were saying, 'Well, I don't mind.' And as everybody seemed to be waiting for John to do something, he thought he had better begin. But words and energy failed him, and in despair he decided to recover, if he could, his lost poem, which he was certain would touch the heart of the Princess. His head was swimming, but at last he thought he remembered it, and sinking on his knees before the reclining lady he murmured:

'You're fatter than butter,
You'd melt by the fire;
You're very much fatter
Than I could desire.
When I see you my courage
Commences to ooze,
But I've come to propose,
And I hope you'll refuse.'

The Princess yawned in his face.

As nothing else whatever happened, he rose to his feet, made his way outside, stood his horse up on its four legs, clambered on to its back, and ambled back to Workaday. 'I don't think that *could* have been the poem,' he said to himself several times on the way.

The Ministers were awaiting him with eagerness. 'Is everything arranged?' they asked. 'Are you and the Princess of the South of one mind?'

'Entirely,' said John.

The Ministers beamed with satisfaction. 'And when does she become your bride?'

'Never!' said John; and went up to his room, and called for Selina to bring him an iced orange squash. She made them very well, and soon had one ready for him in a tall glass with straws in it, and a little ball of orange-coloured ice bobbing on top. While he sucked it up she asked,

'How did you get on with the Princess of the South?'

'I didn't,' said John.

'Didn't take to you, didn't she?'

'Mind your place, Selina!'

'Oh, all right. Is that all for now?'

'No. Tomorrow I am going to see the Princess of Eastmarshes.'

'You'll want your goloshes and your mackintosh,' said Selina, picking up his bag and preparing to take it away.

'Wait, Selina!' said the King.

Selina waited.

'Where do you put what you find in my waste-paper basket?'

'It goes in the dustbin,' said Selina.

'Has the dustbin been emptied this week?'

'I sent for the dustman on purpose,' said Selina. 'It seemed extra full of rubbish.'

Her answer vexed the King so much that when she came in to tell him she had got everything ready in the bathroom for a nice cold shower, he just drummed on the window with his back to her, and hummed a little tune as though she wasn't there.

V

The journey to Eastmarshes was a very different one from those to Northmountains and Southlands. As the road shortened, the young King was met by a harsh and noisy wind that nearly blew him out of his saddle. It seemed, indeed, to be an assembly of winds, all blowing and bellowing, cutting and buffeting, roaring and whistling, at one and the same time. They beat the branches of the trees against each other, and knocked down posts and hoardings. Such a din and clatter beset John's ears, and such ado had he to keep his hat on his head and himself on his horse, that he could hardly look about him to see the nature of the land. He was only aware that the countryside was bleak and damp, and that the city was built of grey stone without any beauty.

'But you can't call *this* quiet!' said John to himself, comparing it with the silence of the North and the slumber of the South; and indeed you could not. Everybody in the city seemed to be rushing here and there, doing vigorously whatever he *was* doing; windows rattled, doors banged, dogs barked, carts thundered through the streets, and people shouted at the tops of their voices as they stamped about their business.

I wonder if I am expected? thought John, for here, too, a messenger had preceded him; and as he neared the palace, which was built of square blocks of granite, he was gratified to see the doors fly open, and a crowd of people stream towards him. They were led by a girl in a short skirt, flying hair, and a stick in her hand, who rushed up to the King, seized his horse by the mane and shouted:

'Can you play hockey?'

Before John could answer, she bawled, 'We're one man short! Come along!' and pulled him to the ground. A stick was thrust into his hand, and before he knew where he was he found himself dragged to a great open field behind the palace, ankle-deep in mud; it stood at the edge of a cliff, and below him he could see cold, grey, angry waves lashing rocks, while up above the wind smacked the people in much the same way.

The game began, and whose side he was on, and what it was all about, John never found out; but for an hour he was slapped by the wind, hacked at by sticks, and stung with the salt spray of the sea. Voices yelled in his ear, hands hurled him violently hither and thither, and mud spattered him from top to toe. At last the game seemed to be over. He sank down exhausted. But even then he was not allowed to rest; for the same girl thumped him on the back and said, 'Get up! Who are you?'

John answered faintly, 'I am the King of Workaday.'

'Oh, indeed! And what have you come for?'

'To woo the Princess.'

'You don't say so! Well, go ahead.'

'But *you* aren't—' began the young King feebly.

'Yes, I am. Why not? Quick fire!'

John made a wild effort to muster his thoughts, and get hold of his lost poem; but what tumbled out of his mouth was this:

'You're louder than thunder,
You're harsher than salt;
We're made as we're born,
So it isn't your fault.
My tastes are not yours,
And your manners aren't mine;
But I've come to propose,
And I hope you'll decline.'

'Well, I never!' bawled the Princess; and lifting her hockey-stick high above her head, she made for him. Behind her came her crowd of indignant courtiers, each with his stick raised. John gave one glance at the muddy, rowdy crew, turned, and fled. He had only just time to scramble on to his horse's back and put it to the gallop, before the sticks descended on him. He did not slacken speed until the shouts of the Eastmarshers were lost on the wind. That, too, died down in time, and at last the young King came, muddy, weary, and breathless, to his own door. The Ministers were waiting for him on the steps.

'Greeting, sire!' they cried. 'Are you and the Princess of the East agreed?'

'Absolutely!' gasped John.

The Ministers danced for joy. 'And when will she name the happy day?'

'Never!' bawled John; and rushed up to his room, and shouted for Selina to come and turn down his bed. She was very quiet and deft about it, and soon had it looking invitingly restful and ready for him. As she put out his dressing-gown and bedroom slippers she asked:

'What do you think of the Princess of the East?'

'I don't!' scowled John.

'Hadn't any use for you, hadn't she?'

'You forget your place, Selina!'

'Oh, all right. Will that do, then?'

'No, it won't,' said John. 'It won't do at all. *Nothing* will do until—'

'Until what?'

'Until I find my poem.'

'Your poem? That bit of poetry, do you mean?'

'Of course I do.'

'Well, why couldn't you say so before?' said Selina, and took it out of her pocket.

VI

The young King stamped with exasperation.

'You've had it all the time, then!' he cried.

'Why shouldn't I? You threw it away.'

'You said you'd emptied it in the dustbin.'

'That I'm sure I never did.'

'You said you couldn't remember what it was about.'

'No more I can. I never *could* learn my poetry lesson.'

'But you kept it all the same.'

'That's *quite* another thing.'

'Why did you?'

'That's *my* business. A *nice* way to treat your work,' said Selina severely. 'A person that can't respect his work doesn't deserve to *do* any.'

'I do respect it, Selina,' said the young King. 'I do really. I was sorry I crumpled it up and threw it away. I only did, because you didn't like it.'

'I never said so.'

'Well—*did* you?'

'It was all right.'

'Oh, Selina, *was* it? *Was* it, Selina? Oh, Selina, I've forgotten it! Read it to me.'

'That I shan't,' said Selina. 'Perhaps it'll teach you another time to *remember* what you write, before you throw it away.'

'I do remember it!' cried the young King suddenly.

'Oh, yes, I remember it perfectly now. Listen!' And seizing her hand he said:

'You're nicer than honey,
You're kinder than doves,
You're the one sort of person
That every man loves.
I can't live without you,
I cannot say less,
So I've come to propose,
And I hope you'll say yes!'

There was a pause, while Selina fiddled with her apron.

'Wasn't that it?' asked the young King anxiously.

'More or less.'

'Selina, say yes! Say yes, Selina!

'Ask me tomorrow,' said Selina, 'in Westwoods.'

'Westwoods!' exclaimed John in surprise. 'You know it's forbidden.'

'Who forbids it?'

'Our fathers and mothers.'

'Well, I never had any,' said Selina. 'I came out of an Orphanage.'

'Then do *you* go to Westwoods?' asked the King.

'Yes, regular,' said Selina. 'On all my days out. Tomorrow's my Half Day. If you care to meet me at the back door, we'll go there together.'

'How do we get in?'

'There's a hole in the fence.'

'And what shall we want,' asked the King, 'to take with us to Westwoods?'

'Just this,' said Selina; and put the poem back in her pocket.

VII

The next day, after lunch, when Selina's work was done, and she had made herself tidy, and put on her pink blouse trimmed with lace and her hat with ribbons on it, the young King met her at the back door, and they set off hand-in-hand for the fence that divided Workaday from Westwoods.

As usual, there was a little crowd of children peeping and prying up and down, and they looked inquisitively at the King and Selina as they, too, began to follow the slats of the fence, each of which Selina tapped with her finger, counting under her breath. It was so odd to see these grown-ups behaving just like themselves, that the children all trooped after them to see what would happen next. But the King and Selina were much too excited to notice. When they came to the Seven-Hundred-and-Seventy-Seventh slat, Selina said, 'Here it is!' and slipped her finger through a hole in the wood, and nicked down a little catch on the inside. The slat swung back like a narrow door, and Selina and the King squeezed through, and all the children squeezed after them.

Once inside, the King rubbed his eyes, for he could hardly believe them. There, as before, was the barrier of branches, leaves, and flowers; but the branches were living and full of singing birds, the leaves were growing and full of happy light, and the flowers—oh, he had never seen or smelt such flowers before! It was easy to find a way through the flowers and leaves to what lay beyond, for Selina led him by the hand. And once again the King rubbed his eyes. For instead of a grey stretch of desert sand, the greenest of swards lay stretched before him, filled with gay streams and waterfalls, and groves of flowering trees; among the groves stood little brown cottages and milk-white temples, the mossy earth was blue with violets, birds of every feather flew in the air, dappled fawns drank at the streams, and squirrels gambolled on the sward. And nothing seemed to fear John, or Selina, or the crowd of children.

Beyond the groves a golden seashore lay, a lovely bay of glittering sand and shining shells and coloured pebbles; a blue-and-emerald sea, transparent as glass, ran the length of it in ripples, until it met the point of a gleaming cliff, in which were alabaster caves and hollows. Gulls, swans, and seabirds wheeled like silver streaks over the water, or stood preening their feathers on the sand. And they, too, were as fearless as the creatures of the wood.

Everything was bathed in radiant light, like mingled sun and moonshine, and was as it is in the loveliest dreams.

'Oh, Selina!' sighed the King. 'I never saw anything like this before!'

'Are you quite sure?' said Selina.

And the King wasn't sure. Yes, he had smelt such flowers, and seen such streams, and wandered on such shores, in—when was it?—oh, in his very earliest childhood. And one by one he had lost sight of them, as they had seemed to die or be less beautiful; and someone, he supposed, had tossed them over the fence as he began to grow up in Workaday.

But there were other things besides the magic glades and shores in Westwoods. For the children who had followed through the fence were now running eagerly hither and thither, racing on the moss, paddling in the streams and in the sea, playing with the sand and flowers and shells, and trooping through the caves and cottages. And out of these they came running again with a multitude of treasures—dolls and trumpets, tea-sets, picture and story books: such dolls, as beautiful as fairies, trumpets that sounded like the clarions of angels, tea-sets that filled themselves with feasts for kings, books from whose covers sprang elves and heroes to be the children's playfellows. At sight of them the King gave a shout, as though he remembered something else he had forgotten; he, too, rushed into a little temple near at hand, and came out with his first humming-top. He set it spinning on the grass, and it gave forth music as lovely as the murmur of the lullabies his mother had sung before he was born.

'Oh, Selina!' cried the King. 'Why did our parents forbid us to come here?'

'Because they'd forgotten,' said Selina, 'and only knew that in Westwoods there is something that is dangerous to Workaday.'

'What is it?' asked the King.

'Dreams,' said Selina.

'Why did I not see all this when I came before?' asked the King.

'Because you didn't bring anything or anyone with you.'

'And this time I've brought my poem,' said the King.

'And me,' said Selina.

The King looked at Selina for the first time since they had entered Westwoods, and he saw that she was the most beautiful girl in the world, and that she was a Princess. There was a light in her eyes and on her hair and in her look that he had never noticed in anybody else, or even her, till now. Her smile was so lovely, the touch of her hand so gentle, the tone of her voice so sweet, that they made his head swim. And she was wearing such beautiful things—a dress like pink rose-petals and silver frost, and round her head a sort of rainbow seemed to float.

'Selina,' said the King, 'you are the most beautiful girl in the world.'

'I am,' said she, 'in Westwoods.'

'Where is my poem, Selina?'

She gave it to him, and he read aloud:

'I know you are sweeter
Than grassfields in June,
And bright as the single star
Watching the moon.
I long for my grass,
And I dream of my star,
Though I haven't the faintest
Idea who you are.'

'Oh, Selina!' cried the King. 'Are you a Princess?'

'Always,' said Selina, 'in Westwoods.'

'And will you marry me?'

'Yes,' said Selina. 'In Westwoods.'

'And out of it too!' cried the King; and seizing her hand he pulled her after him, through the hedge of birds and flowers, to the other side of the fence.

'*Now*, Selina!' he said breathlessly. 'Will you?'

'Will I what?'

'Marry me, Selina?'

'Oh, all right,' said Selina. And she did. And as she had always been good at her work, a very good Queen she made him.

But on the day of the wedding the King removed for good and all the Seven-Hundred-and-Seventy-Seventh slat in the fence between Workaday and Westwoods, for any child or grown-up to slip through for ever after: unless it had grown too fat, which often happens.

THERE was once a Traveller who had a long way to go. He couldn't manage to get there by nightfall, so he walked all night.

His way lay through woods and over hills, where there were no towns and no villages, and not even houses all by themselves. And as it was a dark night he couldn't see his way, and after a while he lost it in the middle of a wood.

It was a night as still as it was dark, and he could hear as little as he could see. So for want of company he began to talk to himself.

'What shall I do *now*?' said the Traveller. 'Shall I go on, or shall I stop still? If I go on I may go the wrong way, and by morning be further off than ever. Yet if I stop still I shall certainly be no nearer than I am now, and may have seven miles to walk to breakfast. What *shall* I do now? Supposing I stop still, shall I lie down or shall I stand up? If I lie down I may lie on a prickle. Yet if I stand up I shall certainly get a cramp in my legs. *What* shall I do?'

When he had got this far in his talk, which was not very far after all, the Traveller heard the sound of music in the wood. No sooner was there something else to listen to, than he stopped talking to himself. It was surprising music to hear in that place. It was not somebody singing or whistling, or playing a flute or a fiddle—sounds which anybody might expect to hear in such a place at such a time. No, the music the Traveller heard in that dark wood on that dark night was a tune on a barrel-organ.

The sound of the tune made the Traveller happy. He no longer felt that he was lost, the tune made him feel as though he was quite near now, and his home was just round the corner. He walked towards it, and as he walked he seemed to feel the grass flutter under his feet and the leaves dance against his cheeks. When he came close to the tune he called out, 'Where are you?' He was sure there must be somebody there, for even a barrel-organ in a wood can't turn its handle by itself. And he was right, for when he called out, 'Where are you?' a cheerful voice answered, 'Here I am, sir!'

The Traveller put out his hand and touched the barrel-organ.

'Wait a bit, sir,' said the cheerful voice, 'I'll just finish this tune first. You can dance to it if you want to.' The tune went on very loud and jolly, and the Traveller danced very quick and gay, and they both finished with a flourish.

'Well, well!' said the Traveller. 'I haven't danced to a barrel-organ since I was ten years old in a back street.'

'I expect not, sir,' said the Organ-grinder.

'Here's a penny for you,' said the Traveller.

'Thank you,' said the Organ-grinder. 'It's a long time since I've taken a penny.'

'Which way are you going?' asked the Traveller.

'No way in particular,' said the Organ-grinder. 'It's all one to me. I can grind my organ here as well as there.'

'But surely,' said the Traveller, 'you need houses with windows in them, or how can people throw the pennies out?'

'I've enough for my needs without that,' said the Organ-grinder.

'But surely,' said the Traveller again, 'you need the back streets with children in them, or who's to dance when you play?'

'Why, there you've hit it,' said the Organ-grinder. 'Once upon a time I played to the houses with windows every day till I'd got my twelvepence, and then for the rest of the day I played in the back streets. And every day I spent sixpence and saved sixpence. But one day it happened I caught cold and had to lie up, and when I came out I found another organ in one of my back streets, and a gramophone in a second, and a harp and cornet in a third. So I saw it was time to retire, and now I grind my organ wherever I please. The tune's the same, here or there.'

'But who's to dance?' asked the Traveller again.

'There's no want of dancers in a wood,' said the Organ-grinder, and turned his handle.

As soon as the tune started, the Traveller felt the grass and leaves flutter as before, and in a moment the air was full of moths and fireflies, and the sky was full of stars, come out to dance like children in a back street. And it seemed to the Traveller, by the light of the dancing stars, that flowers came up in the wood where a moment before there had been none, pushing their way in haste through the moss to sway to the tune on their stalks, and that two or three little streams began to run where a moment before they had been still. And the Traveller thought there were other things dancing that he couldn't see, as well as flowers and streams and stars and moths and flies and leaves in the night. The wood was quite full of dancing from top to toe, and it was no longer dark, for the moon had hopped out of a cloud, and was gliding all over the sky.

Long before this the Traveller was dancing too; he danced as he used to when he was ten years old, till the tune of the organ was faint to hear. For he had danced his way through the wood and was out in the road, with the lights of the city at the other end, and his way before him.

THE GIANT AND THE MITE

THERE was once a Giant who was too big to be seen. As he walked about, the space between his legs was so great that nobody could see as far as from one side to the other, and his head was so high in the sky that nobody's eyes were strong enough to see the top of him. Not being able to take him in all at once, nobody therefore knew that the giant existed.

Sometimes men felt his footsteps shake the earth, and then they said:

'There has been another earthquake.'

And sometimes they felt his shadow pass over them, and they said:

'What a dark day it is!'

And sometimes, when he stooped down to scratch his leg, they felt him breathe, and said:

'Phew! what a wind!'

And that was as much as they knew about him.

But little as it was, it was more than he knew about them; for in spite of his size the Giant had no mind. His legs could walk, and his lungs could breathe, but his brain couldn't think. Of this he had no suspicion, and was quite contented to go on walking about all day, or to stop still and sleep all night; and when he was hungry, he opened his mouth and ate up a star or two, pulling them off the sky with his lips as you might pull cherries off a tree.

At the same time, there was a Mite who was too small to be seen. He was so small that even the ants couldn't see him, and perhaps that was lucky; for if they had done so, they might have gobbled him up. A grain of sand was like a mountain to him, and it would have taken him longer than his whole life to walk across a sixpence. So you can fancy what a tiny bit he moved day by day from the spot where he was born. But he himself never knew this; a tiny way to him was as much as a hundred miles to you, and if his body did not go far, his mind went a great way. For the Mite had a mind, and could think; he was indeed almost all Mind, and his thoughts were as big as the Giant, who couldn't think at all.

Now up in the sky and under the earth sat the two Angels who can see all. Nothing is too big or too small for them, or too far away, or too long ago. One day the Angel in the Sky said to the Angel under the Earth:

'What have you seen today?'

'I have seen a Giant,' said the Angel under the Earth, 'who is so strong that his strength could break the world in two.'

'I know him well,' said the Angel in the Sky, 'and one of these days he is quite likely to break the world in two without thinking.'

'And what have *you* seen today?' asked the Angel under the Earth.

'I have seen a Mite,' said the Angel in the Sky, 'whose mind is so powerful that it could make a new world altogether, if it had the strength to do it with.'

'I've seen him often,' said the Angel under the Earth, 'thinking and thinking of worlds that he will never make.'

It happened one day that the Giant lay down to sleep, with the tip of his right forefinger covering the acre of earth that happened to contain the Mite. The following morning, in helping himself up, he carried away the acre of earth under his fingernail, and the Mite with it. A short while after he happened to scratch his ear, and in doing so he dislodged from under his nail the field in which the Mite was hidden, which to the Giant was but a speck of dirt. In the course of time this speck worked its way through the Giant's ear until it reached his brain. As soon as this happened a marvellous change took place.

For the Giant, who had never had a thought in all his life, suddenly began to think; and he did not know that the Mite was thinking for him. And the Mite, who had never had any strength of his own, suddenly felt that he had the power to make worlds and break them; and he did not know that his strength was in the body of the Giant. Each seemed to himself, not two creatures, but one. And the thoughts of the Mite made the Giant long to do all sorts of things, and the strength of the Giant made the Mite able to carry out his thoughts.

Now terrible things began to happen in the world, and all around it. Between them, the Giant and the Mite tore up mountains and let the sea run in, and they scooped up the rivers and flung them into the clouds, and they moved the moons and stars all about the sky, arranging them in different patterns every night, and they took the wind between thumb and finger, held it up to the Sun, and blew the Sun out. Then they poked a hole with a finger into the middle of the earth, fetched up a handful of fire, and lit the Sun up again. At last it began to look, not so much as though the world would come to an end, as that it would never get on to its end at all, but go backwards or forwards, or up or down, or round and round, or inside out, just as the Mite and the Giant might fancy at any moment.

Then the Angel in the Sky said to the Angel under the Earth:

'This will never do. Between them they will mix up earth and heaven till nobody knows which is which.'

The Angel under the Earth replied, 'There's only one thing for it; we must reduce them to the size of a man.'

'Ah, but,' said the Angel in the Sky, 'size is just an idea, like everything else. We must not only make them equal in size to men, we must also make them look at one another for a moment, so that they shall know forever after that they are not one thing but two.'

In a twinkling the thing was done. The body of the Giant shrank till it became that of a splendid man in full strength, and the Mite looked out from his eyes and saw the form he dwelt in, of which he had never before been aware. At the same moment the Giant was given the power to look inside himself, and there he beheld the Mite.

'Hullo!' said the Giant.

'Hello!' said the Mite.

'What are *you* doing in there?' said the Giant.

'I've just looked in,' said the Mite.

'Well, stay a bit,' said the Giant, 'and between us we might manage to do something.'

'No harm trying,' said the Mite.

So they agreed upon it, and the Angel under the Earth and the Angel in the Sky smiled up and down at each other with just the same sort of smile.

From that day forth, the Giant and the Mite did very little; for each wanted to do such different things that they seldom agreed.

Only once in a great while they forgot they were two and not one, and wanted to do the same thing. When that happened, the Angels held their breath until the Giant and the Mite remembered themselves again, and the danger was past.

THERE was once a Little Dressmaker who was apprentice to a Big Dressmaker. But although she was only an apprentice she cut her patterns so beautifully, and took her stitches so daintily, and had such charming fancies about the frocks she made, that she was really the best dressmaker in the kingdom, and the Big Dressmaker knew it. But the Little Dressmaker was so young and so modest, that the Big Dressmaker said to herself:

'There is no need to tell Lotta she is a better dressmaker than I am. If I don't tell her, she will never find out for herself, and if I do tell her she will go away and set up a Rival Establishment.'

So the Big Dressmaker held her tongue, and did not always praise Lotta when she had done something prettier than usual, and quite often scolded her when she had done nothing whatever to deserve it. But Lotta took it all in good part; and she did not suspect her own worth, even when the Big Dressmaker came to her for advice, as, when she had a particularly important order, she always did.

'The Marchioness of Roley-Poley has just been in to order a ball dress, Lotta,' the Big Dressmaker would say. 'She fancies herself in peach-coloured silk.'

'Oh, what a pity!' Lotta would cry. 'She would look so much better in plum-coloured velvet.'

'Exactly what I told her,' said the Big Dressmaker. 'She wants seventeen flounces on the skirt.'

'Fancy that!' exclaimed Lotta. 'She ought to have it as plain as plain but with a dignified cut.'

'Precisely,' said the Big Dressmaker. 'As I said to the Marchioness with my very own lips, a dignified cut is the thing, and as plain as plain can be.'

So instead of making the Marchioness of Roley-Poley a flouncy peach-coloured dress, they made her a dignified plum-coloured one; and the Marchioness looked extremely imposing at the Queen's reception, and everybody said, 'The Big Dressmaker is a genius.'

But it was really little Lotta.

Now you must know that the Queen of the country was seventy years old and, being unmarried, had no children to succeed to the throne. But if she had never been a mother, she had at least been, for twenty-five years, an aunt; and her nephew, who was King of the kingdom next door, would in the course of time rule over her country as well as his own. He hadn't visited his aunt for twenty years, but report said he was a charming young man, and, like his aunt, he was unmarried—a circumstance which bothered her so much that she wrote to him about it twice a year: at Christmas and on his birthday. But he always wrote back:

'Dear Aunt Georgey,
Thank you awfully for the jolly pencil-case.
Your loving Nephew,
Dick.
PS There's plenty of time.'

But old Georgina was seventy and young King Richard was twenty-five, and at seventy there does not seem to be quite so much time as there does at twenty-five; so presently the Queen, who was a masterful old lady, wrote a letter in between Christmas and his birthday, to tell him he must come to her Court and choose for himself a bride from among the Court ladies, because she was sick and tired of his stuff and nonsense. As this time she hadn't sent him a pencil-case, the King couldn't put her off with thanks, and the chief part of his letter had to be about the marriage. So he wrote:

'Dear Aunt Georgey,
Just as you like.
Your loving Nephew,
Dick.
PS I won't marry anybody who isn't nineteen-and-a-half years old, and nineteen-and-a-half inches round the waist.'

The Queen immediately summoned all the Court ladies of nineteen-and-a-half years old, and had them measured. There were exactly three whose waists were nineteen-and-a-half inches, no more and no less. So she wrote again to her nephew.

'My dear Richard,

The Duchess of Junkets, the Countess of Caramel, and the Lady Blanche Blancmange will all be twenty next December; the present month being June. They are delightful girls, and their waists meet your requirements. Come and choose for yourself.

Your affectionate Aunt,

Georgina Regina.'

To this the King replied:

'Dear Aunt Georgey,

Have it your own way. I'll come on Monday. Please give three balls, on Tuesday, Wednesday, and Thursday, and let me have each of the ladies in turn for my partner. I'll marry the one I like best on Friday, and go home on Saturday.

Your loving Nephew,

Dick.

PS I'd like the balls to be fancy dress, because I've got an awfully good one.'

The Queen did not get this letter till Monday morning, and the King was coming that very night. You can imagine what a flutter everybody was in, particularly the ladies with the nineteen-and-a-half-inch waists! Of course, they paid a visit to the Big Dressmaker at once.

Said the Duchess of Junkets:

'I positively *must* have the most beautiful fancy dress you can make me, and that on Tuesday in time for the First Ball. And be sure, when it is ready, you send me one of your girls to show me how to wear it.'

Said the Countess of Caramel:

'It is of the utmost importance that you should make me the most fascinating fancy dress you can think of, and deliver it on Wednesday in time for the Second Ball. And let your best apprentice bring it, to set it off for me.'

Said the Lady Blanche Blancmange:

'I shall expire of vexation if you do not create for me the most enchanting fancy dress in the world, to be worn on Thursday night at the Third Ball. And that I may see it is quite perfect, put it on your daintiest model so that I can judge the effect for myself.'

The Big Dressmaker promised them all, and as soon as the ladies had departed she rushed in to Lotta and told her all about it.

'We must think with all our brains, and sew with all our fingers, Lotta, if we are to get them done in time!'

'Oh, I'm sure I can manage,' said Lotta cheerfully. 'We'll take the dresses in order, and the Duchess shall have hers tomorrow night, and the Countess shall have hers the next night, and the Lady Blanche shall have hers the night after that, if I have to sit up all the time and never go to bed at all.'

'Very well, Lotta,' said the Big Dressmaker. 'But now I must consider what the dresses will be.'

'The Duchess would look beautiful as a Sunbeam,' said Lotta.

'Just what *I* was thinking,' said the Big Dressmaker.

'And how entrancing the Countess would look as Moonlight,' said Lotta.

'My idea exactly,' said the Big Dressmaker.

'And as a Rainbow the Lady Blanche would look simply ravishing.'

'You have taken the very words out of my mouth,' said the Big Dressmaker. 'Now to design them, cut them out, and make them.'

So Lotta designed the three dresses, and set about making the first one, a radiant golden gown that would flash and sparkle like light as the wearer of it danced. She sat at it day and night, and saw nothing of the young King's arrival at the palace; and on the Tuesday, an hour before the opening of the First Ball, the bright frock was ready.

'They have sent a coach from the palace to fetch it,' said the Big Dressmaker, 'and one of my girls is to wear it and show it off to the Duchess before she puts it on. But whom can I possibly send? It has only a nineteen-and-a-half-inch waist.'

'That's just my size, madam,' said Lotta.

'How fortunate! Quick, Lotta, slip it on and be off.'

So Lotta slipped on the dazzling frock, the golden shoes and slippers, and the little gold crown twinkling with points of light, and throwing her old black cloak over all ran down to the royal coach that was waiting for her. The coachman flicked his whip and away they went. When she arrived at the palace, a Footman who was passing through the hall conducted Lotta to a little anteroom.

'You are to wait here,' said he, 'till the Duchess is ready for you in the next room. When she is, she will ring a bell. What a charming dress you seem to be wearing under your cloak.'

'It is the Duchess's dress,' said Lotta, 'with which she is to captivate the young King. Would you like to see it?'

'Very much indeed,' said the Footman.

Lotta dropped her black cloak, and stepped like a sunbeam out of a cloud.

'There!' she said. 'Isn't it beautiful! Do you think the King will be able to resist dancing with the Duchess in this frock?'

'I am sure he won't,' said the Footman. And making an elegant bow, he added, 'Duchess, may I have the honour of this dance?'

'Oh, Your Majesty!' laughed Lotta. 'The honour is mine.'

The Footman put his arm round Lotta's waist, and danced with her, and just as he was telling her that her hair was more golden than sunlight itself, the bell rang and Lotta had to go.

The Duchess was delighted with the dress, and when Lotta had shown her exactly how to move and sit and stand and dance in it, she put it on and sailed into the ballroom.

Lotta, wrapping herself up in her old cloak, heard how everybody broke into applause as the radiant little Duchess appeared.

Ah, thought Lotta, the King will never be able to resist *her*! And back she ran, to begin the Moonlight dress.

All night and all day she sewed the slim silver sheath, and she got it done by the following evening, just as the royal coach drew up at the door to fetch her. As before, she slipped on the frock, covered herself with her cloak, and drove away; and as before, the young Footman escorted her to the anteroom and told her to wait.

'And what happened at the ball last night?' asked Lotta.

'The King danced with the Golden Duchess all the evening,' said the Footman. 'I doubt if the Countess will have such luck.'

'Don't you think so?' said Lotta; and opening her black cloak, she stood before him like the moon shining at midnight.

'Oh, Countess!' said the Footman, taking her hand and kissing it, 'will you make me the happiest man in the world by dancing with me?'

'The happiness is mine, Your Majesty,' said Lotta, smiling sweetly.

So once more they danced together in the anteroom, and then they sat down and talked all about themselves and each other; and Lotta told him that she was nineteen-and-a-half years old, and that her mother was a housemaid and her father a cobbler, and she herself an apprentice dressmaker. And the Footman told her that he was twenty-five years old, and that his father was a bookbinder and his mother a laundress, and he himself a footman to the young King, to whose kingdom he would return when the King was married. And this made Lotta thoughtful, and the Footman asked why, and Lotta didn't know. And the Footman took her hand in his, and was just telling her that it was as white as moonlight when the bell rang and Lotta had to go.

The Countess of Caramel was charmed with the frock, and when all its points had been shown off she put it on and entered the ballroom. And Lotta heard the shout of admiration that went up as she appeared; while Lotta herself hurried back in her old cloak to make the Rainbow dress.

All night and all day she sat at it, and her eyes were rather heavy, and her heart was a little heavy too, but she couldn't think why. And just an hour before the Third Ball was to begin, the frock was done and the coach was waiting. Once more Lotta put on a shimmering frock, hid herself in her old cloak, and was driven to the palace. And once more the Footman escorted her to the anteroom, where she sank into a deep chair while he stood before her. And once more Lotta asked, 'What happened at the ball last night?'

'The King danced every dance with the Silver Countess, and never took his eyes off her,' said the Footman. 'I don't suppose there's much chance for the Lady Blanche.'

'You never know,' said Lotta. But she was feeling so tired that she didn't even try to undo her cloak and show him. So the Footman undid it for her, and laid it back against the chair; and when he saw Lotta shining like a little rainbow against a black cloud-bank, he fell on his knees before her.

'Oh, Lady!' he whispered, 'won't you dance this dance with me, and every other dance as well?'

But Lotta shook her head, because she was so tired, and she tried to smile, but at the same time big tears trickled down her cheeks. And the Footman didn't even ask why, since tears seem natural in a rainbow, but he put his arms round her as she sat in the chair and gave her a kiss. And before the kiss was quite finished, the bell rang, and Lotta had to wipe her eyes and go.

The Lady Blanche was ravished with the frock, and after Lotta had turned this way and that way to show her how to wear it, she put it on and ran into the ballroom. Lotta heard a great sigh of wonder go round at the lovely little vision that had appeared. Then she went back to the empty anteroom, put on her old cloak, and stumbled back. She meant to go to bed and sleep and sleep.

But at the door the Big Dressmaker met her with a face of despair.

'What do you think?' cried she. 'An order has just come from the Queen that we must make the finest wedding-dress ever made, for the King's Bride tomorrow. The wedding is to be at noon. Now, think, Lotta, think! What shall the wedding-dress be?'

Lotta thought of a dress as pure as a fall of snow, and as she began to cut it out she said, 'But, madam, we do not know whom it is to fit.'

'Make it to fit yourself,' said the Big Dressmaker. 'For you and the three ladies are all of a size.'

'And which do you think it will be?' asked Lotta.

'Nobody knows. They say the King was equally charmed by the Sun and the Moon, and doubtless he will be by the Rainbow as well.'

'And what dress did the King wear at the balls, madam?' asked Lotta, to keep herself awake.

'A most disappointing dress for a King,' said the Big Dressmaker. 'He wore the livery of his own Footman!'

After that, Lotta asked no more questions. She just bent her tired little head over the pure white stuff, and sewed and sewed till her fingers and her eyes ached.

The night passed, morning came, and an hour before noon the frock was ready.

'The coach is here,' said the Big Dressmaker. 'Put on the dress, Lotta, for the Bride will certainly wish to see how it should be worn.'

'Who *is* the Bride?' asked Lotta.

'Still nobody knows,' said the Big Dressmaker. 'They say the young King is making his choice at this moment, and the wedding will take place as soon as he has decided.'

So Lotta put on the wedding-dress, and went down to the coach, and there, to her surprise, was her own Footman, waiting to hand her in. She looked at him earnestly and said, 'But aren't you the King?' and the Footman said, 'Whatever made you think that?' and shut the door, and away they galloped. And Lotta leaned back in a corner, and fell fast asleep, and dreamed she was driving to her wedding.

When she woke up, the coach was just pulling up at a door; but instead of being the palace door, it was the door of a little church in the country.

The Footman jumped down and handed Lotta out; it all seemed a natural part of her dream as she went on his arm up the aisle in her snow-white gown, and found the clergyman waiting at the altar. In two minutes they were married, and Lotta, with a gold ring on her finger, went back to the coach. But this time the Footman got inside with her, and as they drove off he finished giving her the kiss he had begun the night before, and Lotta went to sleep with her head on his shoulder.

She never woke up till they reached the young King's city and stopped before the young King's palace. And there, all in a daze, she found herself going up the steps on the Footman's arm amid the cheers of the populace, and at the top of the steps, waiting to receive them, with a merry smile on his face—*the young King himself.*

Yes; because, you see, the Footman really *was* the Footman. Only, as the young King didn't want to be married a bit, he had sent his Footman in his place. And as the Footman fell in love with Lotta at first sight, he had made up his mind before the very first ball, and after that there wasn't a ghost of a chance for the Duchess of Junkets, the Countess of Caramel, or the Lady Blanche Blancmange. And this was really very fortunate, because if the Footman had chosen and married one of them, the old Queen would have been greatly annoyed when she found out the trick that had been played upon her by her nephew; and the bride would have been annoyed as well.

As it was, when the facts came to the Queen's ears, she wrote to the young King on his birthday:

'My dear Richard,

I send you the enclosed, with my love. At the same time, I wish to say that I am extremely displeased with you, and shall take no further interest in your matrimonial affairs.

Your affectionate Aunt,

Georgina Regina.'

To which the young King replied:

'Dear Aunt Georgey,
        Thanks awfully.
                Your loving Nephew,
                        Dick.
PS Oh, and thank you for the jolly pencil-case.'

A LADY once lived in a room that was as white as snow. Everything in it was white; it had white walls and ceiling, white silk curtains, a soft white sheepskin carpet, and a little ivory bed with a white linen coverlet. The Lady thought it was the most beautiful room in the world, and lived in it as happy as the day was long.

But one morning she looked out of the window and heard the birds singing in the garden, and all at once she sighed a big sigh.

'Oh, dear!' sighed the Lady.

'What's the matter with *you*, Lady?' said a tiny voice at the window, and there, sitting on the sill, was a Fairy no bigger than your finger, and on her feet she wore two little shoes as green as grass in April.

'Oh, Fairy!' cried the Lady. 'I am so tired of this

plain white room! I would be so happy if it were only a green room!'

'*Right* you are, Lady!' said the Fairy, and she sprang on to the bed, and lay on her back, and kicked away at the wall with her two little feet. In the twinkling of an eye the white room turned into a green one, with green walls and ceiling, green net curtains, a carpet like moss in the woods, and a little green bed with a green linen coverlet.

'Oh, thank you, Fairy!' cried the Lady, laughing for joy. 'Now I *shall* be as happy as the day is long!'

The Fairy flew away, and the Lady walked about her green room gay as a bird. But one day she looked out of the window and smelt the flowers growing in the garden, and all at once she began to sigh.

'Oh, dear!' sighed the Lady. 'Oh, dear!'

'What's the matter with *you*, Lady?' asked a tiny voice, and there on the windowsill sat the Fairy, swinging her two little feet in shoes as pink as rose-petals in June.

'Oh, Fairy!' cried the Lady. 'I made such a mistake when I asked you for a green room. I'm so tired of my green room! What I really meant to ask for was a pink room.'

'*Right* you are, Lady!' said the Fairy, and jumped on the bed, and lay on her back, and kicked at the wall with her two little feet. All in a moment the green room changed into a pink one, with pink walls and ceiling, pink damask curtains, a carpet like rose-petals, and a little rosewood bed with a pink linen coverlet.

'Oh, thank you, Fairy!' cried the Lady, clapping her hands. 'This is just the room I have always wanted!'

The Fairy flew away, and the Lady settled down in her pink room, as happy as a rose.

But one day she looked out of her window and saw the leaves dancing in the garden, and before she knew it she was sighing like the wind.

'Oh, dear!' sighed the Lady. 'Oh, dear, oh, dear!'

'What's the matter with *you*, Lady?' cried the Fairy's tiny voice, and there was the Fairy hopping on the windowsill in a pair of shoes as golden as lime leaves in October.

'Oh, Fairy!' cried the Lady. 'I am so tired of my pink room! I can't think how I ever came to ask you for a pink room, when all the time a golden room was what I really wanted.'

'*Right* you are, Lady!' said the Fairy, and she leaped on to the bed, lay on her back, and kicked at the wall with her two little feet. Quicker than you can wink, the pink room turned golden, with walls and ceiling like sunshine, and curtains like golden cobwebs, and a carpet like fresh-fallen lime leaves, and a little gold bed with a gold cloth coverlet.

'Oh, thank you, thank you!' cried the Lady, dancing for joy. 'At last I really have the very room I wanted!' The Fairy flew away, and the Lady ran around her golden room as light-hearted as a leaf. But one night she looked out of the window and saw the stars shining on the garden, and fell a-sighing, as though she would never stop.

'*Now* what's the matter with you, Lady?' said the tiny voice from the windowsill. And there stood the Fairy in a pair of shoes as black as night.

'Oh, Fairy!' cried the Lady. 'It is all this golden room! I cannot *bear* my bright golden room, and if only I can have a black room instead, I will never want any other as long as I live!'

'The matter with *you*, Lady,' said the Fairy, 'is that you don't know *what* you want!' And she jumped on the bed, and lay on her back, and kicked away with her two little feet. And the walls fell through, and the ceiling fell up, and the floor fell down, and the Lady was left standing in the black starry night without any room at all.

DID you ever hear the tale of the Six Princesses who lived for the sake of their hair alone? This is it.

There was once a King who married a Gypsy, and was as careful of her as if she had been made of glass. In case she ran away he put her in a palace in a park with a railing all round it, and never let her go outside. The Queen was too loving to tell him how much she longed to go beyond the railing, but she sat for hours on the palace roof, looking towards the meadows to the east, the river to the south, the hills to the west, and the markets to the north.

In time the Queen bore the King twin daughters as bright as the sunrise, and on the day they were christened the King in his joy asked what she would have for a gift. The Queen looked from her roof to the east, saw May on the meadows, and said:

'Give me the spring!'

The King called fifty thousand gardeners, and bade each one bring in a root of wild-flowers or a tender birch-tree from outside, and plant it within the railing. When it was done he walked with the Queen in the flowery park, and showed her everything, saying:

'Dear wife, the spring is yours.'

But the Queen only sighed.

The following year two more Princesses, as fair as the morning, were born, and once again, on their christening-day, the King told the Queen to choose a gift. This time she looked from the roof to the south, and, seeing the water shining in the valley, said:

'Give me the river!'

The King summoned fifty thousand workmen and told them so to conduct the river into the park that it should supply a most beautiful fountain in the Queen's pleasure-grounds.

Then he led his wife to the spot where the fountain rose and fell in a marble basin, and said:

'You now have the river.'

But the Queen only gazed at the captive water rising and falling in its basin, and hung her head.

Next year two more Princesses, as golden as the day, were born, and the Queen, given her choice of a gift, looked north from the roof into the busy town, and said:

'Give me the people!'

So the King sent fifty thousand trumpeters down to the market-place, and before long they returned, bringing six honest market-women with them.

'Here, dear Queen, are the people,' said the King.

The Queen secretly wiped her eyes, and then gave her six beautiful babies into the charge of the six buxom women, so that the Princesses had a nurse apiece.

Now in the fourth year the Queen bore only one daughter, a little one, and dark like herself, whereas the King was big and fair.

'What gift will you choose?' said the King, as they stood on the roof on the day of the christening.

The Queen turned her eyes to the west, and saw a wood-pigeon and six swans flying over the hills.

'Oh!' cried she. 'Give me the birds!'

The King instantly sent fifty thousand fowlers forth to snare the birds. While they were absent the Queen said:

'Dear King, my children are in their cots and I am on my throne, but presently the cots will be empty and I shall sit on my throne no more. When that day comes, which of our seven daughters will be Queen in my stead?'

Before the King could answer the fowlers returned with the birds. The King looked from the humble pigeon, with its little round head sunk in the soft breast-feathers, to the royal swans with their long white necks, and said:

'The Princess with the longest hair shall be Queen.'

Then the Queen sent for the six Nurses and told them what the King had said. 'So remember,' she added, 'to wash and brush and comb my daughters' hair without neglect, for on you will depend the future Queen.'

'And who will wash and brush and comb the hair of the Seventh Princess?' they asked.

'I will do that myself,' said the Queen.

Each Nurse was exceedingly anxious that her own Princess should be Queen, and every fine day they took the children out into the flowery meadow and washed their hair in the water of the fountain, and spread it in the sun to dry. Then they brushed it and combed it till it shone like yellow silk, and plaited it with ribbons, and decked it with flowers. You never saw such lovely hair as the Princesses had, or so much trouble as the Nurses took with it. And wherever the six fair girls went, the six swans went with them.

But the Seventh Princess, the little dark one, never had her hair washed in the fountain. It was kept covered with a red handkerchief, and tended in secret by the Queen as they sat together on the roof and played with the pigeon.

At last the Queen knew that her time had come. So she sent for her daughters, blessed them one by one, and bade the King carry her up to the roof. There she looked from the meadows to the river, from the markets to the hills, and closed her eyes.

Now, hardly had the King done drying his own, when a trumpet sounded at his gate, and a page came running in to say that the Prince of the World had come. So the King threw open his doors, and the Prince of the World came in, followed by his servant. The Prince was all in cloth of gold, and his mantle was so long that when he stood before the King it spread the whole length of the room, and the plume in his cap was so tall that the tip touched the ceiling. In front of the Prince walked his servant, a young man all in rags.

The King said:

'Welcome, Prince of the World!' and held out his hand.

The Prince of the World did not answer; he stood there with his mouth shut and his eyes cast down. But his Ragged Servant said, 'Thank you, King of the Country!' And he took the King's hand and shook it heartily.

This surprised the King greatly.

'Cannot the Prince speak for himself?' he asked.

'If he can,' said the Ragged Servant, 'nobody has ever heard him do so. As you know, it takes all sorts to make the world: those who speak and those who are silent, those who are rich and those who are poor, those who think and those who do, those who look up and those who look down. Now, my master has chosen me for his servant, because between us we make up the world of which he is Prince. For he is rich and I am poor, and he thinks things and I do them, and he looks down and I look up, and he is silent, so I do the talking.'

'Why has he come?' asked the King.

'To marry your daughter,' said the Ragged Servant, 'for it takes all sorts to make a world, and there must be a woman as well as a man.'

'No doubt,' said the King. 'But I have seven daughters. He cannot marry them all.'

'He will marry the one that is to be Queen,' said the Ragged Servant.

'Let my daughters be sent for,' said the King, 'for the time is now come to measure the length of their hair.'

So the Seven Princesses were summoned before the King. The six fair ones came in with their Nurses, and the little dark one came in by herself. The Ragged Servant looked quickly from one to another, but the Prince of the World kept his eyes down and did not look at any of them.

Then the King sent for the Court Tailor, with his tape-measure; and when he came the six fair Princesses shook down their hair till it trailed on the ground behind them.

One by one they had it measured, while the six Nurses looked on with pride—for had they not taken just as much care as they could of their darlings' hair? But, alas! as neither more care nor less had been spent upon any of them, it was now discovered that each of the six Princesses had hair exactly as long as the others.

The Court held up its hands in amazement, the Nurses wrung theirs in despair, the King rubbed his crown, the Prince of the World kept his eyes on the ground, and the Ragged Servant looked at the Seventh Princess.

'What shall we do,' said the King, 'if my youngest daughter's hair is the same length as the rest?'

'I don't think it is, sir,' said the Seventh Princess, and her sisters looked anxious as she untied the red handkerchief from her head. And indeed her hair was not the same length as theirs, for it was cropped close to her head, like a boy's.

'Who cut your hair, child?' asked the King.

'My mother, if you please, sir,' said the Seventh Princess. 'Every day as we sat on the roof she snipped it with her scissors.'

'Well, well!' cried the King. 'Whichever is meant to be Queen, it isn't you!'

That is the story of the Six Princesses who lived for the sake of their hair alone. They spent the rest of their lives having it washed, brushed, and combed by the Nurses, till their locks were as white as their six pet swans.

And the Prince of the World spent the rest of *his* life waiting with his eyes cast down until one of the Princesses should grow the longest hair, and become his Queen. As this never happened, for all I know he is waiting still.

But the Seventh Princess tied on her red handkerchief again, and ran out of the palace to the hills and the river and the meadows and the markets; and the pigeon and the Ragged Servant went with her.

'But,' she said, 'what will the Prince of the World do without you in the palace?'

'He will have to do as best he can,' said the Ragged Servant, 'for it takes all sorts to make the world, those that are in and those that are out.'

THIS is a French 'counting-out-game'—like our 'Eeny Meeny Meiny Mo!'—which I heard sung in Normandy by two little girls, the children of the white inn among the apple-trees, where I stayed once for a few days. The younger child, Yvonne, was a gay little thing, who thought of nothing but playing with her ball, which seemed to satisfy all her wants. The elder, Geneviève, was grave and knowing; she asked me once if there were fairies in England, and when I said I thought so, shrugged her shoulders and murmured, 'Not possible!' Yet in her father's field stood one of those queer little huts, to be found in almost every Norman orchard, which might well belong to a witch; and just across the way there was behind a gate a flower-garden so beautiful that it might well have been owned by a fairy. I never succeeded in getting into either the hut or the garden, and could only guess at their inhabitants.

It was not long after she had put the question that I heard Geneviève singing with Yvonne the song which in English would run something like this:

'Three little Princes
Leaving Paradise,
Mouth hanging open
Until tomorrow noon.
Clarinette, Clarinette!
My wooden shoes make spectacles!
Peach, apple, apricot,
One too many in the pot,
Lift it with the ladle,
And OUT
goes
HE!'

I did not ask Geneviève what it all meant; she could not have told me. All she knew was that she had sung the funny medley of nonsense all her life, when she and Yvonne were playing their games. As for what it meant exactly—who could say? Perhaps it meant that after all, Geneviève, there are fairies in France—not possible?

I

There were once three little Princes who lived in Paradise. Their names were Felix, Crispin, and Theodore; and if you want to know what Paradise looked like, it was a land of apple and apricot, plum and peach-trees, of magical meadows carpeted with flowers, close rows of poplar-trees stretched like a green curtain between one meadow and the next, of corncocks bright as gold, and rivers brighter than silver. Felix, Crispin, and Theodore had their own little white house and their own little garden, which they shared together for sleeping and eating in; but, being free to do what they liked, as often as not one or other would stroll away for a day, or a month, or a hundred years or so, to sleep, play, and eat in one of the numberless little huts which sprang up like mushrooms among the fruit-trees. The huts were so pretty that no little Prince could ever see one without wanting to go into it. Then too there were the meadows which were so flowery that they could not pass by without loitering there to gather magical coloured bunches to bring back to Yvonne. And with the river to swim in, and the whispering poplars to climb in, you would have thought the little Princes must be as happy as the day was long. And so they were.

And small wonder, seeing that they had Yvonne to look after them. She it was who kept their rooms swept, their beds made, and their supper ready in the pot. She did all this by means of one of her three crystal balls, which she would toss into the air, clapping her hands as she cried out a single word of command, such as 'Ladle!' 'Blankets!' or 'Darning-Needle!' Then, as she caught the ball again, the ladle stirred the pot on the fire and dipped out big portions of the delicious fruits that were stewing there for Theodore's supper; and the blankets tucked themselves cosily round Crispin's bed, while the darning-needle threaded itself with wool and mended the hole Felix had rubbed in the knee of his stocking while climbing the tallest tree in Paradise. The one thing that never needed mending was the Princes' shoes, for they all wore wooden sabots that lasted for ever.

There was in all Paradise only one garden they never entered, and only one hut to which they never succeeded in finding the door. The garden was the most beautiful of all, and the hut the queerest. Many a time the Princes pressed their little noses against the gate of the garden and the dingy window of the hut, to see what they could see, but they did not see much beyond the flowers crowding to the gate and the dirt upon the pane.

One day as Theodore sat by his house whittling a boat to sail on the river, he heard a high voice tittering 'Te-he! Te-he! Te-he!' on the other side of the hedge. Looking up, he saw that the sound was made by a queer little woman with very bright eyes and a very sharp nose, whom he had never seen before.

'What are you tittering at?' asked Theodore.

'You,' said the bright-eyed woman.

'Why?' asked Theodore.

'Because the tip of your nose is as black as a little black pebble.'

'So would yours be,' said Theodore, 'if you had rubbed it on a dirty window-pane.'

'I should never dream of rubbing my nose on a dirty window-pane,' said the little woman, 'without a very good reason.'

'Well, I had,' said Theodore.

'What was it, pray?'

'I wanted to find out who lived behind the window.'

'And who does?'

'I couldn't see, so I don't know.'

'What a pity, *what* a pity!' said the little woman.

'Is it?' asked Theodore.

'Ah,' said the little woman, wagging her head, 'catch *me* being content not to know what I wanted to know!'

Theodore looked at the little woman, and all of a sudden it *did* seem to him a pity not to know who lived in the hut. For the first time in his life he felt a twinge in his mind.

'Perhaps *you* can tell me who lives there?'

'Not I, Theodore.'

'Why, you know my name!' said Theodore.

'Certainly. You *are* Theodore, so how can I help knowing it? My name is Clarinette.'

Theodore looked at her again, and saw that of course she was Clarinette.

'Well, Clarinette, why can't you tell me?'

'I can tell you nothing about Paradise because I don't belong here. I live in the greatest City in the world, and know everything about the world that there is to be known. Ah, it is a wonderful thing to know what to believe and what not to believe!'

'What *do* you believe in, Clarinette?'

'Fine clothes, for one thing,' said Clarinette. 'Look and see!' She hopped up on a bench in the road, so that Theodore could see the grand lace frock she wore, and the rich fur cape. She kicked up one little foot, and pointed at him the toe of her embroidered high-heeled slipper.

'Te-he! Te-he! Te-he!' tittered Clarinette. 'That's how we dress in the City, where we know our own minds; but in Paradise—te-he!—you wear wooden shoes and can't see through a window-pane!'

So saying, she hopped down off the bench, and clattered away up the road, tittering as she went.

That evening Theodore came barefoot to supper. The three little Princes sat round the table with their spoons and bowls all ready for what might come out of the pot. Just as Yvonne was about to toss her ball, Theodore asked. 'Yvonne, who lives in the hut in the field?'

Yvonne held her ball very tight and said, 'Must you ask questions, little Prince?'

'I only wondered,' said Theodore.

'Go on wondering,' said Yvonne.

'I'm hungry, Yvonne,' cried Crispin, beating his bowl on the table.

'In a moment!' said Yvonne, and prepared once more to throw her ball. But once more Theodore asked, 'Who *does*, Yvonne?'

Again Yvonne checked herself. 'Do you want to leave Paradise, little Prince?' said she.

'No, of course not.'

'Then don't ask questions.'

'But I only want to *know*,' persisted Theodore.

'Alas!' said Yvonne.

'Yvonne, I want my supper!' shouted Felix, knocking his bowl on the table.

'Just coming!' said Yvonne, and for the third time she started to throw her ball, crying 'Supper!' as she clapped her hands. But at the same moment Theodore called out, '*Who lives in the hut?*' and startled her so that the crystal ball dropped at her feet and smashed to atoms. And instead of the fragrant portions of fruit that the ladle should have brought up from the pot, out popped a single peach all by itself, and fell plop into Theodore's bowl, so that his mouth fell open with surprise. A bright tear formed in Yvonne's right eye, and she said:

'One too many in the pot! Oh, why must you start asking questions? If you must know, a Witch lives in the hut. And so, Theodore, out you go!'

'Out where?' he asked.

'Out of Paradise.'

Theodore grew as red as a turkey-cock, and cried, '*I'll* go! Who cares about old Paradise? I'm going to the biggest City in the world, where they wear fine clothes and fur, and *can* answer questions.'

Yvonne nodded her head sadly, saying, 'Goodbye, little Prince. Put on your sabots before you depart.'

'Not me!' said Theodore. 'Clumsy old wooden shoes! *I* shall have embroidered shoes, with golden heels.'

'Yet wear your wooden shoes till you get there,' begged Yvonne, 'for the road will be rough, going and coming.'

'I shan't come back till tomorrow noon!' cried Theodore. 'And that will be never, because tomorrow never comes.'

'You'll go hungry till you do,' said Yvonne, holding out his sabots. But Theodore pushed them away and stamped out of the house, his mouth still hanging open, because he wanted his supper. Crispin and Felix stared after him till he had disappeared beyond the gate, and then they thumped their bowls on the table, and called, 'We're hungry, Yvonne, we're hungry!'

'On the spot!' said Yvonne; and fetching her second crystal ball, she threw it into the air, clapped her hands, cried 'Supper!' and at once the sweet steam rose from the pot and the ladle scooped out fruit and syrup into the Princes' bowls till they were running over. While they ate, Yvonne stowed the broken bits of crystal into Theodore's wooden shoes, wrapped them up, and put them away on a shelf in the cupboard.

A year later, as Crispin was sitting by the door making arrows for his bow, he heard a tiny giggle on the other side of the hedge. 'Te-he! Te-he! Te-he!' it went, so that he had to look up; and there was a queer little woman, with a very sharp nose and two very bright eyes, laughing at him for all she was worth.

'What's funny?' asked Crispin, eager to join in the joke.

'You are!' said the sharp-nosed woman.

'Why me?'

'Because your forehead is criss-crossed all over with black, like shadows on the road.'

'That must be where I pressed it against the gate to see the person in the garden.'

'What person's that?'

'I never saw, so I don't know.'

'Too bad, *too* bad!' said the little woman.

'Is it?' asked Crispin.

'Not to see what you try to see? I should think so!' said the little woman, throwing up her hands. And Crispin, struck by her action, felt that it *was* too bad not to know who lived in the garden. His mind felt its very first pang.

'*You* tell me!' he urged her.

'Not me, Crispin!'

'How did you know I was Crispin?'

'Because you are. And I am Clarinette.'

'Why, so you are, and so I am! But *do* tell me.'

'I can tell you all manner of things, but I can't tell you that. I can tell you whatever I want to know myself, but I don't want to know who lives in the garden in Paradise.'

'What do you want to know, then?'

'I want to know the affairs of my neighbour in the City, and how much money she has, and if she can afford grander clothes than mine. Look there now!' And hopping on to the bench, she fluttered her laces and furs, and showed him the tip of her rich slipper. 'Te-he! Te-he!' giggled Clarinette. 'These things are worth knowing, these are! These are What's What in the world! But *you* clump about Paradise in sabots, and don't know how to open a shut gate!'

Saying which, she stepped down from the bench, and went clicking up the road in her high-heeled shoes.

Crispin kicked his sabots off at once, and kept them off for the rest of the day; and as he sat barefoot at the supper table, while Yvonne prepared to throw her ball, he suddenly asked her, 'Who *does* live in the garden over the road, Yvonne?'

Yvonne clutched the ball, and said, 'Why ask questions, little Prince?'

'I just wondered.'

'Go on wondering,' said Yvonne.

'Isn't supper coming?' asked Felix, bumping his bowl on the table.

'Just ready,' said Yvonne; but before she could throw the ball Crispin urged again, 'No, but you might tell me!'

Yvonne held on to her ball and said, 'Don't you like living in Paradise, little Prince?'

'Of course I do.'

'Then no more questions.'

'But why—who—what—?' stammered Crispin.

'Alas!' sighed Yvonne.

'What about supper?' shouted Felix, rolling his bowl round and round on the table.

'Immediately!' said Yvonne, tossed her ball, clapped her hands, and cried, 'Supper!' But Crispin at the same moment began to exclaim, 'Why, why, why, why, why,' and upset her so that she missed the ball, and it smashed into smithereens at her feet. Then out of the pot jumped a single apple, and dropped with a splash into the middle of Crispin's bowl, so that his mouth made a round, startled 'O!' A big tear welled up in Yvonne's left eye, and she said:

'One too many in the pot. If only you wouldn't ask questions! If you will have it, a Fairy lives in the garden. And now, Crispin, out you go!'

'Why!' asked Crispin.

'Because nobody asks questions in Paradise.'

'But why?'

'Because then it isn't Paradise.'

'But you might tell me *why*, Yvonne.'

'That's enough,' said Yvonne.

'Oh, all right!' said Crispin, strutting about. 'Then I'll go to the City and ask Clarinette, and she'll give me such fine clothes to wear that I'll be grander than her neighbour!'

Yvonne shook her head sorrowfully, saying, 'Goodbye, little Prince. Don't forget to put your sabots on.'

'Why?' asked Crispin.

'The road is hard, going and coming,' said she.

'I'm going, but I'm not coming,' declared Crispin. 'I shall come no sooner than tomorrow noon, which never does.'

'You'll go unfed till you do,' said Yvonne, offering him his sabots. But Crispin wouldn't look at them, and ran out of the house with his mouth still making an O. As soon as he was out of sight, Felix banged the table with his bowl, and bawled, 'I'm hungry, Yvonne, I'm hungry!'

'There you are, then,' said Yvonne; and fetching her third and last crystal ball, she tossed, and clapped, and called out 'Supper!' In a moment the big ladle had filled Felix's bowl to overflowing; and while he was gobbling, Yvonne filled Crispin's sabots with the crystal splinters, and put them away in the cupboard beside Theodore's.

It was just a year later that Felix, sitting by the door making mud pies, heard a high cackle on the other side of the hedge, that made him look up; and there was a queer little woman, bright of eye and sharp of nose, saying, 'Te-he! Te-he! Te-he!' as though she never could stop.

So Felix began to laugh too, and then she did stop.

'Why are you laughing?' said she.

'Because *you* are,' said Felix merrily.

'Well, don't you want to know why I am?' asked the little woman.

'Laughing's nice,' said Felix.

'That all depends,' said the little woman tartly. 'Shall *I* tell you why I laughed?'

'If you like.'

'I laughed because one of your cheeks has a big smudge on it, and the other is all streaked with black.'

'How funny!' said Felix, and laughed more heartily than ever.

This appeared to vex the little woman. She asked in an irritated way, '*Why* are they so dirty?'

'I expect it was when I was listening at the window and the gate.'

'Ah, there we are, then! What were you listening for?'

'Just listening,' said Felix, turning out another mud pie.

'I suppose,' coaxed the little woman, 'you wanted very much to know who lived behind the gate and the window. Was *that* it?'

Felix looked at her with big eyes, and said mysteriously, 'I didn't hear a *sound.* Not one *single* sound. Here's a cream ice-pudding for you.'

'That's not a cream ice-pudding, little silly. It is a mud pie.'

Felix laughed gleefully. 'It's got green nuts on it, and sticky cherries, and chocolate sauce, see?'

'No, I *don't* see, Felix,' said the little woman crossly.

'Oh, *poor* Clarinette!' said Felix.

'How did you know I was Clarinette?' snapped she.

'Because you *are,*' said Felix, and offered her another pie. 'Here's a chicken cooked in cream.'

'It's nothing of the sort!'

'And here's a bee-yu-tiful brown soup, with red wine in it.'

'It's *not*, I tell you! It's nothing but mud.'

'Um-um-um!' said Felix, smacking his lips and rubbing his stomach.

'Come with me, and I'll give you *real* soup, and *real* chicken, and a *real* ice-pudding, as I do your two brothers; and I'll dress you in fine clothes and show you the world.'

'Oh, I *am* so full!' sighed Felix, rolling blissfully over on to his face.

'Little idiot!' cried Clarinette shrilly, as she sprang on to the bench. 'Don't you *want* to know about your brothers? Don't you *want* to find out about fine food and grand clothes? Don't you *want* to know what the world is like? Do you *never* ask questions? Why do *I* ask all the questions?'

'I expect because you want to know,' said Felix.

'Know what, pray?' cried Clarinette, beside herself with annoyance.

'I expect you want to know who lives behind the window and the gate.'

'WHO DOES, then?' screamed Clarinette.

Felix looked at her with big eyes, lifted his finger, and whispered, 'I didn't hear a *single sound*.'

With a yell of rage Clarinette sprang off the seat, and went clicking up the road as fast as a trotting pony.

That evening Felix sat at table with his empty bowl held ready, and just as Yvonne was about to toss the ball for supper he remarked, 'I expect I'm going to leave Paradise, Yvonne.'

Yvonne caught her ball to her heart. 'Felix! Are you too going to begin asking questions? What do *you* want to know?'

'I think,' said Felix, 'I will go to my brothers.'

'You also!' sighed Yvonne.

'And bring them back again,' said Felix. As he said it, an apricot popped out of the pot all by itself, and fell plump into his bowl; he opened his mouth to eat it up, but Yvonne said gaily:

'Not yet, not yet! Still one too many in the pot! Out you go, Felix. Have you got your sabots? It's a stony road home.'

'They're on my feet, Yvonne. I expect I'd better take my brothers' sabots too.'

'Here they are then, and goodbye, little Prince,' said she. 'Come back soon, for you'll be hungry till you do.'

'I'll be back by tomorrow noon for certain, Yvonne.' And so the third little Prince left Paradise, with his mouth open.

II

It is a quick step from Paradise to the world, once you decide to take it, and Felix was at the City gates in a brace of shakes. It was still evening when he arrived. A river spanned by fine bridges ran through the middle of the City, dividing it into two halves; in one half the banks were bordered with trees and flower-beds, ornamental lakes and palaces, and gay places where people sat and ate, or danced in the open air. This side of the City was lit with thousands of golden lamps; the other side was darker. Felix wandered among the trees, wondering on which side he would find his brothers. All round him rolled carriages with prancing horses driven by coachmen who cracked their whips and never stopped shouting. This seemed great fun to Felix, and he stood still in the middle of the road, enjoying the noise and lively movement going on about him. Suddenly the shouts and excitement grew twice as loud as before, and Felix felt his shoulder seized by a tall man with a stick in his hand.

'Now then, my little fellow, do you want to get run over?' he demanded.

'No,' said Felix.

'Then don't stand in the middle of things. You'd better run along home.'

'I can't yet,' said Felix.

'Why not? Are you lost?'

'Not at all,' said Felix. 'I know quite well that I am in the world, and that it is not Paradise.'

The tall man shook with laughter. 'That's something to know, that is!' said he. 'Well, and what are you doing in the world tonight?'

'I am looking for my brothers,' said Felix.

'Then you *are* lost,' said the man.

'Not at all,' repeated Felix. 'I have only lost *them*, and it is very important to find them by tomorrow noon. Where are they?'

'How should I know?'

'I ought to have told you,' said Felix, 'that they are Theodore and Crispin.'

'Oh, I see!' said the man, winking at the crowd that had collected. 'Theodore and Crispin! Well, you will no doubt find them on the top of the Eiffel Tower.'

'Thank you,' said Felix. A dozen laughing voices told him that he must cross the water by the next bridge, so he followed the river through the trees and lights, and the crowd followed Felix.

Before he reached the bridge his nose was assailed by the most tempting of smells, and he remembered that he had had no supper and was very hungry. So he stopped at the place the smells came from. It was the gayest of places, as gay as any in that gay City. Many tables spread with delicious food stood under coloured umbrellas among the trees; lights flashed among the leaves, music played from a white pavilion where waiters were moving to and fro with platters of fruit, dishes of ices, and decanters of wine. Round the tables sat men and women in brilliant dresses, with jewels on their hands and in their hair. Some danced, some ate and drank; snatches of song and ripples of talk and laughter filled the air. You would have thought that there was no such thing as sorrow in the world. Yet just beyond the riches and the gaiety, in the deep shadows of a tree outside, three beggars crouched unnoticed, an old woman and her two sons, taking in the lights and sounds and smells so near at hand. As the mirth and music sounded louder, one of the beggar-boys said:

'Ah, it's a gay life!'

And the other, 'Who'd live anywhere but in the City?'

And the ragged old woman nodded her head and chuckled, 'Didn't I tell you, eh? What did I tell you?' And she peered at the scene through an old pair of spectacles, which she lent now and then to the boys. They seemed to have no other idea than to look on.

But Felix did not think of doing that. He went straight up to a table laden with good things, and reached out his hand for a bunch of grapes. Before he could take it, his wrist was seized by a man who was sitting with a party of people at the table.

'Here, here, what are you doing?' asked the man.

Felix wondered at the simple questions that people kept on asking, but he answered very nicely all the same. 'I am taking some grapes,' he explained.

'What for?' asked the man.

'Because I haven't had my supper.'

'Did you ever!' exclaimed the man. One of the party said, 'Never in my life!' and a lady laughed, and another snorted, and the Master of the Pavilion came running out to see what was the matter. All sorts of voices told him at once. 'This little boy came right up to our table, and tried to take some grapes!' 'He said he was doing it because he hadn't had supper!' 'There's a reason for you!' 'The idea!'

The Master of the Pavilion addressed Felix, who stood there with his mouth open. 'You can't come taking grapes like that,' he said.

'I do at home,' said Felix.

'Well, this is not your father's vineyard. If you

want grapes here you must pay for them. What have you got in your pockets?'

Felix drew forth the two pairs of sabots saying, 'These. But I am taking them to my brothers, and I see you have some shoes already on your feet, so you will not need them.'

At this the people began to laugh so loud that Felix was obliged to laugh with them; and then their laughter changed to a sweeter sound, and a lady put the grapes into his hand, saying, 'Where are your brothers, and who are they?'

'They are Theodore and Crispin, and they are on the top of the Eiffel Tower.'

'Who told you that?' asked the Master. Felix looked at the crowd behind him, and said, 'Those kind people.'

'It is a shame!' cried the lady who had given him the grapes; and a man stepped out of the crowd and said:

'You are right. It was just a joke. But we will help the child to find his brothers.'

'We too!' cried the party who had been feasting.

'And we! And we!' cried all the rest of the diners and dancers.

'Thank you,' said Felix. 'It will be quite easy, because they live with Clarinette, who wears a lace dress, and a fur cape, and has embroidered shoes.'

'Clarinette? It is this Clarinette, then, we must find,' cried the lady. She took Felix by the hand and led him on, and everyone followed them. For they all began to feel how important it was for Felix to find his brothers.

Now began a search all over the City; they hunted

on this side of the river and on that. They went to the top of the Hill of Montmartre, and all round the foot of the Eiffel Tower. Some said, 'Let us go to the Triumphal Arch,' and others, 'Try the Woods of Boulogne,' and others, 'They may be in the Circus of Lutetia.' Everybody knew some part of the City to suggest, and they tried them all. Wherever they went, the crowd gathered and grew; people ran out from the shops and houses and places of amusement to see what was afoot, and were told, 'We are looking for Clarinette who dresses in furs and laces, and has charge of Theodore and Crispin, the brothers of this child.' And whoever looked at Felix exclaimed at once, 'Yes, yes, the child must find his brothers; such a child must not be lost in the City.' And Felix explained over and over again, 'I am not lost; I have only lost my brothers. I know quite well that I am not in Paradise.' In the end, the whole of the City turned out to follow Felix in his search for his brothers; there was not a soul who felt he could be at peace till they were found. But Felix wondered more and more that none of them knew Theodore or Crispin or Clarinette.

'For that is who they *are*,' he said. And someone answered, 'Ah, my child, no matter who you are, it is only too easy to pass through the world unknown.'

'In Paradise,' explained Felix, 'everybody knows everybody.'

So they went on till daybreak; and at last, weary and out of breath, the whole City halted under the trees where the search had begun, and the grey light fell upon the tables littered with food, and on the three beggars still crouched under the tree.

'It is useless,' said the Master of the Pavilion. 'We had better have breakfast.'

'Alas, yes,' sighed the lady who had Felix by the hand, 'we must give it up and have breakfast.'

'Let everybody enter!' said the Master, waving his hand generously towards the Pavilion; for he had come to feel that night as though the great search had made them all brothers. And the crowd began to melt away beyond the door, eager for coffee and fresh rolls. As they moved off among the tables with the gay umbrellas, even the three beggars crept out from under the tree; for the Master had said 'Everybody!' But when his eye fell upon the only three people in the City who had not joined in the search, he said roughly, 'Not you! Not you!' and thrust them back again.

Then, as all eyes turned upon them, Felix dropped the lady's hand, and ran up to the old woman and the ragged boys, crying joyfully, 'Theodore! Crispin! Clarinette!' and he threw his arms around their necks, embracing them.

You should have heard the crowd begin to murmur then! 'Theodore, he said, and Crispin!' 'Are those the famous brothers?' 'And Clarinette, who wears fine furs and laces? Do but look at her rags, and theirs!' 'Yes, and even this boy, whom we have been following all night—he's not much better than the rest.' And as the light of dawn grew greyer, and the morning air more nippy, they rubbed their eyes and saw that Felix was but a little boy with rough hair and holes in his stockings from climbing trees. Of a sudden, the whole City felt ashamed of itself for the manner in which it had been led away.

'Who are you, you three boys?' cried the people.

And Felix, with his arms about his brothers' necks, explained, 'We are little Princes, in Paradise.'

The crowd roared at him. 'And who is the old witch?' they cried through their laughter.

But Felix had done with answering their questions. He smiled at Clarinette and lifted his finger, as though he might be listening at a window.

Then the crowd shrugged its shoulders, and said 'Pooh!' and went into the Pavilion, leaving the four of them alone. Soon through the trees floated the fragrant smell of coffee, and the three hungry boys sat with open mouths, breathing it in. Clarinette did likewise, chuckling, 'Ah, it's a fine life in the City! Here we *do* know What's What!'

'Yes,' said Theodore, shivering in his rags, 'how glad I am I came.'

'And I,' said Crispin. 'Only smell the coffee! Lend me your spectacles, Clarinette, so that I can see what's on the tables better. The food looks just like so much mud without them.'

'You can't have them,' grumbled Clarinette. 'I want them for myself. You boys are always snatching.'

'When I am rich, I'll have a gold pair of my own,' boasted Theodore.

'Me, too,' said Crispin, 'with diamonds in them, when I'm rich.'

'Then I'll be able to see the world for myself,' said Theodore.

'Just as it really is,' said Crispin.

'You can see it now, with your own eyes,' said Felix.

'What can we see, I'd like to know?' asked Theodore.

'You can see me.'

'What of it? Who are you?'

'I am Felix,' said Felix, wondering.

'Who's Felix?' asked Crispin.

'Your brother.'

'Not possible!' said Theodore.

Felix grew in wonder. 'And you can see Paradise.'

'There is no Paradise,' said Theodore.

'Not possible!' said Crispin.

'I've come to take you back,' said Felix, 'to the apple and poplar trees, and to Yvonne with her ball, and to the Witch's hut and the Fairy's garden.'

'There *are* no witches,' said Theodore.

'There *are* no fairies,' said Crispin.

Clarinette glanced at Felix with her sharp bright eyes. 'Witches in Paradise?' said she.

'Witches *are* fairies, in Paradise,' said Felix.

And Clarinette muttered, 'Is it possible!'

'Do come,' said Felix. 'Look, I have brought your sabots, but don't put them on till I've emptied out the glass.'

He drew the wooden shoes from his pockets, and turned them upside down; but to his surprise they were already empty. Only in the sole of each shoe a little hole had been worn, no bigger than an eyeball, and in each hole was fitted a round glass, as clear as crystal.

Theodore and Crispin snatched the shoes from his hand. 'Are these my sabots?' cried one. 'Are these mine?' cried the other. And both together shouted, 'Now we've got spectacles at last! Clarinette, Clarinette, our sabots make us spectacles! Now we can see things for ourselves!' In high glee they held the wooden shoes up to their eyes, and stared through the crystals in the soles.

'Oh, oh!' cried Theodore. 'I can see my favourite apple-tree!'

'I can see the tallest poplar!' cried Crispin.

'And there's the silver river!'

'And the golden corncocks!'

'There's the Witch's window!'

'And the Fairy's gate!'

'And the fruit-pot steaming!'

'And Yvonne throwing her ball!'

Then both cried together, 'There's our brother Felix!' And the three boys fell into one another's arms.

In a flash, Theodore and Crispin had their feet in their shoes; and when the people of the City came out of the Pavilion, all they could see was a trio of ragged boys, as the three little Princes went running back to Paradise. But of Clarinette, the old woman they had called a witch, there was never a trace—no, not a single sound.

III

The little Princes arrived on the very tick of Tomorrow Noon. Yvonne was watching for them at the door, and how she laughed to see them coming with their mouths hanging open.

'We're hungry, Yvonne! We're hungry!' they clamoured. 'Is dinner ready?'

'Half a jiffy!' laughed Yvonne. 'While I prepare it you'd better eat up what you left in your bowls.'

Each fell on his own bowl at table, and ate the fruits of Paradise, Theodore his peach, Crispin his apple, and Felix his apricot.

'None too many in the pot!' sang Yvonne; and she tossed her ball, clapped her hands, called out 'Dinner!' and in a moment the ladle had filled the bowls as full as they could hold.

The boys gobbled away for dear life. But between two big mouthfuls Theodore suddenly paused and cried, '*I* know something!'

'What do *you* know, then?' laughed Yvonne.

'I know that a Witch lives in the hut, because you told me so.'

'And *I* know something!' shouted Crispin with his mouth full.

'What do *you* know, then?' asked Yvonne.

'I know a Fairy lives in the garden, because you said she did!'

'We don't know their names though,' said Felix.

'They have only one name between them,' said Yvonne. 'And it cannot be said; it can only be heard.'

The three Princes cocked their ears and Felix, lifting his finger, said, 'I *think* I can hear something.'

'Something squeaky,' said Theodore, 'like a rusty window-hinge.'

'Something sweet,' said Crispin, 'like a drop of honey in a flower.'

'Something,' said Felix, 'like a sort of—a sort of flute.'

'It's possible,' said Yvonne.

'Oh,' cried the little Princes, 'I wonder what it *is*!'

'Go on wondering,' said Yvonne, and tossed her crystal ball for second helpings.

Down in the valley was the village, where John and Mary lived with their Mother and Father in a little cottage and went to school when the bell rang in the little schoolhouse on weekdays; and to church when the bells rang in the little church on Sundays.

And up on the hill was the great mansion, where the Little Lady lived all by herself with her servants, and paced up and down the long flight of stone steps between the cypresses and orange-trees, or walked in her rose-garden, which was the loveliest in the world.

The hill was high and the valley was deep, so people seldom went up or came down; only a silvery river flowed between the high mansion and the low cottages, and seemed to bind them together.

When they were out of school, Mary helped her Mother in the kitchen, and before she was ten could bake little pies fit for a queen. And John dug in the garden with his Father, and before he was twelve could raise cabbages fit for a king. In their free time the children played in the fields with their school-fellows, or paddled in the shallow pools of the river as it flowed down the middle of the valley.

One hot June day as they were splashing in the shallows they saw in the distance two tiny specks floating towards them.

'Here come the boats!' cried John.

'With red and white sails,' said Mary.

'I'll have the red one,' said John; and Mary said, 'I'll have the white.'

But as the tiny craft came nearer, the children saw they were not boats, but roses.

They had never seen such roses for colour, size, and perfume. John captured the red rose and Mary the white one, and home they ran with their prizes.

When their parents saw the roses, the Father said, 'By my Shovel and Hoe! If I could grow roses like *that* in my garden I'd be a proud man!' And the Mother cried, 'Dear bless my Cherry Tart! If I could have roses like *them* in the home I'd be a glad woman!'

Then the Father asked, 'Where did you get 'em, children?'

'They came down the river from the top of the hill,' said John.

'Ah!' sighed the Father. 'Then they came from the Little Lady's rose-garden, and are not for the likes of us.'

And he went out to hoe cabbages, while the Mother rolled her paste.

But John and Mary stole out of the cottage, and John said to Mary, 'Let us find the Little Lady's rose-garden, and beg her for a rose-tree to make our parents proud and happy.'

'How shall we find it?' said Mary.

'We'll take the road up the hill that the roses took down.'

'What road is that?' said Mary.

'The river,' said John.

So they followed the river uphill till they came near the top, and were stopped by a big iron gate, that led to the longest flight of steps they'd ever seen. On the steps the Little Lady herself paced slowly up, and when she reached the fountain at the top she turned, and paced slowly down again. At the bottom of the steps she saw the little faces of John and Mary pressed against the bars.

'What are you doing?' said John.

'Counting the steps,' said the Little Lady.

'Why?' said Mary.

'Because I've nothing else to do,' said the Little Lady.

'Why don't you go and hoe cabbages?' said John.

'My Head Gardener won't let me.'

'Why don't you go and bake pies?' said Mary.

'My Head Cook would be cross with me.'

'Father lets *me* hoe cabbages!' said John.

'Mother lets *me* bake pies!' said Mary.

'How lucky you are!' said the Little Lady. 'Who are you?'

'John,' said John.

'Mary,' said Mary.

'Where do you come from?'

'The village in the valley.'

'What have you come for?'

'A red rose-tree for Father,' said John.

'A white one for Mother,' said Mary.

'OH!' cried the Little Lady. 'Did *you* find the roses I sent down the river? How glad I am!'

'Why did you send them down?' asked John.

'To bring someone back. You can't think how dull it is with nobody to play with. If you'll stay and play with me, you shall have a rose-tree apiece, and my Head Gardener won't know the difference.'

So John and Mary stayed all day with the Little Lady, playing in her rose-garden and her grand rooms till they were tired. And she sent them home with a rose-tree apiece, which they took to their parents, saying that they had had the happiest day of their lives.

But next morning the Little Lady found counting the steps duller than ever, so when she reached the gate she opened it for the very first time and ran down the hill. On reaching the village she went straight to John and Mary's cottage, walked in, and said, 'I want to bake pies and hoe cabbages.'

'Bless my Apple Dumpling, so you shall!' said the Mother.

So first the Little Lady got her hands as white as flour, and then as black as earth; and when she went home she took a cabbage and a pasty with her, and said it was the happiest day of *her* life.

After this, whenever she was lonely, she knew she had only to run down the hill herself, or set a rose sailing to bring up a child. A white rose brought a girl, but a red rose brought a boy.

And sometimes she gathered a whole skirtful of roses and set them afloat; and on those days every child in the village was seen to be running up the hill to the Little Lady's rose-garden.

In *these* days a certain Councillor of a certain country passed on his walk a certain spot. And there he saw a sentry marching up and down, up and down, so many steps this way, so many steps back again. The Councillor watched him for a little while, and he looked at the spot where the sentry marched. There was no building near, no gate in sight, there was nothing and nobody to guard.

'What are you doing here?' asked the Councillor.

'Obeying orders,' said the sentry.

'What are they?' asked the Councillor.

'To walk so many paces in this direction, and then so many paces in that.'

'What for?' asked the Councillor.

'I don't know,' said the sentry.

The Councillor went to headquarters.

'Why is there a sentry guarding such and such a spot?' he asked.

'There always has been one,' he was told.

'But why?'

'The order is on records.'

'Who gave the order?'

Nobody knew.

'When was it given?'

None could remember.

'How stupid,' said the Councillor. 'It must be changed.'

So they held a meeting and changed it, and the sentry was taken away and put on guard somewhere else. For what's the use of guarding nothing at all?

Now I will tell you the story.

In *those* days, and this is true, there was a Queen who walked in her garden, and there she saw growing, what do you think? A flower.

Did you say, 'Well, I'm not surprised'? I dare say not, for what would grow in a garden, if not a flower?

Weeds, did you say? Oh yes, very likely! *I* know gardens where there are more weeds than flowers, but these gardens belong to little girls and boys, who forget to look after them, however much they promise. But this garden was the Queen's garden, with a Chief Head Gardener, and a Chief Head Weeder, and a Chief Head Mower, and all. So you'd expect to see flowers in it. And all the same, when the Queen saw this one she *was* surprised, because it surpassed every flower she had ever seen before.

What sort of flower? Oh, that doesn't matter a bit. It might have been a rose, and it might have been a lupin, and it might have been a clematis with its head in the air, or a pansy with its chin on the ground. All that matters is that whatever sort it was it was the best of its sort, and it took the Queen's breath away with joy.

She came to see it every day, and every day she felt the same delight. Then one morning as she walked in the garden she saw the Chief Head Flower-Cutter lavishly cutting flowers.

'What are you doing?' she asked.

'So please Your Majesty, I'm cutting flowers for Your Majesty's ball tonight.'

The Queen's heart jumped at that, and she hastened to the corner of the garden where her flower grew, and oh joy! there it was still. When she had calmed down from her fright, she sent for her General and said:

'General, I want a special sentry ordered to guard this spot night and day.'

'Dear me, dear me!' said the General. 'Is there danger?'

'Great danger,' said the Queen.

The General stooped down and examined the spot cautiously. 'Is there gunpowder buried here? Is there a secret tunnel the enemy may come by? Has Your Majesty hidden the Crown Jewels under the ground? No? Then what is it?'

'General,' said the Queen, 'why are there sentries posted around my palace day and night?'

'Because Your Majesty's person is precious to the heart of the nation.'

The Queen pointed to the flower. 'Did you ever behold,' she asked, 'a more beautiful flower than this one?'

'Never, madam.'

'Nor I,' said she. 'This flower is precious to the heart of the Queen. Therefore let a soldier be posted here at once, to see that no harm befalls it.'

Her will was done; the order was placed upon the records, and in less than an hour a fine young sentry was marching up and down, up and down, so many steps this way and so many steps back again. All through that summer a sentry stood on duty, and when the Queen came daily to enjoy her flower, he presented arms and stood at attention while she stooped down to smell it.

Summer passed and autumn came. The petals of the flower fell on the earth, and the leaves died down. But still all day and all night a sentry was posted at that corner of the palace garden, because the order had gone forth and never been recalled.

Winter passed and spring came. The garden once more put forth its buds, and once more the Queen walked in the garden to see its beauty growing day by day.

Did she go again to see her flower? Perhaps she did, and perhaps she didn't. But whether she did or not, the sentry took up his post there as regularly as the sun came up in the morning and went down at night. For that was the order.

The years went by, the Queen died, there was another Queen in her place, or perhaps a King instead. There was a new General for the old one, the gardeners were replaced by their sons and then their grandsons. In the garden the flower-beds were changed, lilies grew where pinks had been, and wallflowers took the place of snapdragons. In the city the streets were changed, streets that had been grand had grown poor, and poor streets had become fine thoroughfares.

In the country the land itself was changed, meadows were built on, woods had disappeared, hills had been levelled, and the course of rivers altered.

In the world the very countries were changed. This one was now a part of that one, that one had shrunk to a mere nothing, t'other had spread across the continent like floodwater.

And in the thoughts of men the very world was changed. What once was right, now was wrong. What once was foolish, now was wise. What once was there, was there no longer.

The only thing that wasn't changed was the order in the records; the order the Queen had made in *those* days for a sentry to guard the spot where her flower was growing. And as long as an order stands in the records, it must be carried out. That is why, year in, year out, on a spot of barren ground, a sentry marched up and down, up and down, so many steps this way, so many steps back again.

Until somebody said 'How stupid!' and took him away. For what is the use of guarding a beautiful thing, if you don't even know it is there?

ONE morning just as usual, Danny O'Toole's mother buttoned on his coat, pulled his green beret over his ears, and saw him as far as the door. The rest of the way to school Danny went by himself. He was seven years old, and there was only one crossing.

'Be careful over the road,' said Mrs O'Toole. 'Look both ways, mind.'

'I will so,' promised Danny.

'Isn't that the best advice in the breadth of the world,' called Mr O'Toole from the kitchen, where they all had breakfast. 'If you look both ways you'll be missing nothing so, from a stray cat to a king.'

'Never mind cats and kings,' said Mrs O'Toole. 'You look out for motor-cars and bicycles.'

'I will so,' promised Danny, and set out for Larchgrove Road Junior and Infants' Mixed.

Mrs O'Toole went back to the kitchen, where Mr O'Toole was packing his first pipe of the morning.

'What a lot of nonsense you tell the child,' she smiled. 'You stuff him as full of tales as you stuff your pipe with baccy.'

'What else would ye stuff a pipe with, or a child?' asked Mr O'Toole. He was Irish and she was English, and that was the difference. But the English either smile or scold at what they don't exactly understand, and Mr O'Toole, when he came to live in England, had been careful to pick a smiling one. She was smiling now as she piled up the breakfast-cups. Mr O'Toole got ready to go to work. He worked at the Coronation Theatre round the corner. At home he wore his shirt-sleeves like other men, but at work he wore a touch of splendour on his uniform that set him apart. Last Christmas Danny had been to see his first pantomime at the Coronation Theatre, and he had lost his heart to the beautiful Dick Whittington, and to his wonderful Cat, the Seven Fairy Belles, and the Programme Girl who brought him a vanilla ice after Part One. But when he lay awake at night thinking about it, till he fell asleep and dreamed about it, what he remembered as much as anything was the look of his own little father, opening the doors of motor-cars and whistling to taxis, dressed in something he never wore at home.

'My father has gold on his coat,' he told the children in school.

'Ho, very likely!' scoffed Albert Briggs, who was not Danny's favourite person at all. 'Tell that to the Marines.' Albert had heard his uncle say this lately, and he had faith in everything his uncle said, just as Danny had faith in everything his father told him. 'Gold on his coat, hoo!' scoffed Albert. 'You tell that to the Marines.'

'I will so,' said Danny stoutly. 'My father *does* have gold on his shoulders and all down his fronts.'

'Tell us where your father was born, Danny,' giggled Maisie Bonnington.

'My father was born in Connemara!' shouted Danny fiercely. This was the question which always ended the talk about Danny's father. The children screamed with laughter at the funny word, ever since Danny first said it. The school poet had made up a little chant about it:

> 'Danny's father! Danny's father!
> Doesn't live in Connemara!'

'No he does not then,' shouted Danny, 'but he did before that.'

'Before what?' teased Maisie. 'There isn't such a place as Connemara.'

'There is then!'

'You made it up.'

'I did not then! And my father does have gold on his coat.'

'Tell that to the Marines,' repeated Albert Briggs rudely.

'The Marines *knows*,' said Danny, inspired. For all Albert Briggs knew about the Marines was that they were told things, and now Danny had collared them as if they were old friends. The school bell put an end to the talk, which happened after the Christmas holidays, when the pantomime was in full swing. But the day when Mr O'Toole said that about the cats and kings was in the summer, as far away as it could be from Christmas and pantomimes. It was summer holidays coming, and everybody was telling where they were going, or would like to go, or where they went last year.

At the crossing Danny looked both ways very carefully, and when the road was quite clear he scuttled across and in another minute was in the playground of Larchgrove Road Infant and Junior Mixed. And how funny that his father should have picked that very day to talk of cats, for there was Maisie Bonnington with a kitten in her arms. The other children were crowding round her, all trying to touch the kitten, who had a purple bow tied round its pale grey neck. It was mostly very soft whitey-grey, with dark markings and scared blue eyes, and when the children fondled it it pushed its nose under Maisie's armpit and tried to hide itself. 'It's a chinchilla kitten,' said Maisie proudly.

'Let me see!' said Danny O'Toole.

'Let Danny see!' mimicked Albert Briggs. 'He ain't never seed a chilla kitten before; they don't have chilla kittens in Connemara.'

'They has other things,' said Danny stoutly.

'What has they then?'

'I shan't tell you.'

'You don't know,' scoffed Albert Briggs.

This was only too true. Danny hedged till he could get information at the source. 'I'll tell you tomorrow.'

'No you won't.'

'I will so.'

'You won't, because,' crowed Albert triumphantly, 'there ain't no such a place as Conny-onny-mara!'

The children shrieked with delight, bringing Miss Daly to the door to see what it was all about. She was the new junior mistress, nice to look at, and very popular. She clapped her hands at them.

'Come along, come along, what's the joke? What have you got there, Maisie?'

'It's my chinchilla kitten, Miss. It was give me last night.'

'Given me, Maisie. How sweet. But I don't think you can bring it to school, you know.'

'Oh, Miss!'

Miss Daly shook her head. 'It's not school-age yet.' The children giggled. 'We'll make it cosy and find it some milk. Aren't you the little sweet.' Miss Daly snuggled the soft grey ball under her chin. 'Gracious, look at the time! Get a move on, quick!'

'S'pose it gets out and is lost, Miss,' quavered Maisie.

'I promise it won't. You can take it home at dinner-time.'

The thought of the chinchilla kitten permeated the lessons that morning. Maisie Bonnington basked in the glory of ownership, fawned on and envied by her school-fellows.

At tea-time Danny asked his father, 'What does they have in Connemara, Dad?'

'In Connemara is the greenest hills in Ireland, and the blackest bogs, and lakes like looking-glass you can see the clouds go by in.'

'Is there kittens, I mean?'

'Just wait till you get there!'

'When?'

'Some day or other.' Mr O'Toole sugared his tea. 'Some day you an' me'll go to your grandfather's farm where I was born.'

This was a standard promise, often repeated. Suddenly Danny was curious about the farm he had never seen. 'Is there cats and kittens?'

'Cats and kittens is it? You couldn't step for kittens.'

'Of your very own was they?'

'If I'd wanted. But why me, with a donkey of my very own?'

'A donkey!'

'As white as pear-blossom.'

'A *donkey*.'

'And two eyes like red rubies.' (*Terence!* from Mrs O'Toole.)

Danny said, 'Maisie's chilla kitten's got blue eyes. She bringed her kitten to school today.'

'Did she so?' Mr O'Toole sugared his tea again, absent-mindedly. Out of the corner of his eye he was watching Danny's quivering lower lip.

'Albert says there's no chilla kittens in Connemara.'

Mr O'Toole stirred his cup of tea. 'You tell Albert Briggs, with me very best Sunday compliments, you've got a donkey of your own in Connemara.'

'*Me?*'

'Who else? Amn't I giving you him this very minute?'

'*I've*,' breathed Danny, 'got a donkey!'

'You have so.' Mr O'Toole stood up. It was time to get back to the Coronation, two turnings away, very convenient for slipping home to tea. Danny followed him down the street.

'How big is he, Dad?'

'About so big.' Mr O'Toole's hand sketched the air. 'Just the size for a boy the like of you.'

'Will I see him?'

'Some day or other.'

'Will I ride on his back?'

'Will you not!'

'Does he go quick?'

'As the four winds in one.'

'Does there be a saddle?'

'Sky-blue plush with silver knobs like stars. You turn back now. Herself won't wish you to be crossing twice.'

'Does there be reins?'

'Scarlet leather,' called Mr O'Toole from the middle of the road.

'Dad, Dad!' Mr O'Toole paused on the far pavement. 'What's his name, Dad?'

'His name,' shouted Mr O'Toole, 'is Finnigan O'Flanagan. Go home now I'm saying.'

'Let's have a look at you,' said Mrs O'Toole, when Danny came dancing in, cheeks flushed, eyes shining. 'You haven't got a sore throat, have you?' She searched him anxiously for signs of fever.

'Finnigan O'Flanagan!' cried Danny.

Mrs O'Toole suspected delirium at once.

'My donkey's name is Finnigan O'Flanagan, Ma!'

'Get along!' she laughed. *It's his father's delirium he's got a touch of.* 'Up to bed with you, and don't forget to say your prayers.'

Danny went to bed, and took his donkey with him. His prayers first and last were for Finnigan O'Flanagan.

He ran breathless to school next morning, but only managed to clutch Albert Briggs in the passage leading to their different classrooms.

'In Connemara is donkeys.'

'Wossat?'

'One's mine.'

'Wossat?'

'A donkey. I've got one of my own. It's Finnigan—'

Education parted them, but somehow before the morning break a dozen children knew that Danny O'Toole was the owner of a donkey in Connemara. At least, he said so. But if there was no such place as Connemara, how could there be a donkey in it? This was put forcibly to Danny in the playground. Danny piled on the circumstantial evidence.

'He's got a blue saddle.'

'Coo!' from the Believers.

'And red reins and silver knobs.'

'Hoo!' from the Unbelievers.

'He's a white donkey.'

'There's no white donkeys,' asserted Albert Briggs.

'There is so. He's got rubies for eyes. His name is Finnigan O'Flanagan.'

'Finnigan O'Flanagan!' Derision reached its peak in Albert's voice. 'Tell that to the Marines.'

The Disbelievers had it by an overwhelming majority. The children scampered about the playground shouting the ridiculous syllables. Finnigan O'Flanagan! A white donkey with ruby eyes. The Marines would never swallow it. His Muse took the school poet by the throat. 'Danny's wonky! So's his donkey!' chanted the poet.

'Danny's wonky, so's his donkey!' yelled the school as one child. They plugged this theme song till lessons were resumed.

In class Miss Daly said smiling, 'Handkerchief, Danny!' Sitting right under her nose on the front bench, he was trying to wipe his own without being noticed. He used the back of his hand. It isn't easy to suffer a broken heart in full view of teacher's bright blue eyes. Danny pulled out his handkerchief, and contrived to smear his own eyes with it while blowing his nose. There is nothing shameful about a good hard nose-blow, but eyes are a different matter. Miss Daly smiled again encouragingly, and went on with the lesson, wondering what was upsetting Danny O'Toole. For a reason of her own he was one of her pets, but if you have favourites it doesn't do to show it; and when children are numbered by the score, one must expect tears now and then. At dinner-time she beckoned Danny to her, and tucked a scrap of green in his button-hole.

'Shamrock for luck, Danny.' It had come to her by post only that morning.

'Thank you, Miss. Miss.'

'Yes, Danny?'

'Did you see a white donkey?'

'A white donkey! Where?'

'Isn't there white donkeys, Miss?'

'Indeed and there is then. I don't think I ever actually *saw* one, Danny. They're a rare kind of donkey, you know.'

'What's rare?' asked Danny.

'Special,' said Miss Daly.

Danny strutted out into the playground, fortified with lucky green shamrock. Passing Albert Briggs he shouted, 'White donkeys is special, Miss Daly says. Finnigan O'Flanagan's *special*, do you hear?'

Next day he had specialities to impart. 'His four hoofs shine like gold. He swings a rose on his tail.'

'Coo!'

'Hoo!'

From then on there were tidings every day, gleaned from Danny's father every night. Believers and Unbelievers crowded to hear that Finnigan O'Flanagan had run in the races and beaten all the colts by seven necks. Finnigan O'Flanagan had met a mad bull in the lane and hee-hawed at him till he turned tail, thus saving the life of the Princess of Galway, for which he got a medal from the Mayor. Finnigan O'Flanagan could bray so loud it frighted all the Banshees out of Connemara. Brave as a lion was Finnigan O'Flanagan, gentle as a dove, and wise as an ould barn owl. He would carry a sleeping baby ten miles and never wake it, but he could smell out a villain among twenty honest men, and if that one mounted Finnigan he'd find himself on his back in a bog before you could say 'Whisht!'

'Coo!' breathed the Believers, while the Unbelievers hooted 'Hoo!'

But they were all greedy for more, for a good tale is a good tale, whether it's true or not. If Finnigan O'Flanagan wasn't an accepted fact in Larchgrove Road School, he was at least an accepted legend.

The end of term approached. Interest in the Connemara donkey became somewhat submerged in the excitement of the holidays. 'Where you going?' 'Where *you* going, Maisie?' 'You goin' anywhere, Bert?'

'Southend. Two weeks.'

'Lucky boy!' called Miss Daly, scurrying by with her arms full of copybooks.

'Where *you* going, Miss?'

'Ballynahinch!' Miss Daly scurried on, followed by the children's gleeful laughter.

Pressed to say where *he* was going, on the day before school broke up, Danny said he wasn't going anywhere.

'Then you're going to Connemara,' sneered Albert Briggs, 'cos shall I tell you why, cos Connemara ain't nowhere.'

'I'll fight you!' Danny doubled his small fists.

'You shut up,' said Maisie surprisingly to Albert. Wasn't she spending the holidays with her auntie at Shoreham, and wasn't Bert going to Southend for two whole weeks? Well, then! She chose Danny to go with as the children clattered through the gates, and asked him consolingly, 'What's Finnigan been up to?' Danny took the bait.

'One time Dad was lost and it was as black as pitch and so his lantern blowed out and there was bogs and so Finnigan's eyes shined red like traffic lights all the way a hundred miles Dad was ever so hungry and he would of starved to death if Finnigan—'

'He could have shot some rabbits,' shouted Albert in the rear.

'He could not then, he didn't have a gun.'

'Why didn't he?'

'He was only as little as me.'

'When your dad was lost?'

'Yes, and Finnigan—'

'How old's your dad?' demanded Albert Briggs.

Danny dashed at it. 'Fifty-two.'

'Hoo! Finnigan's dead then.'

Danny turned and stared at him. Albert grinned round the group of home-going children. 'Donkey's don't live *twenty* years. Finnigan's a deader. Danny ain't never had no donkey. He's wonky.'

'So's his donkey!' chanted the poet.

'Danny's wonky, so's his donkey!' yelled the children.

It wasn't true, it wasn't true, it *couldn't* be true. His father would know. Danny doubled his fists again, wavered, then rushed out of earshot, rushed home with streaming eyes. At the crossing he forgot to look both ways.

It was Maisie who brought word to school next morning why Danny was absent on the last day of the term.

That evening Miss Daly appeared on Mrs O'Toole's doorstep. 'I've come to ask after Danny, Mrs O'Toole. We're all so dreadfully sorry. Is he—?'

'Oh, Miss, he's very poorly. Would you like to see him?'

But Danny didn't know who Miss Daly was. He

seemed to be speaking to somebody who wasn't there, somebody he called Finnigan. Suddenly he stared at Miss Daly and doubled his fists. 'Finnigan's *not* a deader. I'll fight you!' he cried.

'I'd better go,' whispered Miss Daly. 'Don't come down. I'll find my way out.'

She went downstairs feeling very much upset. Mr O'Toole was hanging about the passage. He looked at her vaguely. 'Is it the nurse ye are?' Miss Daly recognized her native accent, and her heart went out instantly to Danny's father, as it had gone out instantly to his son.

'I'm Danny's schoolmistress, Kitty Daly,' she said. 'Mr O'Toole, who's Finnigan?'

Mr O'Toole told her. He told her everything, from the rose on Finnigan's tail to his non-existence. 'It's an ould fool I am to be stuffin' the child's brain with legends,' he mourned, 'but such store he set by that lily-white ass I went on and on with it, like a man follows a wandering light in the dark.' Then Mr O'Toole cried, and Miss Daly cried too.

'I'll write,' she said. 'I'll be going home tomorrow, but I'll write. I'll want to know.'

Miss Daly did write, but not as soon as she meant to. When you return home after quite a long time there's so much to catch you up from moment to moment, and then that business of crossing the Irish Channel is more than just putting a space between you and England, it's putting one life in place of another. To make things worse, it happened that a young naval officer, called Frank, arrived in her village the day after she did. He had been on the same ship as her brother, so once she had met him, and now, by a funny chance, he had turned up to spend a holiday where she was spending hers. They spent the first week saying how curious it was. Frank's hobby was taking snapshots, and he took them by the reel of everything she showed him about her home. The only thing he didn't take was Miss Daly. He wanted to, but something got into her, and the more he urged the more she wouldn't let him. It wasn't till the seventh day, when they were leaning over a gate, feeding thistles to Paddy the peat-cutter's old grey donkey, that Miss Daly exclaimed, 'Oh dear!'

'What's the matter?' asked Frank, rather anxiously.

'I never wrote!'

'To whom?'

'To Danny, the darlint.'

'Who's Danny?' asked Frank, rather fiercely.

'He's my pet pupil, and he had an accident. I'll write this very day.'

Three days later, Frank found Miss Daly crying her eyes out over a letter from England.

'Kitty! Kitty dear—what is it?'

'Danny—' she choked.

'He isn't—?'

'No, but he's very bad indeed, he's in hospital, and he keeps crying and crying for Finnigan.'

'Finnigan?'

Miss Daly told Frank everything about Finnigan, everything that Mr O'Toole had told her; and how Danny's whole heart was set upon his Connemara donkey, white as snow, with ruby eyes and gold hoofs and a rose on his tail, his very own donkey whom he had never seen. 'And of course,' sobbed Miss Daly, 'there's no such donkey at all, and never was, and there's Danny crying out that Finnigan's died, and nothing his father tells him makes any difference. Wouldn't I be giving him a white donkey the like of Finnigan if I had one?'

Miss Daly felt her hand pressed gently. 'Indeed it's good of you to feel so for poor Danny,' she sighed, 'but it's only the sight of his donkey will do him any good.'

'Why not?' said Frank, whose only thought was to stop the tears flowing from Miss Daly's beautiful blue eyes.

The tears did stop flowing, and the blue eyes looked with great surprise into his brown ones. 'What do you mean by that?' asked Miss Daly.

'You'll see what I mean,' said Frank, 'if you'll be in Mike's paddock at twelve o'clock tomorrow—and Kitty—'

'Well then?'

'Pray for a sunny day with all your might.'

Miss Daly must have spent the whole night praying, for the day was one of the sunniest ever seen. She couldn't wait till noon to get to the peat-cutter's paddock, but Frank was ready for her. And so was Paddy—but no! this was never Paddy? Mike had surely got himself a brand-new donkey, gleaming like snow on the top of a sunshiny mountain. As she came near, Frank was just finishing tying a big pink cabbage rose to the tail of this white wonder with a ribbon the colour of Kitty Daly's eyes.

'Allow me to introduce you,' said Frank gravely, 'to Finnigan O'Flanagan. Don't come too near, I'm not sure if he's quite dry yet. What do you think of him?'

'Oh, he's beautiful!' whispered Miss Daly. 'Where's your camera now?' She had jumped to it without being told. 'You must photograph him against Mike's old black shed, he'll show up like an angel so.'

'I hope he'll stand still,' said Frank. 'He's tried to kick me twice, and he's kicked over the whitewash can already.'

'He'll not kick me,' said Miss Daly. 'We're old friends, aren't we, Paddy boy?'

'Splendid!' said Frank. 'Then if you'll just stand by him and keep him still—'

'Ah, get away with you! I'll not be photographed.'

'Not even to please poor little Danny?'

'It's not me he's crying after.'

'No,' said Frank, 'but if you're in the picture he'll know that Finnigan is as alive as you are.' Miss Daly wavered. Frank had an inspiration. 'I tell you what! Lift up the donkey's tail, and be smelling the rose.'

Miss Daly gave in. With a face full of laughter she lifted Finnigan's tail daintily and sniffed the cabbage rose. The camera clicked. 'Right!' cried Frank. 'Just one more to make sure.' The camera clicked again. 'We'll have an enlargement made of the best of them, and send it by air.'

'Oh,' cried Kitty Daly, 'I could hug you!'

'Why not?' said Frank.

But it was two enlargements he ordered of the Connemara donkey with a rose on its tail.

When the autumn term started at Larchgrove Road Junior and Infants' Mixed, Danny O'Toole was not there. But halfway through the term he was well enough to come. Everybody knew he was coming, and Miss Daly, who had visited him already at home, knew what he was bringing to school with him. She hovered in the background while he displayed the flat brown-paper parcel he carried so carefully under his small armpit.

'Wossat?' demanded Albert Briggs at sight.

'It's my donkey,' said Danny, 'it's Finnigan O'Flanagan.'

The children crowded round to see as he took off the outer wrapping, and opened the large stiff envelope which contained the photograph of a donkey as white as pear-blossom, as snow on the mountain-tops, or as whitewash. The children gasped with wonder; the black shed threw up the angelic donkey into dazzling relief, but as well as that his eyes glowed as red and his hoofs as gold as luminous paint could make them. And if anyone had still been inclined to doubt, there at Finnigan's rump stood their own Junior Mistress, smelling the rose on Finnigan's tail with a smile as bright as the mischievous sunshine on the paddock grass.

'Coo!' gasped Believers and Unbelievers in one breath.

'It's Miss Daly!' said Maisie Bonnington. She called eagerly to the Junior Mistress, 'Miss, Miss! That's you in the picture.'

'To be sure it's me.'

'And that's—is that akshually Finnigan?'

'Who else would it be? There was never a donkey the like of Finnigan O'Flanagan.'

And she started to tell them wonders that outstripped the stories of Mr O'Toole, yet they carried a conviction his had not. For his were tales of fifty years ago, but here was Miss Daly telling of a donkey she had seen with her own eyes only last month. Among the group of excited listeners, Albert Briggs chewed the bitter cud of thought. When Miss Daly paused for breath, he broke in.

'Miss.'

'What is it, Bert?'

'Danny said his donkey was in Connemara.'

'It is so!' declared Danny.

'But, Miss—you said you was going to Ballyninch.'

'Well then, goofy! Ballynahinch is just another name for Connemara,' laughed Miss Daly.

'Is there really such a place as Connemara, Miss?' asked Maisie.

'Well I should think there is! Wasn't I born there?'

Then Albert knew he had staked all and lost; and so did the rest of the Infants and Juniors of Larchgrove Road School. The fickle poet, seeing how the land lay, began to chant:

'Bert's wonky!
Bert's a donkey!'

And the school took up the chant.

Danny's triumph did not end even there. It had been noticed that Miss Daly came back from Ireland with a ring on her left hand that hadn't been there during the summer term; and one day the exciting news ran round that Miss Daly had been called for by a naval officer, a Lieutenant in the *Marines*! He came down presently from the staff room, where he had been talking to the mistresses; and now he wanted to talk to the children—as many of them as could get near him, and weren't too shy to touch him. And the *things* he told them about Finnigan O'Flanagan! Things which outstripped all Mr O'Toole's and Miss Daly's tales put together. The Marines, it appeared, could tell even more things than they were told. But one thing he told made them all rather sad; it seemed that their Junior Mistress wouldn't be coming back to teach them next term. 'She's going to teach me instead,' groaned the Marine. 'Won't it be awful to be a class of one? I shan't ever be able to escape her eye.'

That made the children laugh. Maisie Bonnington reassured him. 'She's ever so nice, sir, she's scarcely never cross.'

'I'm relieved to hear it,' said the Marine Lieutenant. Then he told them something that brightened them up again. As a Christmas Treat he was going to take them to the Pantomime at the Coronation Theatre one Saturday in January, when he and Miss Daly would collect them all in a bunch.

The Marine was as good as his word, and *Aladdin* at the Coronation was past all expectation. But among the golden wonders of Aladdin's cave, none stuck more vividly in Albert Briggs's mind than the glitter on the coat of an important little man who helped to usher the party of children to their seats; a little man who, catching sight of Danny, winked solemnly, while Danny whispered in passing, 'Hullo, Dad!'—a little man who was Danny O'Toole's father, and who wore gold on his fronts.

EXACTLY a hundred years ago, or more, or less, there was a happy village in the very middle of England, if it wasn't a bit to the north or the south. And the reason it was so happy was that the Tims lived in it.

There were five Tims all told, Old Tim, Big Tim, Little Tim, Young Tim, and Baby Tim, and they were all born wise. So whenever something was the matter in the village, or anything went wrong, or people for some cause were vexed or sorry for themselves, it became their habit to say, 'Let's go to the Tims about it, they'll know, they were born wise.'

For instance, when Farmer John found that the gypsies had slept without leave in his barn one night, his first thought was not, as you might suppose, 'I'll fetch the constable and have the law on them!' but, 'I'll see Old Tim about it, so I will!'

Then off he went to Old Tim, who was eighty

years old; and he found him sitting by the fire, smoking his clay pipe.

''Morning, Old Tim,' said Farmer John.

''Morning, Farmer John,' said Old Tim, taking his clay pipe from his mouth..

'I've had the gypsies in my barn again, Old Tim,' said Farmer John.

'Ah, have you now!' said Old Tim.

'Ay, that I have,' said Farmer John.

'Ah, to be sure!' said Old Tim.

'You were born wise, Old Tim,' said Farmer John. 'What would you do if you was me?'

Old Tim put his clay pipe in his mouth again and said, 'If I was you I'd ask Big Tim about it, for he was born wise too and is but sixty years old. So I be twenty year further off wisdom than he be.'

Away went Farmer John to find Big Tim, who was Old Tim's son, and he found him sitting on a gate, smoking his briar.

''Morning, Big Tim,' said Farmer John.

''Morning, Farmer John,' said Big Tim, taking his briar from his mouth.

'I've had the gypsies in my barn again,' said Farmer John, 'and Old Tim sent me to ask what you would do if you was me, for you was born wise.'

Big Tim put his briar in his mouth again and said, 'I'd see Little Tim about it if I was you, for he was born wise too, and is but forty year old, which is twenty year nigher to wisdom than me.'

So off went Farmer John to find Little Tim, who was Big Tim's son, and he found him lying in a haystack chewing a straw.

''Morning, Little Tim,' said Farmer John.

''Morning, Farmer John,' said Little Tim, taking the straw from his mouth.

Then Farmer John put his case again, saying, 'Big Tim told me to come to you about it, for you was born wise.'

And Little Tim put the straw back into his mouth and said, 'Young Tim was born wise too, and he's but twenty year old. You'll get wisdom fresher from him than from me.'

Off went Farmer John to find Young Tim, who was Little Tim's son, and he found him staring into the millpond, munching an apple.

''Morning, Young Tim,' said Farmer John.

''Morning, Farmer John,' said Young Tim, taking the apple from his mouth.

Then Farmer John told his tale for the fourth time, and ended by saying, 'Little Tim thinks you'll know what I'd best do, for you was born wise.'

But Young Tim took a new bite of his apple and said, 'My son who was born last month was born wise too, and from him you'll get wisdom at the fountain-head, so to say.'

Off went Farmer John to find Baby Tim, who was Young Tim's son, and he found him in his cradle with his thumb in his mouth.

''Morning, Baby Tim,' said Farmer John.

Baby Tim took his thumb out of his mouth, and said nothing.

'I've had the gypsies in my barn again, Baby Tim,' said Farmer John, 'and Young Tim advised me to ask your advice upon it, for you was born wise. What would you do if you was me? I'll do whatsoever you say.'

Baby Tim put his thumb in his mouth again, and said nothing.

So Farmer John went home, and did it.

And the gypsies went on to the next village and slept in the barn of Farmer George, and Farmer George called in the constable and had the law on them; and a week later his barn and his ricks were burned down, and his speckled hen was stolen away.

But the happy village went on being happy and doing nothing, neither when the Miller's wife forgot herself one day and boxed the Miller's ears, nor when Molly Garden got a bad sixpence from the pedlar, nor when the parson once came home singing by moonlight. After consulting the Tims, the village did no more than trees do in a wood or crops in a field, and so all these accidents got better before they got worse.

Until the day came when Baby Tim died an unmarried man at one hundred years of age. After that the happy village became as other villages, and did something.

COMING out of school, Johnny Moon found a penny. Only Mabel Barnard saw him pick it up.

'Oh, you lucky!' she said. 'What you goin' to do with it, Johnny?'

Johnny Moon had no doubt whatever on that point. 'Chocklit,' he said.

II

Johnny Moon did not go home to dinner, and he did not go home to tea; by bedtime Mrs Moon was in a 'state'. She had been round to the school when Johnny did not return at midday. Her house was only five minutes away, and Johnny's goings and comings in that Sussex market-town were no anxiety to her. Several of the children came and went the same way, and anyhow, he was five and getting quite a big boy.

After enquiries had reached as far as Mabel Barnard, Mrs Moon made the round of the sweetshops. Johnny had been to none of them. If he had, they would have remembered. What could have happened to him? An accident? No, the Police Station knew nothing; the Cottage Hospital knew nothing. Gypsies? Soon it got all over that quarter of Horgate that Johnny Moon had been kidnapped by the gypsies.

Johnny Moon had not been kidnapped by the gypsies. He was getting his Pennyworth.

III

Anybody can go into Porter's Confectionery Stores, or Mrs Wettham's Emporium, or the Cabin Cake-Room, and push a penny over the counter and get back a bar of chocolate. But once—ever so long ago—Johnny Moon had been trundled up to the Station outside the town, to meet his Uncle Tom from Portsmouth. That was an event, because Johnny had never been to Horgate Station, before or since; but more than the rush-and-bustle, more than the greeting from a big new red-faced Uncle, who met them just inside the dim booking-hall (Mrs Moon had so much to do that she was always just a little late for everything, and they had arrived in a panting hurry), more, even, than the great engine that was panting still harder than Mrs Moon, beyond the barrier, and the thrill of seeing another train race the other way without stopping, letting out a glorious shriek and a banner of thick white smoke: the memory was branded on Johnny's mind of seeing a boy post a penny in a tall machine, and pull a handle, and be miraculously rewarded with a bar of chocolate. How very different must this chocolate be from the penny-chocolate anybody could get at the Stores, or the Emporium, or the Cabin! It remained Johnny's burning wish to post a penny of his own in that machine one day, and pull the handle, and find the wonderful bar. The thrill of pulling the handle alone was worth a farthing, and the chance of hearing one engine pant and another one scream worth quite two farthings more. So when Johnny Moon found a penny to spend as he pleased, without oversight or enquiry, he turned his fat short legs at once in the direction of the Station, and reached it just as Mrs Moon was saying, 'Drat the child, why *can't* he come in to time?'

IV

There were the machines! His burning wish was about to be realized. Johnny Moon rushed at the nearest, and with a pounding heart posted his lucky penny. Then he grasped the handle with his fist and tugged. It came easily; and with it came a little cardboard ticket.

He couldn't believe his eyes. What horrid trick had the magic machine chosen to play him? He pushed the handle back, and tugged again, and it did not open. His penny had vanished; his chance was over; there was no magic chocolate for him after all. There was, in fact, nothing to do but burst into tears.

V

A lady came up to him. She bent down, looked at the little ticket, and dabbed his eyes with her handkerchief. 'What's the matter, dear? Don't cry! Are you afraid to go on the noisy platform by yourself?

Come along with me. I'm going to meet my little girl from London. Who are *you* going to meet?'

'Uncle Tom from Porssmouf,' said Johnny Moon.

His tears dried like magic. What was happening was almost too good to be true. Clutching the lady's hand he found himself passing in a small crowd through a little gate into a great palace, with a roof but no walls—the palace where the engines lived. It was another world, with smells and sights and sounds of its own. Full of little shops, and doors into strange places, and stairs that went up to the glass roof, and down into stone caverns, and pavements stretching one beyond another before his eyes, with dips in between where, far off, a train stood still, and very close, with such a roar that Johnny gasped, another train came snorting and pulled up, blocking out the sight of all the pavements beyond.

The lady squeezed Johnny's hand, and waved her other one, crying, 'There's my little girl! Gladys! Gladys! Porter! Gladys darling, here we are! Porter! There's a trunk in the van—oh, Porter! where does the next Portsmouth train come in?'

'Platform 5,' said the Porter; and the lady said to Johnny, pointing, 'Down there, dear, and then run along till you see Number Five—you can read the numbers, can't you?'

'Yes,' said Johnny; and trotted quickly down the stone stairs into the mysterious cavern below, afraid that somebody might stop him before he found out where it led.

VI

He stayed in the cavern for quite a long time. It was too good to leave all at once. Your feet sounded different down there, and it was lovely and dark and cold. You could strut and stamp and run from end to end, pretending to be an engine with a train behind you; and when you shrieked '*Hoo-hoo-hoo-hoo!*' your voice sounded different too. You got confidence, and ran up and down three times without stopping, shrieking a little louder, stamping a little harder, running a little faster, each time. A man looked at you and laughed, but nobody bothered you as they jostled to and fro. Sometimes you had the cavern all to yourself. The journey back and forth carried you past openings where daylight came down new staircases, and every staircase had a big number, and you chanted, 'ONE! TWO! FREE! FOUR! FIVE! SIX!' as you passed them. The numbers rang back at you, in a strange new voice, after you had said them.

Presently a Porter pushing a truck said, 'Out o' the way, young 'un!' and stared at Johnny rather hard; Johnny loitered a moment to let him pass, and then scuttled up the first staircase he was near.

Daylight and warmth again; but not the same pavement as before. He could see across two pavements the gate he had come in by; but now he was in the middle of the new world. A lot of people were waiting by piles of luggage, or sitting on seats. A little way off a calf lay under a net. Johnny strutted up to it and said 'Moo-oo!' and poked his finger through the netting to feel its soft nose. The calf shrank under the netting, and said 'Moo-oo!' back at Johnny, like the echo in the tunnel underground.

There was a little house in the middle of this pavement, full of glass jars of food, and cups of tea. Suddenly Johnny felt that he hadn't had his dinner. He went in and stared at the buns in the glass cases till the girl behind them stopped talking to a sailor and said, 'Make up your mind then!' and Johnny moved slowly away. The sailor called, 'Here, mate!' and before Johnny knew it, a sticky sugary bun was in his hand. He hurried outside to eat it, before the girl could snatch it back. He thought perhaps he had better eat it on a further pavement still, and went down into the cavern again.

At the foot of the stairs he bumped into a very small girl, grasping a spade and pail, trailing after a large family of parents and brothers and sisters. She said, 'Oh sowry!' though Johnny had done the bumping. 'All right,' said Johnny. 'I been to Lillamton,' explained the little girl. 'I'm goin' back to Clapham. I got some peppmince.' She pulled out a paper bag of peppermints, and offered them to Johnny. He helped himself to two. 'My name's Dorinda. Well, goodbye I must go now.'

'Goodbye,' said Johnny Moon, and went round to Platform Six while Dorinda trailed back to Platform One.

Platform Six was in the open air. A very small train was standing still. Nobody was about, so Johnny climbed into a carriage with a dusty red-carpet seat, and sat in the further corner, and ate his bun and sucked his peppermints, staring out at a mountain of coal with green trees beyond. While he was sucking his second sweet the coal and the trees got mixed up together, and changed into his red-faced Uncle Tom talking to the Bun-Girl in Johnny's own schoolroom, only the Bun-Girl was Dorinda, and the calf was trying to teach them lessons.

Then Johnny sat up with a jerk, because the little train was moving. It moved slowly till the coal-mountain was out of sight, and the green trees turned into a green field with a glorious rubbish-heap in it. Then it stopped.

'Porssmouf!' cried Johnny Moon, and tried to get out to the rubbish-heap, where there was a lovely twisted bicycle wheel all handy; but that door was locked, and before he could cross the carriage the train backed as slowly as it had gone forward. The coal-mountain came in sight again. Some men were on it, filling trucks on the other side. Johnny climbed out of his carriage, and got over the railway lines by a wooden way down and up, and went and watched the men. Some other boys were watching too. Presently one of the bigger boys chucked a lump of coal into a truck. The men only laughed. Then another boy chucked a lump, and then Johnny did. When he had chucked five lumps, one of the men sang out, 'Run along 'ome, you blacklegs!' and the boys scampered off laughing, and Johnny, wondering why the coalmen hadn't said black-hands, went back to his engine palace. He played the train-game in the tunnels again, and went up Staircase Number Four, and found a paper bag dropped under a seat. In it was one whole ham sandwich, and the edges of two others, with fat between them. He ate the sandwich and the edges, leaving the fat, which looked quite black after he had taken it out. He went back to the calf-pavement, to give the fat to the calf, but it was no longer there.

Then he noticed how much darker it was. The trains running this way and that were more exciting. He went up on a bridge under the roof, and looked down on red sparks flying. Far out in the black country he could see a fiery glow which meant a train was coming. He could not tear himself from that glorious sight.

A hand grasped his collar. He wriggled and turned, and looked up into the face of a Porter. 'Here!' said the Porter. 'I've seen you before. What's your game?'

'Uncle Tom comin' from Porssmouf,' explained Johnny Moon.

'Portsmouth train's just gone,' said the Porter. 'You'd better hop it or *some*body'll be in a stew. Off you go!'

Then Johnny knew his Pennyworth was up.

VII

In the dim booking-hall the lamps were lit. As he came out of it, a man was hurrying and a boy was lingering by the tall machines, posting a penny. 'Come on!' shouted the man. 'But, Daddy, I just—' 'Come *on*, I tell you! we'll be late!' The man grabbed his son by the hand and rushed him away.

Johnny went up to the machine where the boy had posted the penny, and tugged the handle. It came easily. Inside was a bar of chocolate.

Slowly, contentedly, Johnny Moon trudged back home, sucking chocolate and coal-dust as he went.

GRISELDA CURFEW lived with her Great-Grandmother in the last cottage in the Lane. She was ten years old, and her Great-Grandmother was one hundred and ten years old, and there was not as much difference between them as you might suppose. If Griselda's Great-Grandmother had been twice, or thrice, or four times ten years old, there would have been a great deal of difference; for when you are twenty or thirty or forty, you feel very differently from when you were ten. But a hundred is a nice round number, and it brings things home in a circle; so Griselda's ten seemed to touch quite close the ten of Great-Grandmother Curfew, who was a hundred years away, and yet so very near her.

Great-Grandmother Curfew liked the things that Griselda liked. She did not, as middling old people do, pretend to like what Griselda liked, she really liked what Griselda liked. When Griselda sat threading bead-necklaces, Great-Grandmother Curfew liked sorting the bead-box into little heaps of different sizes and colours, and giving them to Griselda as she wanted them. When Griselda put her doll to bed, Great-Grandmother Curfew liked helping to undo the buttons, and talking in whispers with Griselda till Arabella had been 'got-off'; and when Arabella was naughty, and wouldn't go off, Great-Grandmother Curfew liked singing 'Hush, hush, hush!' to her, rocking the restless one against her shoulder until she was quiet and good. Above all, when Griselda was making cakes, Great-Grandmother Curfew liked picking the currants or grating the nutmeg; and as for the cakes, she liked them so much, that out of a batch of seven she always ate four.

Great-Grandmother Curfew had six teeth left, and all her faculties. She could see, hear, smell, taste, talk, feel, and remember. She could misremember, too. She misremembered the things that had happened last week, and she remembered the things that had happened a hundred years ago. She could not walk very much, so on fairly fine days Griselda sat her at the open window, looking out on the Lane where the world went by; and on very fine days, she sat her in the garden at the back, where the bees hummed. In summer, Great-Grandmother Curfew liked to sit near the currant-bushes, or the raspberry canes, or better still among the green peas. She said she could wag her finger at the starlings, when they came stealing. But when Griselda came to take her in, there would always be quantities of little strings stripped of their currants on all the currant-bushes within reach; or a host of little white fingers robbed of their raspberries poking out all over the canes; or dozens of empty pea-pods hanging open on the green-pea-vines. And Great-Grandmother Curfew, seeing Griselda observing all this, would shake her old head and say, 'Oh them starlings, them starlings! I must of dropped off for forty winks, and then how them starlings do nip in!'

And Griselda pretended not to see that Great-Grandmother Curfew's withered finger-tips were stained bright red, or that there were green specks under her crinkled finger-nails.

But in autumn, Great-Grandmother Curfew preferred to be set down by the hazel-hedge, and at those times the ground round her chair would be littered with green shells. When she heard Griselda coming, she would stare at the shells, and mutter, 'Oh them squirrels, them squirrels.' And Griselda said nothing till bedtime, when she mentioned, 'I'm going to give you a dose tonight, Gramma.'

'I don't want no dose, Grissie.'

'Yes, Gramma, you do.'

'I don't like doses. They're that nasty.'

'They're good for you,' said Griselda, getting the bottle.

'I won't take no dose, I tell you.'

'If you don't, you'll wake up in the middle of the night with the collywobbles.'

'No, I won't, Grissie.'

'I think you will, Gramma.'

'Why do you think so?'

'Well, I just do think so. And I think the squirrels will too, if somebody don't give *them* doses.'

'Oh,' said Great-Grandmother Curfew. But when

Griselda put the medicine under her nose, she shook her head and cried, 'No, I won't! I won't unless Bella has one too!'

'All right, Gramma, and you see how good she is about it.' Griselda tilted the glass against her doll's china mouth. 'You'll be as good as Bella, *I* know.'

'No I won't! No I won't!'

'Come along.'

'Can I have a sweetie after?'

'Yes.'

'Two sweeties?'

'Yes.'

'And will you tell me a story?'

'Yes.'

'And sing me to sleep?'

'Yes, Gramma. Come along, now.'

Then at last Great-Grandmother Curfew drank down the nasty physic, and made a funny face as though she was going to cry; but Griselda popped the first sweet so quick into her mouth that her funny face turned into a smile instead, and her old eyes grew bright and greedy for the second sweet. When she was tucked up cosily in bed, under the patchwork quilt, Great-Grandmother Curfew said, 'What tale will you tell me tonight, Grissie?'

'I'll tell you the tale about a giant, Gramma.'

'The giant who had three heads?'

'Yes, that one.'

'And he lived in a brass castle?'

'Yes, that one.'

'I like that one,' said Great-Grandmother Curfew, nodding her old head, her eyes bright with anticipation. 'Now then, you tell it to me, and mind you don't go and leave any of it out.'

Griselda sat down by the bed, and held her Great-Grandmother's little thin hand under the quilt, and began.

'Once upon a time there was a Giant, and he had *Three Heads*, and he lived in a BRASS CASTLE!'

'Ah!' breathed Great-Grandmother Curfew. There was a little silence, and then she asked, 'Have you told me the story, Grissie?'

'Yes, Gramma.'

'*All* of it?'

'Every word of it.'

'Didn't you leave a bit out?'

'Not one bit.'

'I like that story,' said Great-Grandmother Curfew. 'Now you sing me to sleep.'

Then Griselda sang a song that Great-Grandmother Curfew had sung to her son, and her son's son (who was Griselda's father). And her own great-grandmother, who had sung it to her mother and to her, when she was a little baby, had had it from the mouth of her grandmother, for whom the song was written.

'Hush, hush, hush!
And I dance mine own child,
And I dance mine own child,
Hush, hush, hush!'

This was the song that had come down to Griselda from her great-grandmother, who had had it from her great-grandmother, who had had it from her grandmother, who was the child in the song. Griselda sang it over and over, fondling her Gramma's hand under the quilt. Now and then she stopped singing and listened, and Great-Grandmother Curfew opened one bright eye and said:

'Now don't you go and leave me, Grissie. I aren't asleep yet.'

Griselda sang once more:

'Hush, hush, hush!
And I dance mine own child,
And I dance mine own child,
Hush, hush, hush!'

Stop and listen again. Again the old eyelid quivered. 'I aren't asleep yet. Don't go and leave me, Grissie.'

So again over and over:

'Hush, hush, hush!
And I dance mine own child!'

Stop. Listen. '*Hush, hush, hush!*' Very very softly Griselda crept her little hand out of the bed. Great-Grandmother Curfew was fast asleep, breathing like a child.

You see how very near is a hundred-and-ten to ten years old.

All this was in the year 1879, when little girls of ten paid twopence a week to go to school, and old women of a hundred-and-ten did not have the pension. You may wonder what Griselda and Great-Grandmother Curfew lived upon. Taken all round, it may be said that they lived on kindness. Their cottage was rented at a shilling a week, which was little enough, but even a shilling had to be obtained somehow; and then there was the twopence for Griselda's schooling. The cottage-rent was due to Mr Greentop, the Squire, and when Griselda's father died, leaving Griselda and her great-grandmother alone without anybody to earn for them, everybody said:

'Of course old Mrs Curfew will go to the Almshouse, and Griselda will go into service.'

But when this was proposed, Great-Grandmother Curfew kicked up a rare old fuss. 'I won't go to no Almshouse!' she declared. 'I am but a hunderd-and-nine, and I aren't ripe for it. I will stay where I be. Aren't I got Grissie to look after me?'

'But what will you do while Griselda is at school?' asked Mrs Greentop, who had come to look into matters.

'Do? I'll do a heap o' things. I'll set in the garden and weed where I'm set, and I'll watch the pot that it don't boil over, and I'll mind the kitten don't get into the milk, and I'll make the spills, and tidy the kitchen drawer, and I'll sharp the knives, and I'll scrub the pertaties for supper. Do? What d'ye mean, do? If I can't get about on my legs no more, that aren't no reason for setting with my hands in my lap.'

'But, Mrs Curfew, suppose you were taken ill?'

'Why should I be took ill? I've never been took ill yet, and I aren't going to begin at my time o' life.'

'But, Mrs Curfew, what about the cottage rent?'

For this old Mrs Curfew had no answer, and Mrs Greentop went on persuasively, 'Come now, you'll be much more comfortable at the Almshouse, and Griselda can come and see you there quite often. I'll take her into my house to help with the children while I train her for kitchen-work.'

'She knows kitchen-work already,' said Great-Grandmother Curfew. 'She can make and bake and sweep and clean like a little woman—and I aren't going to no Almshouse. Leave that to lazybones like Em'ly Deane, who want to get out of doing, though she's no more 'n a hunderd, *if* that. Some people talk more 'n the Gospel—and I'll stay where I be.'

Mrs Greentop sighed, and wondered what to say next to soften the blow, because she was quite sure that old Mrs Curfew could not possibly stay where she was. She turned to Griselda, who was sitting very quiet by the fire, busy with her crochet, and asked, 'What do *you* say, Griselda?'

Griselda stood up and bobbed, and said, 'If you please, 'm, I can do Gramma before morning school, and I can come back and do her dinner at noon, and I can come to you afternoons and do the children and that till bedtime, and do Gramma's bedtime when I come back—if you think Mr Greentop 'ld be satisfied to let Gramma keep on in the cottage. I'd do my very best, 'm. I can shine brasses, and fill lamps, and turn sheets sides to middle, and I could do the darning and buttons, and I'd love to bath baby, 'm, best of all I would.'

'And what about your Granny while you were with me?' asked Mrs Greentop.

'The Lane 'll keep an eye on her, 'm,' said Griselda, who knew the kindness of poor neighbours as even the Squire's wife did not.

'And the twopence for your schooling?'

'I can earn that too, 'm.'

'And what about your food? You must eat, you know, Griselda.'

'There's the hens, and the bees, and the garden-stuff, 'm. And all the firing we want from the woods.'

'But who'll see to all that, Griselda?'

'I can do the hens in the morning before I do Gramma, and the garden in the evening, after she's tucked up.'

Griselda seemed so sure about it all that Mrs Greentop could only murmur, 'Well, I'll speak to the Squire, and see.'

She did so, and it all got arranged as Great-Grandmother Curfew and Griselda intended it to. Mr Greentop allowed them the cottage and garden in return for Griselda's daily services in the nursery. The twopence for her schooling she got from the mothers of the very small scholars who lived a mile and more distant from the school. Griselda undertook to collect and deliver these little ones every day. The garden would have been a problem, but here the Lane stepped in. The Lane not only kept an eye on Great-Grandmother Curfew while Griselda was out, but on the bees and chickens too; the Lane supplied her with seed; one planted for her, one hoed for her, a third got in her firing. The women stripped her currants and raspberries, and cut up her marrows, for jam. Clothing happened in oddments at all times, from all over the place. Somehow or other, Griselda and Great-Grandmother Curfew managed, and because they could go on living together, they were perfectly happy.

Just before she was eleven years old, Griselda Curfew was taken ill. She got out of bed one morning feeling dreadfully queer, but she said nothing to her Great-Grandmother. She made up the fire, put on the kettle, went outside and fed the chickens, said a word to the bees, and got a panful of potatoes for dinner. Then she came in, and hotted the teapot, and wetted the tea, and set it on the hob. Then she got her great-grandmother up and dressed, brushed what was left of her thin white hair, and gave her her breakfast.

'Don't you want nothing to eat this morning, Grissie?' asked Great-Grandmother Curfew, crumbling her bread into her teacup.

Griselda shook her head, and sipped a hot cup, and felt a little better. Great-Grandmother Curfew took no particular notice, because Griselda often said she didn't want anything to eat for breakfast, but this was usually because there was barely enough for one, let alone two. Before she left the house, she put Great-Grandmother Curfew in the sunniest window with the pan of potatoes, a bowl of water, and a good sharp knife.

'That'll be a great help for me, Gramma, if you can get them done,' she said.

'I'll get 'em done all right,' said Great-Grandmother Curfew. 'And when Ebenezer Wilcox goes by, I'll call him in, and he can put the saucepan on the fire.'

'That *will* be a help,' said Griselda. 'I'll leave you Bella for company, and two peppermint drops to suck, one for each. Don't you go giving Bella both drops now!'

'She's that greedy, she'll want 'em both,' said Great-Grandmother Curfew, her eager eyes glancing from Griselda to Arabella. 'Mebbe you'd better leave *three* pep'mint drops.' She smiled her sweet greedy smile.

'She'll only be sick,' said Griselda, feeling oh so sick herself, but keeping it down bravely. She sat Bella up in the window-seat, and Bella flopped over with her head in her lap.

'She looks sick to me already,' said Great-Grandmother Curfew beginning to scrape her potatoes. 'Mebbe I'd better have both pep'mint drops arter all, to spare her stomach.'

Griselda reached for a book to prop Bella up with. Great-Grandmother Curfew had only two books in the world, the Bible that Griselda read in every Sunday, and another one she never read in at all, because it was so old, with funny print, and wrong spelling. But it came in useful to put under a broken chair-leg, or, as today, to support Bella. With its help, Bella sat up looking quite lifelike.

'There, that's better!' said Griselda, feeling that her Gramma was not quite alone while she had Bella to talk to. 'Goodbye, Gramma, till dinner.'

But it was goodbye for longer than that.

For when Griselda had trudged a mile to fetch one of her tiny scholars, she fell down on the doorstep, and was found all of a heap by the tiny scholar's mother.

'Bless me, Griselda Curfew, how ill you do look!' exclaimed the mother. 'As sure as I stand here, you've took the fever.'

And Griselda had, and was whisked away to hospital without knowing anything about it. She had the fever very badly, with two relapses and a long convalescence. The first time she was clear in the head, she asked, 'How's my Gramma managing?'

'Don't you go worrying after your grandmother,' said the pleasant nurse who looked after her. 'Everything has been arranged for her, you may be sure of that.'

And so it had, for they had taken Great-Grandmother Curfew to the Almshouse at last.

Three months later, when Griselda left the hospital, very pale and thin and with her hair cropped short, Mrs Greentop's own carriage came to fetch her. Griselda could hardly contain her excitement as the horses trotted nearer and nearer to the village. She did not yet know the truth, and expected in another minute to have her Gramma in her arms. Great was her disappointment when the high-stepping horses passed the top of the Lane, and trotted on towards the stone gate-posts of the Squire's house.

'Please, please!' cried Griselda, kneeling up on the seat, and tapping the coachman's broad back as though it were a door she wanted opened. The coachman looked over his shoulder and said, 'It's all right, little 'un, you're to go up to the Big House to have tea with the little masters and misses.'

Griselda sank back. Tea with the little Greentops—Harry, Connie, Mabel, and Baby—would have been a treat at any other time; but just now, when all she longed for was to hug her little Gramma, it was a mistaken kindness. She supposed kind Mrs Greentop just didn't understand. Suppose Mrs Greentop had had the fever, and was going to see her baby for the first time for three months?

Mrs Greentop understood more than Griselda imagined. She met her on the big front steps, put her arm round her, and said, 'Come along, Griselda, the children are dying to see what you look like with your hair cut short. I wonder if Baby will remember you.'

'I hope so, 'm,' said Griselda meekly.

She went with Mrs Greentop into the nursery, where the children came clamouring about her.

'I say, doesn't Grizzel look funny!' cried Harry.

'I want my hair short too!' shouted Connie, whose hair was straight.

'I don't,' said Mabel, who had curls.

Baby was the only one who noticed nothing different. He crawled and grabbed Griselda by the ankle, buzzing, 'Gizzie-gizzie-gizzie!'

'He *does* know me!' cried Griselda. 'There, 'm, he *does* know me, don't you, my sweet?' She caught him up in her arms, chanting, 'I dance mine own child!' Then she turned quickly to Mrs Greentop. 'Please, 'm, is anything the matter with my Gramma!'

'No, Griselda, of course not,' said Mrs Greentop. Her voice was a little flustered, and so especially kind that Griselda faltered, 'Oh what is it, please, 'm?'

'Now, Griselda,' Mrs Greentop sat down and drew Griselda to her. 'I'm sure you'll see it's all for the best. While you were away there was nobody to look after Mrs Curfew properly, and such a nice comfortable room fell vacant in the Almshouse—'

'The Almshouse!' Griselda stared aghast.

'One of the corner rooms, behind the rose-beds. Your Gramma has a lovely fire, and warm blankets, and tea and sugar, and everything possible,' went on Mrs Greentop smoothly, as though she were covering up Griselda's looks and feelings with a cosy quilt. 'And the village is so proud of her, Griselda. She's far the oldest inhabitant in the place, and all the visitors who come insist on seeing her, and talking to her, and they always leave her something nice. Tomorrow you shall go to see her too, and take her a little present.'

'*Tomorrow*, 'm?'

'Yes, Griselda, it's too late tonight.'

'I see, 'm. Then tomorrow I can go and fetch her away.'

Mrs Greentop hesitated. 'Where to, Griselda?'

'To the cottage, 'm.'

'Well, you see, Griselda, Mr Greentop is thinking of selling the cottage, now that Mrs Curfew is settled so nicely where she is, and is so well looked after—and really, dear, you aren't strong enough to do what you used to do.'

'Grizzel's crying,' observed Mabel. 'Grizzel, what are you crying for?'

'Be quiet, Mabel, and don't tease. Grizzel's going to stay here and be Baby's little nursery-maid, and you children are going to be very kind to her, and soon we'll all be going away to Whitstable together, for six whole weeks. Think of that, Griselda!'

'Grizzel,' said Connie, pulling at her hand, 'there's teacake for tea.'

Griselda turned her head aside, and swallowed hard. It didn't do to let children see the sorrows of life, she knew that. Those responsible for children must keep them cheerful and happy. But not in her worst moments at the hospital had she felt as bad as this. Teacake and Whitstable were nothing to her.

Mrs Greentop was as good as her word, and the next day Griselda was taken to see Great-Grandmother Curfew in her new quarters at the Almshouse—the new home that was so much older even than she was. Many a time Griselda had passed under the ancient archway into the square garden enclosed by the dwellings of old men and women who sat sunning themselves at their last doors. It was pretty and peaceful in that sunny courtyard. Every diamond window had its pot of geraniums, or petunias, or nasturtiums, every open door showed a crackling fire with a teapot on the hob, every old man had his pipe of tobacco, and every old woman her paper of snuff. The garden in the middle of the courtyard was divided into little plots, one for each almsman and almswoman. A young gardener was there weeding the cobbles, and trimming the edges, but the old men and women had a finger in their own patches, and those that had relatives were helped by sons and daughters to make their gardens pretty and productive. Already, as she followed Mrs Greentop along the path, Griselda wondered which of these plots belonged to her Gramma, and she planned to put in a few pea-sticks and currant bushes with the first pennies she could scrape together.

There were one or two visitors strolling about, stopping to say a word to the most interesting-looking inmates. A pleasant-looking lady and a clever-looking gentleman had paused by the door of Emily Deane, who was airing a grievance. Emily Deane, aged one-hundred-and-one, had for long been the show-piece of the famous old Almshouses.

'Don't you b'leeve her!' chattered old Emily. 'Don't you b'leeve one word of it. Not a day more 'n ninety-nine she ain't. Did you look at her teeth? Six she got, and me only with two. *She* older 'n me? No, sir, and no, ma'am. She got her six teeth, and I got my two. Why, it stands to reason!'

'Good morning, Emily. What is the trouble?' asked Mrs Greentop.

'Goo' morning to you, ma'am. Ol' Mrs Curfew, she's what's the trouble. An 'underd-and-ten? Not a day more 'n ninety-nine! Hello, Grissie, you come to fetch yer grammer 'ome? Sooner the better.'

Griselda thought so too, but Mrs Greentop only smiled. 'No, Emily, Griselda has just come to see her Gramma, and how nicely off she is here.' Then she turned to the lady and gentleman, whom she evidently knew. 'Well, Margaret, well, Professor, and have *you* been to see Mrs Curfew yet?'

'Wonderful old body,' said the Professor.

'Didn't I tell you so?'

'Not a day more 'n ninety-nine,' mumbled Emily Deane.

The pleasant lady called Margaret looked down kindly at Griselda. 'And this is her little great-granddaughter who has been ill? Mrs Curfew told us all about her, and how sweetly she sang. How are you now, my dear?'

Griselda bobbed, and said, 'I'm quite well, thank you, 'm.'

'And will you sing for us, Griselda?'

'Yes, 'm,' whispered Griselda shyly, for really she only sang for her Gramma and Baby Richard.

'Some other day,' added Mrs Greentop, to Griselda's great relief. 'For now we must go and see her great-grandmother. They haven't seen each other for three months, you know. Don't forget you're coming to us tonight, Margaret. If you come early, you can see Richard in his bath.'

Then she moved on with Griselda down the sunny

path, and stopped in a corner, and there, in her own little old rocking-chair, sat Great-Grandmother Curfew nodding by the fire. Griselda could contain herself no longer. She flew in and hugged her Gramma tight in her arms, and Mrs Curfew opened her eyes and said, 'Hello, Grissie, so you got back then. What they been and done to your hair?'

'They shaved it, Gramma, when I was ill.'

'I don't like it,' said the old lady. 'They didn't ought to of done it without asking me. Are we going home now?'

'Oh Gramma!' whispered Griselda. Again Mrs Greentop came to the rescue, saying, 'Not today, Mrs Curfew. Now you must show Griselda how nice and comfortable you are here. Look, Griselda, your Gramma might almost be at home, mightn't she? She's got her own chair and quilt, see, and her hassock, and her books and teapot, and the flowers in the window came out of your own garden.'

'Oh, and Bella!' exclaimed Griselda, catching sight

of her doll peeping out of Great-Grandmother Curfew's shawl.

'Yes, you've been taking care of Bella for Griselda, haven't you, Mrs Curfew?'

'Has she been good, Gramma?'

'On and off,' said the old lady.

'I brought you some pep'mint drops, Gramma.'

Griselda put the packet into the thin little hand, that hid it at once under the thick shawl. Great-Grandmother Curfew's eyes grew suddenly bright, and her face puckered into its sly sweet smile. 'That Em'ly Deane!' she chuckled.

'Em'ly Deane, Gramma?'

'Jealous. She wur the oldest till I come. She aren't now. She've only turned a 'underd, the chit. Never mind that. She kin 'ave it 'er own way tomorrer, when you fetch me 'ome.'

'Oh, Gramma!' whispered Griselda.

'I'll be ready for you in the morning,' said Great Grandmother Curfew; and then, as suddenly as a baby or a kitten, she fell asleep.

'Come along, Griselda,' said Mrs Greentop very kindly. 'I expect you'd like to take Bella with you, wouldn't you?'

'No, 'm,' said Griselda, 'I'll leave Gramma Bella. I've got Baby.'

She followed Mrs Greentop through the door and in and out of the cobbled paths, keeping her face turned aside into her sun-bonnet all the way.

Griselda applied herself very hard to Baby Richard all that day, and nobody interfered with her. Mrs

Greentop understood so well what she was feeling that she talked it over with her husband when they were dressing for dinner. 'I suppose it *isn't* possible, John?'

'Let well alone, my dear,' advised the Squire. 'They'll both shake down to it soon, and the old dame will want more and more care every day now. That child could never earn the cottage rent, and look after the old thing into the bargain. Besides, I don't want the rent, the sale of the cottage will mend the fences, and re-thatch the two roofs in the Hollow, with a bit over towards the new barn. Farmer Lawson's offered me thirty for it, but I think he'll go to thirty-five. Anyhow, the cottage isn't worth repairing, and it will have to be sold.'

'Hush,' said Mrs Greentop, for Griselda was going by the door, crooning to Richard as she took him to his bath.

'You're too soft-hearted,' said Mr Greentop, pinching her ear. 'Now don't dally, for that's the doorbell, if I'm not mistaken.'

Their dinner-guests had arrived, and the first thing Margaret said to Mrs Greentop, after they had kissed, was '*Can* I see Richard?'

'He's just having his bath,' said Mrs Greentop.

'Oh, the blessing!' exclaimed Margaret, and ran upstairs to the nursery without another word. Mrs Greentop ran after her, because she wanted to see Margaret see her perfect baby; and she called over her shoulder to the Professor, 'Don't you want to come too, James?' She was quite sure that everybody wanted to see her baby in his bath.

'Of course he doesn't, my dear,' said Mr Greentop

impatiently. But the Professor very agreeably said, 'Of course I *do*!' So the two gentlemen went upstairs after the two ladies; and at the nursery door found Mrs Greentop holding it ajar with her finger to her lips; for above the splashing and crooning of Baby Richard in his bath rang the honey-sweet voice of Griselda Curfew:

> *'Hush, hush, hush!*
> *And I dance mine own child,*
> *And I dance mine own child,*
> *Hush, hush, hush!'*

'Oh, how perfectly charming!' whispered Margaret.

But the Professor pushed his way quickly through the door and went straight up to the bath-tub, and said to Griselda, 'What song is *that*, child? Where did you get the tune? Do you know what it is you're singing?'

Griselda looked up very startled, and she turned very red, and as she lifted the kicking baby out of the water she said, 'Yes, sir. It's what I sing Gramma to sleep with. Don't scream, duckie! You be a good little boy. Look now, "I dance mine own child, I dance mine own child!"' sang Griselda, dancing Richard, rolled in his towel, up and down on her knee.

'Who taught you that song?' demanded the Professor.

'What *is* the matter, Jim?' asked Margaret.

'Be quiet, Peggy,' said the Professor. 'Who taught you the words and the tune, Griselda?'

'Nobody did, sir. Gramma used to sing it to my grandad and to my dad, and then to me, and now I sing it to her and baby.'

'And who sang it to your Gramma?'

'*Her* Gramma did.'

'And who sang it to your Gramma's Gramma?'

'Don't be absurd, Jim!' laughed Margaret. 'How *can* the child know? You must have got back to the days of William and Mary.'

'I want to get back a bit further than that,' said the Professor. 'Now, Griselda—Griselda! Dear me! And your great-grandmother spoke of you as Grissel!'

'Grissie, sir.'

'Well, Grissie will do. What is your grandmother's name?'

'My Gramma's name is Griselda, and so was *her* Granny's. We're all Griselda, because of the song. It's called Grissel's song, sir.'

'Yes, I know it is,' said the Professor, rather surprisingly.

'And it's *our* song,' said Griselda, drying Richard carefully in all the creases.

'Little precious!' said Margaret, stooping to kiss them.

'Don't interrupt, Peggy,' said the Professor. 'What do you mean, Griselda, by *our* song—*your* song?'

'I mean it was written for us,' said Griselda. 'For one of us Griseldas, ever so long ago, but I don't know which of us.'

'Do you know who wrote it?'

'Mr Dekker wrote it, sir.'

'Exactly!' said the Professor triumphantly.

'What *are* you so excited about, James?' demanded Margaret.

'Shut up, Peggy. Now, Griselda, how do you come to know Mr Dekker wrote that song—and for "one of you", too?'

'Because it's in the book, sir.'

'What book?'

'Gramma's book. The one with the funny print and bad spelling.'

'Oh, a *printed* book.' The Professor's voice sounded a little disappointed.

'Yes, sir. But the song is in writing too, inside the cover, and under it he's written "To mine own Grissel Thos. Dekker", and the day of the month and the year after.'

'What month? What year?'

'The Eleventh Day of October, One Thousand Six Hundred and Three,' said Griselda.

'Eureka!' said the Professor.

'Are you out of your mind, James?' enquired Margaret.

But the Professor merely asked another question. 'Where is that book now?'

'Bella's sitting on it, I expect, sir.'

'Bella?'

'My doll, sir. It props her up beautiful.'

'And where *is* Bella?' The Professor's eyes darted about the room.

'I left her in the Almshouse, sir, with Gramma, for company.'

'So you gave up your own child to another, did you, patient Grissel? Tomorrow we'll go together to the Almshouse, to see your Gramma.'

Griselda's eyes shone, as she buttoned the linen buttons of Richard's swansdown-calico night-suit; but all she said was. ' "Patient Grissel" is the name of the book, sir.'

'Yes,' said the Professor, 'I know it is.'

* * *

The following day the Professor called for Griselda, and bore her off to the Almshouse. He came before she had done giving Richard his first bottle, and Mrs Greentop said, 'Well, you *are* an early bird, James!' To which the Professor answered, 'I have a worm to catch.'

They found Great-Grandmother Curfew still in bed, propped up with pillows, and Bella beside her, peeping out of the patchwork quilt. She glanced at Griselda eagerly, saying, 'Grissie! Are we goin' 'ome now?'

'This gentleman wants to see your book, Gramma.'

'Well, there it is, on the window-ledge, if he want to hev a look at it.'

The Professor picked up the old leather book, and with great care opened it, and looked first at the title-page, and then inside the cover. Both times he nodded as though he was pleased, and then he sat down by Great-Grandmother Curfew, just like the doctor, and said, 'Tell me about this book, Mrs Curfew. Can you remember anything you were told about it?'

'Remember!' cried Great-Grandmother Curfew indignantly. 'In course I remember! I remember what my Gramma told me her Granny told her as though 'twas yesterday. What d'ye take me for? A poor old piece like Em'ly Deane, who've got a mind like a sieve?'

'Of course not, Mrs Curfew. Tell me exactly what you remember,' said the Professor.

Great-Grandmother Curfew's eyes became brighter than ever as they looked back into the past. 'My Gramma,' said she, speaking more clearly than Griselda had ever heard her speak before, 'were born when

King William of Orange sat upon the throne, God bless him, and *her* Granny was then ninety-three year old, though she didn't live beyond one-hunderd-and-four, poor soul, but for eleven year *she* sang *my* Gramma the song in this book, which was the song her own Daddy made for her the year she were born, and put down in print and in handwriting too.'

'Mr Thomas Dekker,' said the Professor.

'The very same, sir.'

'Your great-great-great-great-grandfather?'

'I dessay, sir.'

'He was a famous man, Mrs Curfew.'

'I shouldn't wonder, sir.'

'What was your Gramma's Granny's name, Mrs Curfew?'

'Griselda, sir.'

'And your name, Mrs Curfew?'

'Griselda, sir.'

'And this little girl is Griselda too.'

'Well of course she is. Oh deary me!' chuckled Great-Grandmother Curfew. 'What a lot of questions about one and the same name.'

'Mrs Curfew, you ought to know that this is a very valuable book. Will you sell it to me?'

Great-Grandmother Curfew looked at him with her sly sweet greedy smile. 'How valuable is it? Ten shilling?'

The Professor hesitated. 'Much more valuable than that, Mrs Curfew.'

Suddenly Griselda plucked up her courage to speak. 'Is it as valuable as thirty-five pound, if you please, sir?'

The Professor hesitated again, and said, 'I think it is quite as valuable as fifty pounds, Griselda. At all events, I'll give your Gramma fifty pounds for it, if she likes to sell it to me.'

'Oh!' breathed Griselda. 'Thank you, sir!'

'What you thanking the gentleman for, Grissie?' demanded Great-Grandmother Curfew, tartly. 'It's my book, not yours.'

'Yes, I know, Gramma,' said Griselda anxiously.

'And I won't sell it to him—' said the old lady obstinately.

'Oh Gramma!'

'—under ten shilling,' said Great-Grandmother Curfew.

The Professor laughed; but Griselda nearly cried for joy.

'Now, Grissie, be done wi' all this flummox,' said Mrs Curfew. 'Why don't ye get me up and dress me? What they been and done to yer hair, child?'

'They shaved it, Gramma, when I was in hospital.'

'Was you in hospital?'

'Yes, Gramma, don't you remember?'

Great-Grandmother Curfew fixed a dull eye on Griselda's cropped head. 'I don't like it,' she said. 'They shouldn't a done it without my leave.' Suddenly she looked very tired. 'Get me up and dress me, Grissie. I want to go 'ome.'

'This afternoon, Gramma, this very afternoon!' promised Griselda; and she thrust into the Professor's hands the book of Patient Grissel, by Mr Thomas Dekker, and ran out of the cottage as fast as her legs could carry her. It was a very breathless Griselda who fell into the Squire's study without knocking, and cried, 'Oh please, sir, please, Mr Greentop, if Farmer Lawson'll give you thirty pound for our cottage, we'll give you thirty-five, oh please, Mr Greentop, we'll give you fifty!'

There is not much more to tell. When the Professor arrived soon after Griselda, the matter was made clear; and when Mr Greentop understood that Great-Grandmother Curfew really did have as much as fifty pounds in the world, and when he heard Griselda herself laughing and crying and pleading all in one breath to be allowed to bring her great-grandmother home, and promising to come and look after Baby Richard for ever, when her Gramma did not need her any more—he gave in all at once, saying, 'All right, Griselda, you shall have the cottage for thirty-five pounds, and I'll take care of the other fifteen for you, and give it you as you and your great-grandmother need it.'

That very afternoon, Griselda drove to the Almshouse in Mrs Greentop's victoria, with one of Mr Greentop's farm-carts following after. Into the victoria she put Great-Grandmother Curfew, and her Bible, her hassock, her teapot, her patchwork quilt, and Bella; into the farm-cart she put her rocking-chair, her clock, and her little wooden box of clothes; and back they all went to the last cottage in the Lane, where the fire was already lit, and the bed freshly made. The hens were clucking, the bees were humming, the roses were all out in the garden, and the first thing Great-Grandmother Curfew said was, 'Ef you was to set me down by the curran' bushes, Grissie, I could fright away them starlings while you wet the tea.'

And that night, as the happy Griselda put her Granny to bed, she washed the red stains off her withered finger-tips, and said, 'Now you shall have a dose tonight.'

'No, I shan't, Grissie, doses is nasty.'

'Yes, you shall, Gramma, and a sweetie after.'

'Two sweeties? And you'll tell me a story?'

'I'll tell you the story about the Giant who had three heads, and lived in a Brass Castle.'

'I like that story. I reckon ol' Em'ly Deane's a happy 'ooman tonight.'

'Now, Gramma, take your dose.'

'Have Bella took hers?'

'Yes, and never a murmur. There's your sweetie, and there's your other sweetie. Let me tuck you up, and now you lie still and listen. Once upon a time there was a Giant.'

'Ah!' said Great-Grandmother Curfew.

'And he had *Three* Heads!'

'Ah!'

'And he lived in a BRASS CASTLE!'

'Ah!' Great-Grandmother Curfew closed her eyes.

'Hush, hush, hush!' sang the happy Griselda. 'And I dance mine own child! And I dance mine own child—!'

At the end of the street stood the School. On the right-hand street corner sat Old Dinah the gypsy, who kept a pair of lovebirds in a cage. And on the left-hand street corner sat Susan Brown, who sold bootlaces. Susan thought she was about nine years old, but she never quite knew. As for Old Dinah's age, it was too great to be remembered, and she had forgotten it long ago.

At half-past twelve every morning, when school was over, the little boys and girls ran out through the gates on the way home, and Susan Brown would remember it was dinner time; and she would begin to eat her bit of bread and dripping, and admire the little girls' hair-ribbons, and the little boys' boots without holes in them. Very often their bootlaces were broken and knotted together, for you know what bootlaces are, but Susan Brown never really expected the little boys to come and give her their penny for a new pair.

Their mothers bought their bootlaces for them in a shop, and they wanted the penny for something else, for a top, or an ounce of bulls'-eyes, or a balloon. And the little girls with their pennies got beads, or pear-drops, or a bunch of violets. But almost every day at least one or two of the little girls and boys would stop in front of Old Dinah's lovebirds, and hold out their pennies and say, 'I want a fortune, please.'

For the lovebirds were such wonderful birds!—they were not only wonderful to look at, with their smooth grass-green bodies and long blue tail-feathers, they were wonderful because they could give you a fortune for a penny; and you can't get a fortune much cheaper than that.

Whenever a child came to buy a penny fortune, Old Dinah said, 'Put your finger in the cage, Ducky!' And when the child did so, one of the two lovebirds hopped on to the finger and was brought out with a flutter of wings. Then Old Dinah held out the fortunes in a little packet of folded papers, pink, and green, and purple, and blue, and yellow, that always hung outside the cage-door. And the wonderful lovebird picked out one of the fortunes with its curved beak, and the child took it. But just how did the lovebird know just which was the right fortune for that child?—the right one for Marion, for Cyril, for Helen, for Hugh? All the children put their heads together over the little coloured papers, and wondered.

'What's *your* fortune, Marion?'

'I'm to marry a king. It's a purple one. What's *yours*, Cyril?'

'A green one. I'm to go a long journey. What's Helen's?'

'I got a yellow one,' said Helen, 'and I'm to have seven children. What's *your* fortune, Hugh?'

'I'm to succeed in all my undertakings. It's blue,' said Hugh. Then they ran home to their dinners.

Susan Brown sat listening with all her ears. How beautiful to have a fortune! If only she had a penny to spare! But Susan Brown never had a penny to spare, and not often any other sort of penny, either.

But one day, when the children had gone, and Old Dinah was nodding in the sun, something lovely happened. The door of the lovebirds' cage had been left open a little by accident, and one of them got out. Old Dinah, asleep on her corner, didn't see. But Susan, awake on hers, did see. She saw the little green bird hop from its perch and flutter to the pavement. She saw it run along the kerb a little way, and she saw a thin cat crouch in the gutter. Susan's heart gave such a jump that it made her body jump too. She jumped before the cat did, and ran across the road crying, 'Shoo!'

The cat turned away as though it was thinking of something else, and Susan put her hand down to the lovebird, and the lovebird hopped on to her finger. Now to have a lovebird sitting on your finger is as lovely a thing as anyone can wish for on a summer day; it was the loveliest thing that had happened to Susan Brown in all her life. But that wasn't all; for just as they got to the cage-door the lovebird stretched out its beak, and picked a rose-pink fortune from the packet, and gave it to Susan. She couldn't believe it was true, but it was. She put the lovebird in the cage, and went back to her corner with her fortune in her hand.

In time Marion and Cyril and Helen and Hugh stopped going to school. They had lost their fortunes long ago, and forgotten all about them. And Marion married the chemist's young man, and Cyril sat all day in an office, and Helen never happened to marry at all, and Hugh never happened to do anything whatever.

But Susan Brown kept her fortune all her life. By day she kept it in her pocket, and by night she kept it under her cheek. She didn't know what was in it, because she couldn't read. But it was a rose-pink fortune, and she hadn't had to buy it—it had been given to her.

CATHY GOODMAN was picking peas in the front garden of the Corner Cottage on the village green. She picked them as though she hated them. For four years, ever since she had been evacuated, her face had been puckered with a scowl. This was a pity, for Cathy Goodman had been born with a nice face.

Old Mrs Vining was peering through her window in the cottage. She had a bad leg, and spent most of her time peering at what went on round the green. Just now she was peering at Cathy, to see she didn't eat too many peas; and she also peered at Mrs Lane, the Doctor's wife, and at Miss Barnes, the schoolmistress, who were standing at the edge of the duckpond on the green, staring into it.

Miss Barnes was saying, 'It's a disgusting sight!'

'And smell,' said Mrs Lane, screwing up her pretty little nose. 'Oh, *mon dieu*!'

Doctor Lane had married her in London, a year ago. Everybody in Little Eggham liked Doctor Lane, and was curious about his French wife. Would she be plain or pretty? She was pretty. Pleasant or stand-offish? She was pleasant. Young or old? She was neither. Mrs Lane was thirty-five, just betwixt and between—a very suitable age, thought Little Eggham, for a doctor of forty-four. Before long they liked her as much as they liked him, for all her funny ways. She was lively, and kind, and practical, and interested in everything and everybody. Her clothes were plain, yet there was something different about them; it was a treat to see her walking up the street. And her cooking—well, she had the same rations as everybody else, but she made *them* different too. What she could do with a cabbage or a pound of veal would surprise you; so Mr Fletcher, the vicar, said. Of course, the way she talked was different again, but she talked very well for a foreigner, for she had come to England soon after the last war. And if her ideas and her manners weren't quite what Little Eggham was accustomed to, Little Eggham found it liked them. Life was somehow a little more amusing in the twelve months that the doctor's wife had lived among them. She was always up to something. Mrs Vining, peering between her lace curtains, wondered, 'What's she up to *now*?'

Mrs Lane was saying, 'How long is it since the pond was cleared out?'

'Not since before the evacuees came in 1939,' said Miss Barnes. 'We'd always been particular about it, and never let it be a dump for rubbish. But some of the evacuees were rather a rough lot to begin with; they were at a loose end, and used to sit on the rails chucking in anything they could get hold of, for the fun of the thing. They settled down, of course, and now they like being here.'

'Not Cathy Goodman,' said Mrs Lane, glancing towards the Corner Cottage.

The schoolmistress knit her brows. Cathy Goodman was a problem. She didn't fit in. She didn't try to. She had no parents and seemed to belong to nobody; ever since she had come to Little Eggham she had got the habit of being unhappy, and resisted all attempts at friendliness. Miss Barnes hated children to be unhappy, but Cathy's case had got her beat, she said.

'It's a pity she was put with Mrs Vining.'

'Can it not be changed?' asked Mrs Lane.

'Who would take her?' Miss Barnes shook her head impatiently, and stared at the pond again. 'Goodness! I'd no idea how much had been thrown in till this drought.'

Little Eggham was suffering badly from the drought. The wells were dry, the gardens were parched, and the ponds were showing their bones. The duckpond had shrunk to a smear of green duckweed on the slime in the middle, with a crust of mud all round, in which was embedded a number of disagreeable objects. Salmon tins, sardine and soup tins, rusty kitchen things, and broken bottles; in one part an old boot, hard as iron, had thrust its wrinkled toecap through the caked mud, and in the very middle a wooden chair-leg stuck up like the mast of an ancient wreck.

'It is not nice!' said Mrs Lane energetically. 'It is not sanitary. And it is very ugly! It's time it is cleaned out.'

'I've spoken to Mr Fletcher about it,' said Miss Barnes. 'But with labour so short there's no men to spare in the village.'

'*Eh bien!*' cried Mrs Lane. 'If there are no men, there are women, I hope! I shall clean out the pond myself.'

'When?' asked Miss Barnes.

'After supper,' said Mrs Lane.

'I'll help,' said Miss Barnes.

'We'll want rakes and shuffles,' said Mrs Lane. 'I shall put on shorts and the doctor's wellingtons. Eight o'clock, after we've had our café.'

'I'll be here,' laughed Miss Barnes. She went off gaily to her cottage near the school, and Mrs Lane crossed to the pretty white house that overlooked the green. They both seemed merry, and walked so full of purpose, that old Mrs Vining asked herself again, 'What *are* they up to?' She called through the window to Cathy, 'What was Mrs Lane doin' by the duckpond?'

Cathy did not answer.

'An't you got a tongue in your head?' rapped out Mrs Vining.

Cathy put it out at her.

'Get on with them peas!' shouted Mrs Vining; and added to herself, 'One might ha' thought she were expectin' to find a treasure in the pond.'

Cathy crammed peas into her mouth to stop herself from crying. A treasure! Only she knew about the treasure in the duckpond. Oh, how she *hated* the duckpond! The duckpond was the reason why, for four years, her nice little face had been puckered with a scowl.

II

The treasure in the duckpond was San Fairy Ann. She lay in the mud under the broken chair in the middle. When it settled on her chest and pushed her deep down, she gave up all hope of seeing daylight again. She hadn't seen the light for nearly four years. Her frock, made of fine old silk, in blue-and-white stripes with rosebuds dotted down the white stripe, by now her lovely frock must be simply ruined. Her sawdust body felt sadly limp and soggy. San Fairy Ann hoped that her face was still all right. She had been born with a shiny pink and white china face, and glossy black china hair, and big blue eyes and a little rosy mouth—born long ago in France. Lying under the mud in the green duckpond, San Fairy Ann had lived upon her memories. She thought she must be nearly eighty years old. She remembered a lovely little château with turrets and a bridge over a dry moat, and rose gardens and peaches that ripened in the sun; a fairy castle, with a lady as pretty as a fairy to live in it. The lady was sewing at a table strewn with bits of brocade and reels of coloured silk, and a fine lace flounce. San Fairy Ann, with nothing on, was lying amongst the finery. The lady was finishing making a blue-and-white striped bed-jacket for herself, with lace ruffles in the sleeves. A scrap of lace, and a piece of the silk, were left over. 'These will just do for Célestine's doll,' she said. She cut the garments deftly, and with exquisite stitches made a petticoat of the lace and a frock of the silk.

Next day the doll was given to the lady's little girl; it was her *jour de fête*, her birthday. The child, seven years old, called the doll Célestine, after herself. She loved the doll better than any of her toys, kept her carefully, and years later gave her to her little girl, who was also called Célestine. Thirty years after there was another child called Célestine, and she in her turn treasured her grandmother's doll in its rich dress of old French silk and real lace. The doll supposed she would go on living for ever in the fairy castle, belonging to one little Célestine after another. Then the time came when she learned that things don't go on for ever.

It was the year of the first Great War. Guns boomed all round the castle, and holes appeared in walls, and some ceilings fell in. One night her little mistress ran and clutched her out of her cradle, saying, 'We're running away, Célestine; maman says we must hurry ourselves, but I won't go without you.'

'Quick, *chérie*, quick!' called her mother from below. The little Célestine of flesh and blood flew down the stairs, clasping the sawdust Célestine in her arms. Out into the starry summer night, through the sweet-smelling gardens, and across the bridge over the moat—suddenly the child stumbled, the doll fell out of her arms, and a servant who followed kicked it into the moat. 'Célestine!' cried the child. 'Hurry!' called her mother. 'But Célestine is down there!' 'Oh, darling, we can't wait . . . ' The last thing the doll heard was her little mistress weeping for her.

She did not know how long she lay in the moat. Her next memory was of a man in a sand-coloured uniform fishing her out of the dead leaves and dusting her off. 'Coo!' he said. 'Just the ticket for my Kitsy!'

The guns were still booming, and the fairy castle was fuller of holes than before, and the rose-gardens were trampled to bits, when the English Tommy carried the doll away. That was her last memory of France.

Next she remembered the soldier unpacking her from his haversack in a little room in England, where his wife was clinging to him, crying for joy, and on his knee was the little girl he called Kitsy.

'See what Daddy brought you all the way from France, ducky!'

'Oo!' said the little girl. 'Ain't she luvverly! Wot's 'er name?'

'Let's see,' said the soldier. He didn't know her name was Célestine, and he said, 'Her name's San Fairy Ann.'

'What's it mean, Dad?'

'Means she's a fairy, see, and'll bring you luck.'

She loved her because she was a fairy, and because no other doll in the world had such a face, or such beautiful clothes. Miss Higgins the dressmaker said about her dress, 'That's a very fine sample of silk,' and about the petticoat, 'Well! I do believe it's *real lace*.' But San Fairy Ann herself was what Kitsy loved most.

And San Fairy Ann she became, first to Kitsy, who loved and treasured her as three little French Célestines had done, and then, many years later, to Kitsy's only little daughter, Cathy Goodman. Nobody, not Kitsy, not one of the three Célestines long ago, had loved her as much as Cathy Goodman did.

Presently, before the second great war broke out, sad things happened in Cathy's life. She was left without parents, and the people who were supposed to look after her neglected her. All she had in the world was San Fairy Ann, and San Fairy Ann was all the world to her.

III

Then, in 1939, came the World War, and just before it came Cathy with a crowd of other children was evacuated. She fell to the lot of old Mrs Vining in Little Eggham, and that was bad luck, because Mrs Vining was selfish and crotchety, and had no notion of making a child happy. Still, Cathy would have found friends in the village, and things would have been very different, but for a bit of worse luck that happened on her very first day.

There was in Little Eggham a boy who was not bright in his wits. Johnny sat in school with the youngest when he was well-grown, and Miss Barnes was especially careful and kind with him. There was no harm in Johnny, but he had a weakness for bright things, and when a child complained of missing this or that, Miss Barnes would take Johnny into her room and say, 'Now then, you squirrel, let's see what you've got in your drey.' Johnny grinned at being called a squirrel, and turned out his pockets readily—and there, to be sure, was Dorrie Carter's hairslide, mixed up with somebody else's ribbon, bright rose-haws from the hedge, and a glass button from goodness knows where. The morning the evacuees arrived they were welcomed with cups of tea in the Women's Institute, where Johnny loitered to gaze at his face in the metal tea-urn. 'Keep an eye on the teaspoons,' whispered Miss Barnes to her helpers. She knew that Johnny's fingers would itch for them. But soon those fingers itched for something else. Johnny had caught sight of Cathy, sitting forlorn in a corner hugging San Fairy Ann. She was miserable in this strange new place, wondering who would choose her to go home with them, but she got comfort from knowing that she and San Fairy Ann would go together, and sleep in the same bed. One day her fairy doll would bring her luck.

Johnny came up and grabbed at the doll's silk dress. 'Gi'e oi 'er!' he said. Cathy could only stare at him and hold San Fairy Ann tighter. 'Gi'e oi 'er!' repeated Johnny, and this time Cathy gave him a violent push, crying, 'Go away, you horrid little beast!'

Lady Bridgewater, who was choosing five children and had paused by Cathy, passed on, remarking, 'I'm afraid you're one of the troublesome little girls.' And somehow her ladyship's words stuck. Nobody wanted Cathy, and in the end old Mrs Vining had her.

That evening Cathy stood inside the gate of the Corner Cottage, showing their new world to San Fairy Ann. It was quiet on the green, everybody seemed to be at supper. Johnny came by, and stared in from the other side.

'Gi'e oi 'er!' he said.

'Go away, or I'll tell the pleeceman on you,' said Cathy angrily.

She never knew how it happened—Johnny had made a long arm over the fence, snatched San Fairy Ann out of her arms, and scampered off. Cathy flashed through the gate after him, and chased him round the green, shrieking, 'I'll tell the pleeceman! I'll tell the pleeceman!'

Was it her threat that frightened him out of his small wits? Suddenly Johnny raised his arm and hurled San Fairy Ann far into the middle of the pond. For one moment she swam on her stiff silk skirt; as soon as it got drenched, she sank out of sight. Cathy's screams brought people to their doors. They saw Johnny lying on his back on the green, being scratched and pounded by a furious little evacuee.

The children were pulled apart. Johnny couldn't, and Cathy wouldn't explain. She would not show her broken heart to these unfeeling strangers. She would suffer in silence—but oh! how she would suffer. Her pain went deep, and shut her lips. She scowled at Johnny. She scowled at the duckpond. She scowled at Little Eggham and everything in it.

It was a bad start for the 'troublesome little girl' from London. It was why Cathy Goodman had never fitted in, and never tried to. But nobody had ever known the reason.

At eight o'clock in the evening, double summertime in July, there are still three good hours of light. Old Mrs Vining, peering as usual, saw children and grown-ups gather in increasing numbers round the duckpond, and heard the jokes and chatter, and the occasional shouts, with which they filled the air. In the middle of the pond stood Mrs Lane, her sleeves rolled up, her cotton shirt tucked into her shorts, her legs encased in the doctor's rubber boots, her capable hands raking the slime as she passed her findings to Miss Barnes, on the hard caked mud. The children framing the banks made rubbish piles, to be carted away tomorrow.

'Biscuit tin, pre-war!' announced Mrs Lane. 'Cricket ball, belonging to William the Conqueror. Tea-kettle used by Noah in the Ark.' Each find was greeted with bursts of laughter and applause. It was as good as a play. 'The wooden horse from Troy!' called Mrs Lane.

'Thur be my owd 'orse!' cried Bobby Maitland. 'I niver knowed what 'ad become of 'e.'

On the edge of the crowd, staring with all her heart in her eyes, stood Cathy Goodman. If Bobby Maitland's wooden horse was found, why not San Fairy Ann?

The hunt went on. Nine o'clock chimed. Mothers began to chase their children to bed. Mrs Vining screamed to Cathy to come in. Cathy slipped behind a bush and hid. When ten o'clock chimed there was almost no one left but Mrs Lane and Miss Barnes. The green showed three big dumps, and not a tin was visible in the pond. San Fairy Ann had not come to light. Mrs Lane pushed her hair off her damp forehead with a muddy forearm.

'That is all, I t'ink,' she said, raking idly in the slime. ('*Oh, go on! go on! go on!*' prayed Cathy silently.) Doctor Lane leaned over the garden wall of the white house, smoking his pipe. 'That's quite enough, Tina! Come along in,' he called. ('*Please, please!*' prayed Cathy Goodman.)

'Pouf! It has been fun!' laughed Mrs Lane. She pulled herself slowly out of the sucking mud that dragged at her long boots.

'Great fun,' said the doctor, 'if I have you sneezing tomorrow.'

'And do my shoulders ache!' Mrs Lane wriggled them, and crossed the green to her house.

Miss Barnes said, 'We'll clear the dumps in the morning.' And she too went away.

The green was empty, except for Cathy crouched behind the bush. Old Mrs Vining had given her up as a bad job, and gone to bed.

And San Fairy Ann still lay under the mud in the middle of the pond. No wonder Mrs Lane hadn't raked her up. She had been standing right on top of her all the time.

IV

Twelve o'clock chimed. The doctor was asleep. Mrs Lane slipped out of bed to smell the jasmine at her window and look at the moon on the green. It was one of the prettiest sights in Little Eggham, but not many people bothered about it. Standing in her pyjamas at the window, Tina Lane gazed at the square church tower behind the peaceful elms, the quiet grass where children had played their games for hundreds of years, the darkened cottages, asleep in silver light. Dear Little Eggham! The church tower might almost be the turret of a fairy castle, thought Mrs Lane.

She caught her breath. What was that muffled sobbing sound in the night?—*and what was that in the middle of the pond?* Had a dog or a sheep floundered in? 'Oh, *mon dieu*! It's a child!'

Mrs Lane was down the stairs and out of the house in a flash. In the hall she snatched up the muddy wellingtons as she ran, and thrust her pyjamaed legs into them, scarcely stopping. Within two minutes of seeing her from the window, Mrs Lane was lifting Cathy Goodman out of the slime. They stood clutching each other in the middle of the pond. Cathy was a dreadful sight, soaked with mud, her wet hair streaked with duckweed.

'San Fairy Ann! San Fairy Ann!' she sobbed.

'Cathy—*chérie*—what is it?'

'San Fairy Ann!'

'Tell me, *pauvre petite*.'

'I want San Fairy Ann.'

'Who is she, San Fairy Ann?'

'You never fished her out. You fished out Bobby's horse, but you left San Fairy Ann.'

'She's your doll!' cried Mrs Lane, light breaking on her. 'Stop crying, *chérie*—we'll find her if we have to fish all night.' And in her own language, she added, smiling, '*Ca ne fait rien!*'

Cathy stopped sobbing, and stared. Were people kind, after all, then? Regardless of her pyjamas, Mrs Lane knelt in the mud and groped with both her hands. What was this? Only another tin. She must be careful. Ah! here was something smooth and hard. A stone? She brought it into the moonlight. Not a stone, a china head, with glossy black hair, blue eyes, and a rosy mouth.

Cathy Goodman turned red with happiness. 'San Fairy Ann!' she screamed. But Mrs Lane turned white, and said, 'Célestine.'

Doctor Lane in his pyjamas met Mrs Lane in hers at the front door. She dripped with mud, and clasped in her arms a child and a doll, even muddier.

'Tina! what on earth—!'

'Don't stand asking questions, *mon cher*. Turn on the hot bath and heat some milk.'

They all went into the bath, Mrs Lane, Cathy, and San Fairy Ann, whom Cathy would not let go. Her china face and arms and legs soon shone again—but her poor limp body! And her clothes! But what did it matter? Wrapped in a towel, she was lying beside Cathy in a clean bed, while Cathy sipped hot milk. Mrs Lane, also sipping, sat with her arm round her. Only then did she ask a question.

'Cathy—where did you get my Célestine?'

'She's *not* your Célestine. She's *my* San Fairy Ann.'

'Yes, *chérie*, I know. But when I was a little girl in France, long ago, she was mine. Tell me.'

'My grandaddy bringed her from France for my mummy.'

'Yes?'

'He found her in a castle.'

'Yes.'

'My mummy gived her to me.'

'What do you t'ink, Cathy! My mummy gave her to me. And I cried because I lost her, just like you.'

'She's *mine*,' said Cathy Goodman, very fiercely, very imploringly.

'Yes, she is yours. She always shall be till you give her one day to *your* little girl. Tomorrow I will make her a new body, and a new dress. Can you guess what San Fairy Ann's dress shall be?'

Cathy shook her head. Mrs Lane went to a drawer and took out a lovely little jacket made of blue-and-white striped silk, with rosebuds on the white stripes, and lace flounces in the sleeves.

'Oh!' gasped Cathy.

'This little jacket,' said Mrs Lane, 'belonged to my great-grandmother. It was made from one of *her* granny's dresses. Her granny danced in it when she was a princess in France, and lived in a fairy castle.'

'Oh!'

'Tomorrow,' said Mrs Lane, 'we will cut it into a new dress for San Fairy Ann, with a lace petticoat underneath.'

Cathy stared at her, unable to speak. Suddenly the scowl came unpuckered from her face, and her face was so nice when it smiled that, just as suddenly, Célestine Lane's eyes filled with tears. She put her arms round the little girl and the doll, saying, 'And Cathy—would you and San Fairy Ann like to stay here and live with me?'

'*Oh!*' gasped Cathy Goodman.

ANNAR-MARIAR lived in a queer old alley in one of the queerest and oldest parts of London. Once this part had been a real village all by itself, looking down from its hill upon the fields and lanes that divided it from the town. Then gradually the town had climbed the hill, the fields were eaten up by houses, and the lanes suffered that change which turned them into streets. But the hill was so steep, and the ways were so twisty, that even the town couldn't swallow the village when it got to the top. It was too much trouble to make broad roads of all the funny little narrow turnings, so some of them were left much as they were, and one of these was the alley where Annar-Mariar lived. It ran across from one broad road to another, a way for walkers, but not for carts and cars. The two big roads met at a point a little further on, so there was no need to turn Annar-Mariar's alley into a thoroughfare for traffic, and it remained a paved court, with poor irregular dwellings and a few humble shops on each side. Being paved, and out of the way of motors, it became a natural playground for the children who lived in it; and even from the other alleys nearby children came to play in Mellin's Court. The organ-grinder, making his way from one big road to another, sometimes made it across Mellin's Court. One day, as he was passing, a group of children were clustered round the little sweetstuff shop that sold bright sweets in hap'orths, or even farthings-worths. The shop had an old bow window nearly touching the pavement—it came down about as far as a little girl's skirt, and went up about as high as a man's collar. To enter the shop, you went down three steps into a dim little room. None of the children had any farthings that day except Annar-Mariar, and *she* had a whole penny. Her little brother Willyum was clinging to the hand that held the penny, and telling her all the things he liked best in the jars in the window. He knew his Annar-Mariar, and so did the other children who were not her brothers and sisters.

'I like the lickerish shoe-strings,' said Willyum.

'*I* like the comfits with motters on,' said Mabel Baker.

'And I like the pink and white mouses,' said Willyum.

'Them bulls'-eyes is scrumpchous,' observed Doris Goodenough.

'And the chocklit mouses,' continued Willyum, 'and I like them long stripey sticks, and them chocklit cream bars with pink inside.'

'Peardrops,' murmured Kitty Farmer.

'And white inside too,' said Willyum.

While Annar-Mariar was puzzling and puzzling how to make her penny go round she saw the organ-grinder, and cried, 'Oo! an orgin!' The other children turned. 'Ply us a chune, mister!' they cried. 'Ply us a chune!' The organ-grinder shook his head. 'No time today,' he said. Annar-Mariar went up to the organ-grinder and smiled at him, plucking his coat.

'Do ply 'em a chune to dance to,' she said, and held out her penny. It was Annar-Mariar's nice smile, and not her penny, that won the day. Annar-Mariar was quite an ordinary-looking little girl until she smiled. Then you felt you would do anything for her. This was because Annar-Mariar would always do anything for anybody. It came out in her smile, and got back at her, so to speak, by winning her her own way. All day long Mellin's Court was calling her name. 'Annar-Mariar! Johnny's bin and hurted hisself.' 'Annar-Mariar! come quick! Bobby and Joan is fighting somethink orful!' 'Annar-Mariar, boo-hoo! I've broke my dolly!' Or it might be an older voice. 'Annar-Mariar! Jest keep an eye on baby for me while I go round the corner.' Yes, everybody knew that Annar-Mariar would always be ready to heal the hurt, and soothe the quarrel, and mend the doll, and mind the baby. She would not only be ready to, but she could *do* it; because everybody did what she wanted them to.

So the organ-grinder refused her penny, and stopped and played three tunes for her smile; and the children got a jolly dance for nothing, and Willyum got a pair of liquorice shoe-strings for a farthing. The rest of Annar-Mariar's penny went in Hundreds and Thousands, and every child licked its finger and had a dip. There wasn't a fingerful over for Annar-Mariar, so she tore open the tiny bag and licked it off with her tongue.

After that the organ-grinder made a point of cutting across Mellin's Court on his rounds, stopping outside the Rat-Catcher's, where it was at its broadest, to play his tunes; and the children gathered there and danced, and sometimes he got a copper for his kindness, but whether he did or not made no difference. He always came once a week.

Christmas drew near, and the little shops in Mellin's Court began to look happy. The sweetstuff shop had a Fairy Doll in white muslin and tinsel in the middle of the window, and some paper festoons and cheap toys appeared among the glass bottles. At the greengrocer's, a sort of glorified open stall which overflowed into the courtyard, evergreens and pineapples appeared, and on one magic morning Christmas trees. The grocery window at the corner had already blossomed into dates and figs and candied fruits, and blue-and-white jars of ginger; and the big confectioner's in the High Street had in the window, as well as puddings in basins, a Christmas cake a yard square—a great flat frosted 'set piece', covered with robins, windmills, snow babies, and a scarlet Santa Claus with a sled full of tiny toys. This cake would presently be cut up and sold by the pound, and you got the attractions on top 'as you came'—oh lucky, lucky buyer-to-be of the Santa Claus sled! The children of Mellin's Court were already choosing their favourite toys and cakes and fruits from the rich windows, and Annar-Mariar and Willyum chose like all the rest. Of course, they never *thought* they could have the Fairy Queen, the Christmas tree, the big box of sugary fruits, or the marvellous cake—but how they *dreamed* they could! As Christmas drew nearer, smaller hopes of what it would actually bring began to take shape in the different homes. Bobby's mother had *told* him he'd better hang his stocking up on Christmas Eve 'and see'. That meant something. And the Goodenoughs were going to be sent a hamper. And Mabel Baker was going to be taken to the Pantomime! And the Jacksons were all going to their Granny's in Lambeth for a party. And this child and that had so much, or so little, in the Sweet Club.

And as Christmas drew nearer, it became plainer and plainer to Annar-Mariar that this year, for one reason or another, Christmas wasn't going to bring her and Willyum anything. And it didn't. Up to the last they got *their* treat from the shop-windows, and did all their shopping there. Annar-Mariar never stinted her Christmas window-shopping.

'What'll *you* 'ave, Willyum? I'll 'ave the Fairy Queen, I think. Would you like them trains?'

'Ss!' said Willyum. 'And I'd like the Fairy Queen.'

'Orl right. You 'ave her. I'll 'ave that music box.'

At the confectioner's: 'Shall we 'ave a big puddin' for us both, or a little puddin' each, Willyum?'

'A big puddin' each,' said Willyum.

'Orl right. And them red crackers with the gold bells on, and I'll tell 'em to send the big cake round too, shall I?'

'Ss!' said Willyum. 'And I'll 'ave the Farver Crismuss.'

'Orl right, ducks. You can.'

And at the grocer's Willyum had the biggest box of candied fruits, and at the greengrocer's the biggest pineapple. He agreed, however, to a single tree—the biggest—between them, and under Annar-Mariar's lavish disregard of money there was plenty of everything for them both, and for anybody who cared to 'drop in' on Christmas Day.

It came, and passed. The windows began to be emptied of their attractions for another year. Mabel Baker went to the Pantomime, and told them all about it. Annar-Mariar dreamed of it for nights; she thought she was a very lucky girl to have a friend who went to the Panto.

Life went on. The New Year rang itself in. At dusk, on Twelfth Night, Annar-Mariar knelt on the paving-stones in Mellin's Court and renewed a chalk game that had suffered during the day. She happened to be the only child about, a rare occurrence there.

She heard footsteps go by her, but did not look up at once; only, as they passed, she became aware of a tiny tinkling accompaniment in the footsteps. Then she did look up. A lady was going slowly along the alley with something astonishing in her hands.

'Oo!' gasped Annar-Mariar.

The lady stopped. What she was carrying was a Christmas tree, quite a little tree, the eighteenpenny size, but such a *radiant* little tree! It was glittering and twinkling with all the prettiest fantasies in glass that the mind of Christmas had been able to invent, little gas lamps and candlesticks, shining balls of every colour, a scarlet-and-silver Father Christmas, also in glass, chains and festoons of gold and silver beads, stars, and flowers, and long clear drops like icicles; birds, too, in glass, blue and yellow birds, seeming to fly, and one, proudest and loveliest of all, a peacock, shimmering in blue and green and gold, with a crest and long, long tail of fine spun glass, like silk.

'Oo!' gasped Annar-Mariar. 'A Christmas tree!'

The lady did an undreamed-of thing. She came straight up to Annar-Mariar and said, 'Would you like it?'

Annar-Mariar gazed at her, and very slowly smiled. The lady put the tinkling tree into her hands.

'This,' she said, 'was for the first little girl that said Oo! and you're the little girl.'

Annar-Mariar began to giggle—she simply *couldn't* say 'Thank you!' She could only giggle and giggle. Her smile, however, turned her giggling into the loveliest laughter, and seemed to be saying 'Thank you,' on top of it. The lady laughed, and disappeared from Mellin's Court.

Willyum appeared in her place. 'Wot's that?'

' 'Ts a Crismuss tree. A lidy give it to me.'

Willyum scampered screaming down the alley. 'Annar-Mariar's gotter Crismuss tree wot a lidy give 'er!'

The crowd collected. They gathered round the tree, looking, touching, admiring, and the 'Oos!' came thick and fast.

'Oo! See ol' Farver Crismuss!'

'Oo! See them birds, like flying, ain't they?'

'Do the lamps reely light, Annar-Mariar?'

'Oo! Ain't that flower loverly!'

'Wotcher goin' to do wiv it, Annar?'

'I shall keep it by my bed ternight,' said Annar-Mariar, 'and termorrer I shall give a party.'

Longing glances flew about her.

'Can I come, Annar-Mariar?'

'Can I?'

'Can I?'

'Let *me* come, won't yer, Annar?'

'You can all come,' said Annar-Mariar.

That night, that one blissful night, the little tree in all its gleaming beauty shone upon Annar-Mariar's dreams—waking dreams, for she hardly slept at all. She kept looking at it, and feeling it when she couldn't see it, running her finger along the glassy chains, outlining the fragile flowers and stars, stroking the silken tail of the miraculous peacock. Tomorrow night, she knew, her tree would be harvested, but she thought her own particular fruit might be the peacock. If so, he could sit on the tree beside her bed for ever, and every night she could stroke his spun-glass tail.

The morrow came. The party was held after tea. Every child in Mellin's Court took home a treasure. Willyum wanted the Father Christmas, and had him. The other children did not ask for the peacock. Somehow they knew how *much* Annar-Mariar wanted it, and recognized that off *her* tree she should have what she prized most. Little Lily Kensit *did* murmur, when her turn came, 'I'd like the peac—' But her big brother clapped his hand over her mouth, and said firmly, 'Lil'd like the rose, Annar-Mariar. Look, Lil, it's got a dimond in the middle.'

'Oo!' said Lil greedily.

So when the party was over, and the little empty tree was dropping its dried needles on the table, Annar-Mariar was left in possession of the magical bird whose tail she had touched in her dreams.

When she came to put Willyum to bed, he was sobbing bitterly.

'Wot's the matter, ducks?'

'I broke my Farver Crismuss.'

'Oh, Willyum . . . you never.'

'Yus, I did,' Willyum was inconsolable.

'Don't cry, ducks.'

'I want your peacock.'

'Orl right. You can. Don't cry.'

Annar-Mariar gave Willyum her peacock. He sobbed himself to sleep, clutching it, and in the night he dropped it out of bed. Annar-Mariar heard it 'go' as she lay beside her little empty tree. All night long the pungent scent of the Christmas tree was in her nostrils, and the tiny crickle of its dropping needles in her ears.

And in the room of every other child in Mellin's Court some lovely thing was set above its dreams, a bird, or flower, or star of coloured glass; to last perhaps a day, a week, a few months, or a year—or even many years.

If you heard tell of a man that all his life had been a stern teetotaller, refusing even the smell of liquor, and, after his prime, had tasted beer and ended a drunkard, you wouldn't be much surprised, I dare say.

Well, then, don't you be surprised at this.

The day that Farmer Robert Churdon dismissed William Stow from the farm for idleness, Will turned at the door and said in a shaking voice, 'Mister Churdon, what you're doing may be the ruin of me and mine. Think twice.'

'I'm not such a fool, man,' said Robert Churdon, 'as to spend two shot on a bird I've winged with one. Who wastes my time, wastes my money. You waste my time. I've thought once, and that's enough.'

'And once will be enough for me,' said poor Will, 'the day that you or yours have need of me.'

'If I'd ever let myself have need of wasters,'

retorted Churdon harshly, 'I'd not have laid up store for my old age. If I'd ever had need of wasters, I wouldn't now have a thousand fat acres, two hundred head of cattle, a shop in Bonemarket, the Inn at Underbone, the mills on the Honey, and a nest-egg in Six-per-cents in Bonemarket Bank. It isn't me that'll have need of the likes of you, Stow; and as for mine, there *is* no mine, and if there were, I could provide for a dozen children, and theirs to come, so that they'd never know the want you'll see this day when you go out of that door. And now you can go and face it.'

Stow went. And that night, in the fifty-odd dwellings and scattered cottages that made up the hamlet of Underbone, nothing else was talked of but the hardness and the prosperity of the farmer in their midst.

There were few who in one way or another had not suffered from him. Those who worked for him he drove to the hilt of time for the lowest wage in the country: those he bargained with parted with more than their money's worth; he never put a penny in the parson's plate; he never subscribed sixpence to the school-treat; he never allowed a half-pint's credit at the inn, which was run for him by an old browbeaten acquaintance with whom he did as he pleased. He turned his labourers out of doors on the slimmest pretext, if he saw he could get labour cheaper. The man to whom he spared skim milk for his pig, mortgaged one part of the pig to him for this benefit. Gleaners were driven from his harvests, and beggars turned from his door. And he prospered. Year by year he laid by more gold, bought more land, and increased his stock. His hay was the best in the shire;

his corn and his fruit did not fail him; and he sold at top prices. Yes, he prospered, and his neighbours and dependants hated and feared him. For while he prospered, the village went down; their gardens dwindled, their homes went unrepaired, their children wanted. He squeezed them all. Not a good word was to be heard of this hard man from Underbone to Bonemarket, or from Bonemarket to Beadon-on-Honey where the Mills turned other men's grain into Farmer Churdon's Six-per-cents.

But if he had not turned off Will Stow with hard words that got their answer, it may be things would have ended different. For among poor Stow's few rejoinders, one phrase stuck in the farmer's mind as a legacy. 'You and yours,' the man had said—'the day that you and yours have need of me.' It was not the day or the need that stayed in Robert Churdon's mind, but 'You and yours' rang now and again in his thoughts as he trod his ploughed fields and turned the pages of his pass-book. Not that he dwelt on the thought. It only came in like a sort of refrain to a song, a song of rich crops and full coffers. If it had not been there, like a pebble sometimes tossed uppermost in the surf of his thinking, his eye might have roved past Jane Flower's face at Bonemarket Cattle Fair. As it was, it rested on that lovely face, and for the first time in his life he wanted something which could not be turned into hard cash. But maybe, he thought, hard cash could buy it.

She was a stranger to him that day, but not that night. Robert Churdon did not shilly-shally when he knew what he was after. And he had not looked twice on that shining light-brown hair, that fresh and smiling mouth, that creamy freckled skin, and those grey innocent eyes, before he felt his heart turn over in his breast. He heard her speak to someone who was looking at the cow she had brought with her, and the sound of her voice in his ears was like water to a parched throat; the difference being, that he'd never known of his own thirst till now.

Stepping forward, he too examined the cow she held by a halter.

'I'm looking for stock,' he said. 'What are you wanting for her?'

'Oh, I am sorry,' said Jane Flower. 'I have just sold her.'

'What price did she fetch?'

Jane named it.

'I'll make it a pound above that,' said Farmer Churdon, to his own surprise.

'You're ever so kind, sir,' said Jane, 'but she is sold already.'

It was the first time man, woman, or child had called Robert Churdon kind.

'Has the money been paid?' he asked.

'I'm waiting for it now.'

'Then the deal's not clinched. You can better the price.'

'It was a fair deal, and I passed my word, sir. I must not try to better the price after that, must I? But thank you all the same.'

'She's a good cow, and he offered too little. I've not seen you here before, have I?' said the farmer.

'I'm John Flower's daughter from Camstock,' said Jane. 'You'll have seen my father, I dare say. But he's ill, and we wanted the money, so I said I'd bring

Beauty to market myself. There's her new master coming for her now. I think he looks like one fond of beasts, don't you? Goodbye, my Beauty,' said the girl, kissing the cow between the horns. She spoke cheerfully, but the look in her eyes made Churdon's heart turn again. For a moment he hated the cow she kissed. The buyer came up and counted his money into Jane Flower's hand. She put it in her pocket, said 'Good-day' to both men, and went away. Churdon stared after her. Not a doubt of it, he thought, she'd brought beauty to market, and now it was gone. Goodbye, my Beauty! By George, no. He turned to the cow's owner and looked the creature over. 'That's a paltry lot you've bought,' he said, thrusting out his hard lip. 'Where were your eyes, man?' He ran over the cow's bad points.

That evening his knock on John Flower's open door brought Jane Flower running to him. He saw her coming down the steep cottage stairs, not knowing him as he knew her, for his back was to the sun; but when she stood before him—'Why, it's you!' she said, and held out her hand. It was said like a welcome, a new sound in Robert Churdon's ears. Then, as he touched her hand, 'Oh!' she gasped, gazing beyond his shoulder, and her hand gripped his like an excited child's.

'Yes, Miss Flower,' said he, 'that's your Beauty. She's come back to you.'

'But how?'

'I've bought her, and she's yours. Put her in her stall.'

Jane looked at him speechless. She ran past him and threw her arms around Beauty's neck. This time

Robert Churdon could stomach it, for wasn't Beauty his proxy?

When Jane had disposed of the cow for the night, she begged the farmer to step in and see her father. 'I told him of your kindness to me today,' she said, 'but I did not know your name. He'll thank you better than I can.' Churdon doubted that. But he stepped in and saw her father. John Flower lay back on his pillow and stared, while Jane poured out the tale of Farmer Churdon's goodness. He stammered his thanks, but Churdon soon cut him short and left him. For he knew enough of John Flower to know that John Flower knew still more of him. Jane walked with Churdon to the gate.

'I don't know what to say to you,' she said simply. 'I feel as though I ought to give you back Beauty's price, but we sold her because we had to have the money.'

'I don't want Beauty's price,' said Churdon. No need to mention that he had got the cow for a pound less than Jane had sold her for.

'Then ought you not to take Beauty to your own farm?'

'We'll see,' said Robert Churdon.

'Well,' said Jane Flower, 'ask for her when you want her, sir, and thank you again for all your kindness.'

Three months from that date Churdon took Beauty to his own farm. John Flower had died in the meantime. Underbone gaped when the farmer drove his bride home. Why, the girl looked happy! Did you ever see the like of her smile? How d'ye figure it out? A poor girl might wed a prosperous man for his long stocking, but does the thought of a long stocking make you look like wild roses in June?

In the eleven months of her married life, Jane Flower, that was, looked nothing else. Churdon kept her close, and outside the house went his own way. But inside he made a secret indulgence of the things that made her say, 'How kind you are!' or look it. And he discovered very soon that such little things sufficed, things that, as often as not, cost nothing at all. He could get the word cheap by merely stooping for the first wild strawberries. Yet even after this discovery he would bring her a coloured kerchief from some fair, or a packet of sweetstuff now and then, for which good pence must be paid out. By these means he kept her in the dark as to himself, and when, before the year was out, she bore him a daughter and died, she had never once in her short married life called him anything but kind.

He called the child Jane Flower after her mother, but always spoke of her as little Jane, and he emphasized the 'little' more than the 'Jane', because it was that word that made the difference, and seemed less to shut his big Jane out.

'How's *little* Jane?' he'd ask of the maid that looked after her. 'Where's *little* Jane?' of the men in the fields. So in a few years she became *Little*jane to everybody, Littlejane, all of a run.

You'd have thought a man like him might have turned against the baby at first, but from the first she took her mother's place in his heart, and carried on her mother's work; though it didn't begin to show until the child could speak. Before then he'd sit and stare at her in her cot, or carry her slung on his back like an

Indian woman's babe, as he went about the fields. He didn't talk much to her, and perhaps as he stared at her and felt her little weight on his broad shoulders his thoughts were no more or less than 'Me and Mine'. But that takes in a lot. 'Da' came to her tongue; and other words followed, a sort of wonder to him—like the little shoots coming out of the earth that was ready for them, and like flowers in spring. Why, those things were a bit of a wonder too, come to think of it, but Farmer Churdon never *had* thought of it like that before the child's new words sprang out like early violets, or the first green signs of corn. He took to listening for the new words, and came to link them up with those other new things that are so old; so when, in the summer just before Littlejane was two, he found the first wild strawberries in the nine-acre field, he brought them to her like a new word from the earth, as two years before he had brought them to her mother. Littlejane took the leaf full of tiny red balls with delight, and looking up at him, '*Kind* Da!' she crowed. And that was a new word for Littlejane. It made Robert Churdon's heart turn again in his breast. For where had Littlejane got *that* word, if not from her mother?

Of all her words, it was this he wanted to hear most. His ears were greedy for it, and he began to plan ways of getting it out of her. He brought her little toys from the markets, he took her more and more about the fields, showing her birds' nests, and this and that. He began to look for things to show her, and to notice what he'd never noticed before, only taken for granted. Now he could no more take for granted anything that might bring that word to Littlejane's lips. And he couldn't take the word itself for granted, unless he heard her say it; say it often. As for what the word stood for, he hardly thought about that at all. He didn't know or care whether he was kind or not. But he wanted to hear Littlejane say he was.

One day he heard a child crying at the gate. He thought it was Littlejane, and ran to stop the sound at all costs. Littlejane was there, but it was another child crying, a girl perhaps a year older than his own. Littlejane toddled towards her father, and pointing to the weeping one explained, 'She lost her penny.' Then she toddled back to the gate, and explained, 'My kind Dad'll give you a penny.' And she looked confidently at her father.

To Robert Churdon's surprise he put his hand in his pocket and gave the tearful child a penny; and another thing that had hitherto been taken for granted went to the wall. For surely one didn't make pennies to give them away for nothing. A great uneasiness came over the farmer as he did it. He felt as though he had just parted with a fortune; and perhaps he had. But his Littlejane was looking at him still with those confident eyes, and the other child had stopped crying and was scampering up the road, clutching her treasure.

'What child's she, Littlejane?' asked the farmer.

'She's Molly.'

'And who's Molly?'

'Molly's Molly,' said Littlejane. 'That's her *name*.'

And Farmer Churdon was no wiser. But that evening the fifty-two houses in Underbone were telling each other how Robert Churdon, for the first time in his life, *had given away a penny*. And, of all people, to Will Stow's Molly.

A few nights later there was more gossip running like wildfire from door to door. A tramp had come away from the farm with bread and a pair of old boots. Some said bread and meat, and boots and a hat. Nay, and a bottle of beer, they do say! Ay, and farmer's old coat. Never! But 'tis true. Sal Winter saw and spoke with him. He'd found Littlejane Churdon playing at the back door, and she marched him in to the farmer herself and said, 'He's hungry, Dad.' Them was her very words. Then the farmer gave him a parcel of food, and other things. What's come to Robert Churdon? He'll be standing the school-treat a shilling next!

He did, two shillings. And Littlejane Churdon went to the Treat, though she was too small for school, and came home crowing. Her father met the party on the road, and picked her out of the mass of children, and carried her home in his arms.

'Well, did ye like it, Littlejane?'

'Oo, I did, Dad!' And she tucked her beaming face

into his neck, repeating, 'I did, my *kind* Dad!' But over the head of his smiling sleepy child, the farmer's face looked out with a queer bother in it.

Next thing the village knew, he sent round word that Littlejane would be giving a party to the village children. Littlejane had so much liked the Treat the children had let her come to, that now she was sure they must come to *her* treat. She sat on her dad's knee and explained this to him, and she told him what cakes and stuff they'd had at the school-treat, and what games they had played, and what songs they'd sung. And she wanted her party to be just the same, only not in the woods but in her dad's own hayfield and the big barn, see, Dad?

Robert Churdon said, 'All right, then,' and thought, It'll not cost less than three-pound-ten.

Underbone couldn't believe its ears. It thought there must be some catch in it, but there was none. The children came, and feasted, and none went short. Littlejane ran among them, too happy to make more than one bite at anything, too happy to play more than one minute with anyone. The children patted her, and not because she was a rich man's child. 'Come over here, Littlejane! I'll make 'ee a haynest.' 'Nay, come and slide down the big haycock, Littlejane—*I'll* hold ye tight.' 'It's Littlejane's turn to skip now—*we'll* turn the rope.' 'Who's *my* baby, Littlejane? You are, ain't ye?' Behind it all brooded Robert Churdon, with that new anxious look in his eyes.

After this not a week passed but there was food for talk. Littlejane now had the run of the village, and was welcome everywhere. In the evening she sat on her kind dad's knee and chattered. Tommy Robinson's mam was in bed and never got up, and Tommy had nothing to eat all day. Susie Moore's bed was wet where the rain came through the wall. Gaffer Jennings cried because a hawk killed his two hens, and what would he do for eggs now? *You'll* give him two of *your* hens I said, of course, Dad. Littlejane related the village sorrows with a cloudless brow. She knew that there was a panacea for all woes in her dad. Her dad could fill larders and mend leaky roofs. There *were* no sorrows for Littlejane while her dad was in the world to put them right. And Robert Churdon, who had never yet seen his child look unhappy, put them right. Underbone, in which his farm alone had had an air of well-being, Underbone bit by bit was put into repair. At last there wasn't a child in it that hadn't as dry a roof as Littlejane's, and that didn't sleep as warm. There wasn't a man without sufficient ground, and good seed of his own. It became the most prosperous hamlet in the shire, and was the talk of it.

But the money it cost! And every penny spent was a penny spent away from Littlejane's future. He knew it, and over and over again swore he would pull himself up, and after this one bout do no more of it. Mustn't a man think of his own child first? Mustn't Littlejane's future be made safe? But tush! there was plenty left. And Littlejane's presence was too powerful for him. So he went on with it, blindly. It had gone, like drink, to his head, you see—or to his heart. Anyhow, once he'd begun, he couldn't stop giving. The village began to speak of him behind his back as Bob Churdon, and to venture a greeting when he passed by. There wasn't one he'd not done something for. And he looked as though he was being dogged.

Littlejane fell ill, and was taken to the Children's Hospital, and cured. Till she came back, Churdon was nearly out of his mind. Soon afterwards a fire broke out in the hospital, and the small patients were got out safe, but the place was gutted. Hard on this news, came the news that Churdon had sold the Mills at Beadon-on-Honey to build up the hospital again. Because it was urgent, he had sold at a loss. The buyer chuckled over his bargain; the village gaped; the hospital blessed Churdon's name; and Churdon hugged his Littlejane to his breast, and saw poverty stalking on them both.

Even then, he'd no cause to fear anything but his own obsession. But he was incurable now. Wherever there were things to be done for children, he did them, and if they didn't come his way naturally, he went looking for trouble, as you might say. You'd have to go deep for the explanation; but I expect the truth was that once this habit of *giving*—giving to Littlejane—had got its grip on him, what he could give straight to her seemed soon finished and done with, for after all there's an end to the benefits you can pour upon any one person by the mere spending of money. The only way to go on giving to his child was to give to all children, so he did, and the queer thing was that the less he had to give, the freer his giving became. Some of the things he did the village knew of; but there were more of which they never got wind at all. And all the while, he was going about with that worried look on him, as though he had a haggard conscience, and what he couldn't help doing put too great a strain on heart and mind. Like a man with a secret vice he tries to rid himself of, and can't. And while his property and savings were shrinking every week, and people were blessing and praising him near and far, he never once tried to tie up even a small sum to make Littlejane safe. Safe? The laughing lovely thing! What danger was she in with that look in her eyes of trust in the kindness of her dad, and of all the world? Would it have mattered to her, even had she known, when the shop in Bonemarket was auctioned, when Churdon sold out his last investments, when the inn was taken over by a new man? Did it matter to her when her father said to her one day, 'How'd you like to live with me in Underbone Cot, instead of this big farmhouse, Littlejane?'

'In the teeny cottage in the wood?' cried Littlejane. 'Oh, Dad, I'd *love* it!'

So they went there, and someone else farmed Bob Churdon's fat acres, and the Bonemarket Orphanage got the biggest cheque it had ever received—from an unknown donor. You see, Bob Churdon began to feel he was breaking up, the worry of it all was wearing him down, and he had a secret pain he told no man of, and grudged the doctor's fee for; and he'd begun to think of his Littlejane left without father or mother—and so the orphanage was enriched.

He and Littlejane lived for about a year in that woodman's cottage. During this time his big schemes dwindled, for he had nothing left to spend on them. But it is a fact that also at this time the furrow smoothed out of his brow, and the anxiety cleared out of his eyes. He hadn't a penny now to cling on to for Littlejane's sake, so when he thought of her future he knew there was nothing for it but to trust in God. And the man who does that takes the heart out of his care.

He hired himself out as labourer on his own farm, and when his wage had provided porridge for two, he and Littlejane went for Sunday walks, and gave away whatever he had left to the beggars on the road. He'd look at her with that new clear look of his as he trudged home with empty pockets, while she danced through the woods ahead of him, knocked at the cottage door, cocked her head to listen, called 'Come in,' to herself, went in, and sat down to wait for his knock.

'Come in, Dad!'

'Good evening, Miss Littlejane.'

'Good evening. Did you have a walk?'

'Yes, and a nice walk too.'

'Who did you see?'

'A beggar or so.'

'What did you give them?'

'A penny or two.'

'What did they say?'

'Thankee kindly, sir.'

'Thankee, *kind* sir, you mean, Dad!' said Littlejane.

After this they supped; and there was nearly always something more than bread and milk, for people liked giving Littlejane a basket of fruit, or a honeycomb. And many a time when a pig was killed, some bit of it was taken along to Bob Churdon—to 'Bob's', as all now called the cottage in the wood. For during this year they'd come to speak of him as Bob, and to hail him by the name. 'Just run down to Bob's with these chitterlings, Tommy'—or, 'Louie, leave this couple of eggs at Bob's as you go by'—became common words on a woman's tongue that year.

Then one morning Littlejane came early to William Stow's house and said, 'I can't wake my dad up.'

'Can't you?' said Stow. 'Sit down and have breakfast with Moll, and I'll go and see.'

Littlejane stayed all that day, and the day after, and the day after that, when Bob Churdon was buried. The whole village walked behind him to the churchyard. By then it was known that he had died penniless, and that no child was ever left more destitute than Littlejane Flower Churdon. I don't know who it was that first mentioned the Bonemarket Orphanage, but you should have seen William Stow flare up at the word.

'Send Bob Churdon's child to the Orphanage?' he cried. 'Not till my own must go too! Littlejane's come to my house, and there she can stay. I'd not think twice about a thing like that.'

Then a woman spoke up. 'Nay, Will, you can't afford another. Let me take Littlejane. I'm better able than you, and I owe her father a debt I'd never hoped to pay.'

'Why, so do I, if it comes to that,' said another, 'and I feel as if the child was one of mine.'

Others chimed in—Bob Churdon had done this, had done that, and t'other. He'd ruined himself for their children. And was his child to suffer because her father had had a kinder heart than one man can support? Why, the whole village was in debt to him. And now he was gone, who was Littlejane's parent but the village?

And so it ended. That village stood father and mother to Bob Churdon's child, the child he couldn't make safe. Each of the two-and-fifty homes put in its claim, and kept her for one week in the year. And there wasn't one, from the parson to the stonebreaker, that wouldn't have rejoiced to keep her the year round. Littlejane passed happily from home to home, and in all she heard her father spoken of as the kindest man that ever lived. 'The kind farmer' was the name his memory went by, there and in distant parts. Underbone became noted for the man, and proud of him, who for the sake of all children had left his child with nothing. Yet in the end, you might say, he had left the whole village to Littlejane Churdon, for every roof and hearth in it was hers.

Dan Searle the shepherd, whose cottage was halfway up the Down, was seldom seen in the village. He lived less in his cottage than in the shepherd's hut stationed hard by the wattled field, where the flocks he tended lived like natives in a hamlet. When Dan did, for any reason, appear in the village, the boys called him 'Old Surly!' and ran away from his threatening crook. No wonder he never cottoned to the farmer's idea that he should have a boy to help him. He couldn't seem to get on with boys at all, and least of all with little Ned Jewel.

Ned was an orphan, and lived with his aunt, looking forward to the day when he could go out to work. Young though he was, he already had a hankering to become sheepboy to any man but Dan. A shepherd's life seemed to Ned to be the best life under the sun, and sheep were his passion. It was through

Dan's finding him prowling one day about the sheepfold that their feud began. The shepherd chased him off with ugly words, and Ned defied him from a distance. After this when Dan passed through the village, Ned's voice was louder than any in shouting, 'Here comes Old Surly!' Then Dan would growl, 'Drat all boys, and you first, Ned Jewel!' In spite of this, Ned more than once went up to the Down again, to prowl around the community of the sheep, and was driven away with harder words each time. The two seemed bound together by their quarrel.

One Christmas Eve, when an early snowstorm had blotted out the features of the hills, Ned's aunt went hastening from house to house to ask if he was there. The boy was missing, and by nightfall a second blizzard filled the villagers with fears for his fate. At dawn when the storm abated, his aunt, going to the door to recommence her search, found Ned standing there like a boy in a dream. His tale was a queer one. Some of the older boys had told the little fellow that there was a bramble-patch full of berries growing in the snow in Blicknell Bottom, and like a silly he had gone to look for it; and then the blizzard came, and he was lost among the Downs. He could see nothing for the darkness and the stinging snow, but presently he stumbled against a little hut. The door opened, and a shepherd, 'bearded like Methusaley', lifted him in.

'My word, his eyes! They was like two stars!' said Ned. 'He made me warm and gave me something nice to drink. And he sat by me all night a-rubbing of me, and the hut was full of the brightness of his eyes. I couldn't see nawthing but his eyes till I fell asleep, and when I woke up, here was I on the doorstep.'

'Who *was* the shepherd?' his aunt asked.

'Nawbody *I* know. I never see him before.'

The same wild night a thing had happened to Old Surly that he never told. The blizzard had blown up, and as he sat smoking in his hut he heard a thud against the door, and on opening found a strange boy lying there. Dan took him in, covered and fed him, and sat for hours chafing his stiff limbs. The boy said nothing, but looked at the shepherd with such eyes as boy never had before or since, thought Dan; eyes like twin stars in the sky, and the hut was light with their shining. Dan fell asleep at last; when he woke it was day, and the unknown boy had disappeared.

On Boxing Day, the shepherd had occasion to go down to the village. A boy or two set up the usual cry, 'Old Surly!' and Ned, who was among them was about to echo the words; but his eyes met Dan's, and for a few moments the old man and the boy stared at each other as though they had been strangers, or friends meeting after a great while. Ned shut his mouth, and Dan passed on in silence to the farm. There, after finishing his business, he mentioned casually that he thought he could do with a boy in the New Year.

'You're welcome, as you know,' said the farmer. 'Who were you thinking of?'

'That young Ned Jewel would do as well as another.'

'Would he go?' asked the farmer, who knew about their feud.

'I think he mowt,' said Old Surly.

To the surprise of everyone, Ned agreed; and on New Year's Day the young and the old shepherd came together.

A MANUSCRIPT of André Chénier begins with this explanation: 'Several young girls surround a little boy, caressing him . . . "They say you have made a song for Pannychis, your cousin" . . . "Yes, I love Pannychis, she is pretty, she is five years old like me." . . . "Oh, do sing us your song." . . .

'Then in a clear voice he began to sing:

'Oh Pannychis, you can't help loving me!
We live together, the same age are we.
Just see how big and tall I am! I did
Stand myself yesterday beside my kid;
By Pollux and Minerva, I declare
His little horn-tip did not reach my hair!
Out of a nutshell I have made for you
A box to keep a beetle in, bright blue;

I've lined it with the very softest wool.
This morning on the seashore in a pool
I found a coloured shell which we will fill
With earth, and plant a flower in it, we will!
I'm going to show you how a navy floats
Upon our pond, with scraps of bark for boats.
The house-dog is so tame; at eventide
I'll lift you on his back to have a ride,
And I will walk in front of you and lead
You home each night safe on your gentle steed.'

SOMEONE—I think it was Palgrave—once wrote that of all French poets André Chénier most nearly approached to Keats. On this account I obtained, when in France, a small paper-covered collection of André Chénier's poems, and amongst them found nothing which to me suggested even a resemblance to those of Keats. But presently I lit on the lines which I have translated above. To me they were by far the most charming lines in the book; in the original they are limpid and child-like, as though they had been breathed in the clear air of the Golden Age. The way in which Chénier introduced them attracted me too—the tiny prelude, scarcely an explanation, less the beginning of an incident than a finger beckoning you upon it while it is happening. It is as though in passing through some sunlit Arcadian scene you behold the group of young maidens kneeling about the child, coaxing his innocent love-tale out of him—and then pass on, knowing not who the maidens are, who is the child, or who Pannychis, the little cousin he adores. Yet you remember this glimpse, and the sound of their voices, as you remember many lovely fleeting moments whose story is never rounded off with a beginning or an end. We do not know the boy's name, or when he lived, or in what isle of Greece. We do not know whether he was an imagination of André Chénier's, or whether the French poet had once read something, a fragment of a legend perhaps, of which he felt impelled to make a picture. He made it in mid-air, as it were, and left it there, suggestive and unattached. Only the name of Pannychis we know, and that she was five years old; but for the rest, who, when, and where?

Her cousin, let us call him Cymon, had grown up beside her from babyhood. Their mothers were sisters, and the two homesteads lay side by side on the fringe of a wood which contained in its midst a beautiful lake. The ground shelved down to it upon three sides; ilex and myrtle and eucalyptus trees descended the slopes to the lake's brink, guarding it like a secret, yet leaving it so open to the sky that the still clear water was sunlit and moonlit by turns. On the fourth side more lightly-scattered shrubs and flowers formed its frame, and the level sandy soil led among willows to a shallow ledge where the water was no more than ankle-deep, and coloured pebbles lay strewn like precious stones. Further in, the ledge dipped suddenly to waist-depth; and in the middle of the lake, out of reach of any but a swimmer, a two-tiered stone was visible, the top tier flat like an altar. Rosemary, violets, wild parsley, and many flowering vines crept to the lake's edge, and groups of golden iris with leaves like spears stood up in the very water, poised on their own reflections. This lake lay in the wood perhaps half a mile behind the homes of Pannychis and Cymon, and here the children often came to play. In front of their home, beyond stretches of sea-pinks and sea lavender, was the sea itself, lying quite still on the silver lap of the sand. Its colour was of so translucent a blue, and it was so motionless, that it seemed to be bewitched. It was as though at a supreme moment the life of sky and sea had been suspended, and they were left forever beneath the spell of their own beauty. Here too the children played their games together.

Although they were the same age, there was a great difference in their size when they were five years old. Pannychis was tiny, a fairy child, her skin was like white silk, her limbs as delicate as the stems of flowers, her hair of fine pale gold, so fine that any breeze could spin its soft mesh like rays about her head. Her mother could pick her up with one hand, and hardly know she held her, so springily she came up in the air. Sometimes she lifted the child suddenly shoulder-high, and Pannychis's little legs curled under her, and the bright hairs flew about her neck and eyes. 'There's my golden fountain,' laughed the mother, and set her down again. And little Cymon, brown, and tall for his age, watched the gold fountain go up in the air and come down again, and when she was down ran and held her, as though he feared she might spring up once more and never return to earth. He watched her as a flower watches the sun, and watched over her as a bird watches over its egg. He never tired of devising little pleasures for her with the pretty toys he found on the shore and in the wood. All the loveliest of the treasures were hers, he kept not for himself the brightest sea-shell, the whitest tuft of lamb's wool, the gayest beetle, the most curious nut, the sweetest flower. He brought them to her saying:

'Look, Pannychis, what I've just found for you.'

'Oh, thank you, Cymon.'

'Do you like it?'

'Yes, it is beautiful.'

'Shall we keep a beetle in this nutshell? It is just the right size for a beetle's home. And shall we plant a violet in this sea-shell? I know where there are some white ones. Would you like it?'

'Yes, I would love it.'

'And do you love me, Pannychis?'

'Yes, I do, Cymon.'

'I'm growing so tall, Pannychis, I'm taller than the kid already, by Pollux and Minerva I am! Will you always love me?'

'Always,' said Pannychis.

And she played with his shell, and planted his violet, and sailed his little bark-boat on the lake; and at bedtime, when he set her on the big house-dog's back ('Would you like it, Pannychis?' 'Oh, yes, I would!') and led her home, she left the shell, the boat, and the flower upon the shore or in the wood, whence they had come. And she did not think she was neglecting them, or that in leaving them there she was not 'keeping' them; because to Pannychis all shells were her shell wherever they lay, all flowers her flower wherever they grew, the world was hers wherever she found it. How could she neglect or lose even the least bit of it? Was it not always there, and always hers? Here was her sunny lake, her blue sea with her evening star above it, here sprang her meadow grass, yonder was her stretch of silver sand, here was her kid, and all the kids upon the hill were hers, here was her Cymon, and hers were all the people in the world.

And if Cymon wanted it to be different—if he wanted her to love *his* shell more than all other shells, find *his* flower sweeter than all other flowers, and prefer *him* to all other people, Pannychis never knew it. She was free, she laughed out to the world, life was her delight, she held nothing, and she had all.

One day, Cymon went apart and made his song for her. His mother listened to him, and told her sister. 'How Cymon loves your Pannychis!' she laughed. She boasted here and there that her little son had made a poem like a poet. Soon afterwards, when he was wandering along the shore looking for pretty stones and seaweed, some girls who had been bathing in the cool of the evening came running out of the water, calling to him.

'Cymon! Little Cymon!'

He stopped, and they surrounded him. Aglaia stooped to kiss him, and her wet hair streaked his cheek.

'They say you have made a song for Pannychis, your cousin.'

'Yes, I love Pannychis, she is pretty, she is five years old like me.'

'Oh, do sing us your song!'

And he sang them his song in a clear voice.

When it was done they praised and petted him. 'Oh, what a pretty song!' 'What a clever Cymon!' 'How you must love your cousin to sing so sweetly about her.'

'Yes, and everything loves her,' said Cymon.

'No wonder. But take care!' said Aglaia. 'Lest when you set her on your big dog's back he runs away with her as the bull did with Europa.'

'What bull? Who was Europa?'

'Oh, you must ask your mother to tell you. We've no time now for tales.' And the girls kissed him, and ran back into the sea.

Cymon asked his mother to tell him the tale, and she told him not only that, but also the tale of Persephone who was carried away underground, of Daphne who was changed into a laurel tree, of Syrinx who changed into a reed, and of Arethusa, who became at last a fountain. Now when he played with Pannychis beside the lake, he held her hand tightly, and would not let her go into the water. Who knew but that she might in one instant become a golden iris or a rush? And in the woods he would hardly let her pull a flower, for fear that from the hole in the ground might rise the King of Hades to carry her away. He began to be afraid of the very sunlight that fell upon her; had not the kiss of Phœbus turned a girl into a green tree? Upon the shore he feared the waves that ran to lap her feet, and at night he set her no more upon the house-dog's back.

'Why not?' asked Pannychis, but he dared not tell her that he feared the dog might be a god in disguise. All the beautiful world, the earth, the sky, the sea, which he had once ransacked for things to please her—all had become dangers to her in Cymon's eyes. If Daphne, Syrinx, Persephone, and Europa had been their victims, how could one so lovely as Pannychis escape? He shadowed her day and night, he laughed no more, he held her by the hand or a fold of her garment, and she looked at him in wonder.

'Why do you follow me so close, Cymon? Oh, don't hold me so hard!' she begged. 'Shall we run races as we used to on the shore?'

'No, no, don't run away from me!'

'Shall we play hide-and-seek?'

'Oh no! Don't hide from me!'

'Let us go and paddle in the lake.'

'No, Pannychis, the lake is very deep.'

'Not at the brim. And you said you would teach me to swim.'

'One day—not today.'

'Why not? Last week I saw a crown of parsley on the stone in the lake. Did you put it there?'

'No, I can't swim as much as that.'

'I wish I could. I wonder who did. It was an offering to the god.'

'Which god?'

'I don't know. I would like to make an offering to him too. Cymon, look happy.'

'I am happy while you are here. You do love me, Pannychis?'

'Yes, I do. Look happy, then.'

Suddenly she broke away from him and ran laughing into the forest. He followed her, damp with fear. 'Look happy! Look happy!' called Pannychis over her shoulder. She ran on laughing, laughing, and vanished among the trees. Oh, how he hated the trees that hid her from him. The sound of her laughter led him to the lake, but when he got there he could not see her. He gazed at the water—there was no ripple on it, but he hated it. What did it conceal? A ray of sunlight struck through an ilex bough across his path. His eye travelled up it, fearing and hating it. Suddenly he knew that he had come to fear and hate the whole world, all the things he had once most loved for Pannychis's sake: trees, flowers and light, and water, all things in which the dreaded god might dwell. How could he live and fear these things—even though he feared them for the sake of Pannychis, she who had always loved them? But where, where was Pannychis?

Suddenly he heard her faint laughter ring from the further side of the lake. He thought he heard her call, 'Look happy!' He ran as hard as he could, crying her name; but did not find her on the further side. Yet the echoing laughter led him on and on, out of the wood, over the flowers, down to the shore of the sea, lapping the silver sand so softly, while in the pale green evening sky the stars came trembling out. All was pure loveliness; but Pannychis was nowhere to be seen.

And she was never seen again. They sought her in every glade, in every cave, they dived beneath the lake and watched the tides. But which had taken her, sea, lake, or wood, they never knew. It might have been the sunlight, or the stars.

Cymon grew up, and when he was a man he loved and married. He loved his wife well, though he made no song for her. She knew the name of Pannychis his little cousin, beautiful as a forest flower or a sea-shell, who had disappeared so strangely when she was a tiny girl. To his children he sometimes sang the song of Pannychis, and they loved it, and they too planted flowers in shells, sailed bark-boats on the lake, and rode upon the back of their big dog. Cymon let them do all these things without fear. He had lost his fear of them, and regained his love, soon after Pannychis had disappeared. But he never told even his wife and children that often, when life seemed too heavy to be borne, as life so often does, the beauty of things rushed in upon him unawares, from the sky and the grass, the trees and the rocks, the fresh water and the salt, the light and the dark, and he heard as clear as in the moment when she broke from him the lovely laugh of Pannychis, and heard her call to him from heaven and earth, 'Look happy! Look happy!'

ELEANOR FARJEON was born in 1881 in London. Although she received no formal education, she and her brothers were encouraged to write stories and poems. Her first book *Nursery Rhymes of London Town* was published in 1916, and she went on to write over 60 books for children, including many collections of verse. As well as the Hans Christian Andersen International Medal and the Carnegie Medal which she was awarded for *The Little Bookroom*, Eleanor Farjeon was also awarded the Regina Medal in 1959 for her complete works. Eleanor Farjeon died in 1965.

EDWARD ARDIZZONE was born in 1900. His family moved to Ipswich in 1905, before moving to London in 1914. After leaving school he worked as a clerk in the City of London and studied life-drawing in the evenings. In 1927 he gave up work to become a full time artist. In 1936 Edward Ardizzone made an illustrated story of a book he had made up for his children, *Little Tim and the Brave Sea Captain*. A much-loved artist, Ardizzone went on to illustrate more than 170 books and was awarded the Kate Greenaway Medal in 1956 and the CBE in 1971. Edward Ardizzone was married with three children and died in 1979.